At Face Value

At Face Value
The Life and Times of Eliza McCormack/ John White

๛

DON AKENSON

McGill-Queen's University Press
Montreal & Kingston • London • Buffalo

© McGill-Queen's University Press 1990
ISBN 0-7735-0765-5
Legal deposit 3rd quarter 1990
Bibliothèque nationale du Québec

Printed in Canada on acid-free paper

Canadian Cataloguing in Publication Data
Akenson, Donald Harman, 1941–
    At Face Value: the life and times of Eliza McCormack/
John White
    Includes bibliographical references.
    ISBN 0-7735-0765-5
    1. McCormack, Eliza. 2. White, John, 1831–1894.
3. Canada. Parliament. House of Commons –
Biography. 4. Legislators – Canada – Biography.
5. Feminists – Canada – Biography. 6. Impersonators,
Male – Canada – Biography. I. Title.
FC27.W44A43 1990   328.71'092   C90-09128-4
F1033.W44A43 1990

To A.S.F.

Contents

Preface

Everyone knows that Agnes Campbell MacPhail was Canada's first female member of Parliament, elected in 1921. That is incontestable. But consider…

When the former member of Parliament for East Hastings died in 1894, his funeral, conducted by the Grand Orange Lodge of Ontario East, "was remarkable above anything else for the number of ladies present." That was what the local newspaper said, and it was what first called John White to my attention. White's obituary mentioned his unusual sympathy for women and quoted his oft-stated dictum, "Give me the ladies on my side and I don't care much for the men." This was not a throw-away line: it was a considered principle of political solidarity. Given that women did not receive the vote in dominion elections until after World War I, it seemed that something more than electoral expediency might be involved here.

As I tracked White down, certain facts about his life made sense while others proved unsettling. The available documentation allows one to trace White from birth in County Donegal before the charnel months of the cholera epidemic of 1832, through a sadly deprived childhood that knew the Great Famine of the 1840s, and then to emigration to Canada. For a time White disappears. It is not until the mid-1850s that he resurfaces, north of Belleville, Ontario, with money in hand. He had entered an alliance with a woman of some means and become a big-time operator in a small-town way: cheese-factory and foundry owner, local politician, Orange Lodge official. In 1871 White surprised everyone by winning a dominion parliamentary election, and from then until 1887 he was a trustworthy Tory backbencher. Not a great career, but an interesting and in some ways puzzling one.

I let White sit for a while in my file of intriguingly elliptical Irish immigrants to Canada. Then I came across Eliza McCormack, a transvestite prostitute who had some high times and legal troubles in central Canada in the late 1840s and early 1850s. Her intersection with Ogle Gowan, the founder of the Orange Order in Canada, is described in *The Orangeman*.

Something clicked. I recalled McCormack was a County Donegal Protestant name (as was White) and that the McCormacks, like the Whites (with whom they intermarried), were poor farmers and artisans who had settled in small Protestant enclaves among the overwhelmingly Catholic and undeniably hostile Roman Catholic peasantry of that part of Ulster. Although the province of Ulster is usually thought to have escaped the worst effects of the Irish famine, parts of it, especially Donegal, were hard hit. Starvation and epidemics of typhus and relapsing fever raged through the population. Mortality records for the time are scarce, but one of the hastily scribbled notes made by an attendant at the temporary fever hospital in Donegal town lists among the dead one "John White, young man, about fifteen or sixteen."

One of the intellectual turning points of twentieth-century historical writing is Joan Kelly-Gadol's 1977 essay "Did Women
Have a Renaissance?" Her work prompts one to ask how any
historical concept might be gender loaded. Inquiry can carry
so many unexamined assumptions about gender that it obscures
more than it illuminates. Historians of women have successfully
argued that a patriarchal society has existed for most of the
duration of Western history and that patriarchy has had con-
sequences for both the position of women and the nature of
the historical record. Evidence about the character and quality
of women's lives is only a small fraction of that available for
men's lives. Consequently, the historical methods that have been
used in male history are inadequate for the task of recovering
female history. New methods and new historiographic canons
must evolve for dealing with women's history, and in my view
these should be fused with the methods that have been applied
to male history.

In biography, a good way to apply this gender sensitivity is
to ask, "How would my view of my subject change if, in an
effort to escape an unthinking gender bias, I assumed that he
is actually a woman, or she a man?" This is not a bad exercise:
if nothing else it prevents our falling into Carlyle's trap of believ-
ing that history is merely the collective biography of great men.
Samuel Johnson was right when he said that "the business of
a biography... is to lead the thoughts into domestic privacies
and display the minute details of daily life," but there is more
to it than that. In his autobiography Mark Twain remarks, "What
a wee little part of a person's life are his acts and his words!
His real life is in his head and known to none but himself." The
biographer must explore domestic and private facts and proceed
from that basis to make a speculative entry into the subject's
heart, mind and soul. This is why the best biographers are
always doing two things at once: setting down the facts, big
and small, and on the same pages and at the same time, writing
a novel. Evaluating the fine work of biographer Richard Ellman,
Edward Mendelson points out that "any attentive reader may
find [Ellman's] novel in the interstices of [the Joyce] book's archi-
val reportage. Its presence announces itself whenever Ellman
(like all recent biographers) tells us what Joyce was thinking in
such-and-such a city or what he felt when such-and-such hap-

pened." This is the way modern biography works. "We have focused our gaze," Mendelson concludes, "on the inaccessible inner reaches of authorial psyche without quite facing the fact that we have no way of making the inaccessible accessible. So we invent what we cannot know and call the result 'biography.'" Good biography always has simultaneously deconstructed and reconstructed perceived historical reality.

It took a long time for the penny to drop, but finally I realized that the best way to make sense of the career of John White in Canada was to recognize that he was actually a she: that Eliza McCormack had taken on the deceased John White's name and much of his persona. What a pinched, pained and heroic life she must have led! At heart she was a loving and generous person, a loyal friend and a devoted provider for her family. Withal she had a straight from the shoulder honesty and a rural shrewdness that made her a character to be reckoned with. She was a postmodern (perhaps even a postfeminist) heroine in what was not yet a postmodern age.

Was John White really a woman? That is a question from male history and an inherently, if unconsciously, hostile one. The known facts of White's life fit the hypothesis, but the reality can never be known and that is just the point: in a culture where most historical records have been made and preserved by males it is very difficult to get at the true stories about women's lives. Heuristic biography can correct in part this historical imbalance. We know with certainty that although the details of all save a very few female lives in the past are lacking, women played major roles in the history of Western society. As historians, we can either go back to stark fact-grinding biographies (which in their selection and arrangement of facts are fictive, but in an unconscious and unexamined manner), or we can try to get inside our subject's mind – and in so doing accept the fact that biography, like many other forms of historical investigation, demands an energetic, self-conscious exercise of imagination. Perhaps we should put a different tag on biography. Stories of individual human lives might better be called speculative history or historians' fiction. In any case, they should be accepted for what they are.

I am grateful for financial support and encouragement in the writing of this book to the Social Sciences and Humanities Research Council of Canada, the School of Graduate Studies and Research of Queen's University, the Directorate of Multiculturalism of the Government of Canada, and the Tyrone Guthrie Centre, Annaghmakerrig, County Monahan. And I am particularly in the debt of two anonymous readers for McGill-Queen's University Press for their constructive and critical assessment of an earlier draft of this manuscript.

Part One
Donegal's Own

1

The Real World

There are many things that tie the world together, and at the time of the birth of Eliza McCormack White the main tie was cholera. In 1826 the disease, endemic to the filthy villages and urban slums of the Indian subcontinent, escaped and traveled to Russia and from thence to central Europe. At the time, no one knew how cholera was spread, although a few sages suggested, correctly, that it was communicated through some discharge of the victim that entered the water supply. But if the causes of the pandemic were unknown, its effects were not. Victims experienced violent vomiting and severe diarrhoea – or rice water, as it was known – wrenching cramps and, more often than not, collapse and death within a few hours. Newspapers in the British Isles, the Canadas, and the United States charted the inexorable march of the dread disease from the

Baltic countries to the Mediterranean basin and into central France. Its every step moved closer to the English Channel. Weekly cholera reports were a matter of general morbid fascination. One can imagine various governmental health authorities, like generals of the late Roman empire, placing flags on their maps and sadly shaking their heads at the inevitable approach of disaster.

Cholera reached England in 1831 and by the fall of that year spread throughout the country. Because so many migrants persisted in emigrating to the Canadas from the British Isles, colonial administrators tried to set up quarantine procedures, but these did little good. In June 1832 a ship arrived at Grosse Isle having lost forty-two passengers to the disease en route. The vessel passed through the quarantine without impediment, and the disease began its westward trek across British North America. Montreal, Cornwall, Brockville, Kingston, Belleville, and York (now Toronto) were stops on this funereal progress. Meanwhile, in almost perfect step with its advance across the Canadian colonies, cholera marched through Scotland and Ireland.

The great Irish cholera panic is the backdrop to the birth of Eliza McCormack White. The disease had first appeared in Belfast in mid-March 1832. A week later it was in Dublin and three days after that, Cork. By mid-June most but not all of the thirty-two Irish counties had reported an outbreak. The terror that ran through the countryside is easy to imagine in theory, but its magnitude is quite beyond anything experienced in the English-speaking world in the twentieth century. This incurable sickness was careening into a largely preliterate, poverty-stricken population that believed in the intervention of the supernatural in everyday life. The epidemic was beyond human explanation and, consequently, it could only be stopped by divine intervention.

Thus the "blessed turf." On Saturday the ninth of June someone visiting the Roman Catholic chapel at Charlesville, County Cork, reported that the Blessed Virgin Mary had appeared on the chapel altar and left some ashes that were a certain protection against cholera. These ashes, she ordered, were to be tied into small parcels and taken to cottages in the area they were to be hidden in the rafters or chimneys. A relieved cottager would then take ashes from his own chimney or hearth, tie them into four parcels, carry them to four cottages that had not yet been visited, and so on. So desperate were the Irish peasants for solace in their hour of peril that in a mere four hours, between midnight and 4 A.M., the message spread across an area of more than forty square miles in the Cork region. And it kept traveling, transformed as it went. By Monday the eleventh of June it had reached Queen's county to the north. Now it involved not ashes but "blessed turf." The fundamental magic was the same, however – follow certain supernatural steps and avoid the plague. In six days, between the ninth and fifteenth of June 1832, the miraculous cure for the pandemic spread across three-quarters of the country. Only the mountainous and most rugged parts of Ireland were excepted. The magical cure reached Ballyshannon, County Donegal, on Wednesday the thirteenth of June. This was just a few miles from where Martha White, in the last days before childbirth, lived.

Martha White was a Protestant by habit. Her husband, John C. White, was one by fervent conviction. Like most Protestants, they scoffed at the superstitions of the Catholic peasantry. Holy water, charms and amulets were already suspect; now the papists had turf and ashes to keep themselves from illness. The Whites feared the twisting indignity of death from cholera just as much as their Catholic neighbours, but being Protestants, that had something more on their mind: they saw the scurrying of their Catholic neighbours from cottage to cottage – clandestine, often nocturnal movements – and concluded that the papists were up to something. The Whites were not alone in this. In places throughout Ireland, Protestants went to the police or to the local magistrates to report a Catholic conspiracy. Many Protestants took to staying up at night in fear of attack. But the Irish Catholics were not like the Hungarian peasantry who, in the belief that the nobility was spreading cholera, murdered members of aristocratic families. There were few recorded instances of violence. One of these was, however, in County Donegal, and John and Martha White resolved to keep alert.

Not that the Whites would have had anything to worry about even if the Catholics had taken to laying waste the nobility and gentry. White was a blacksmith with only a small cottage, an attached workshop that he called a foundry, and two acres of potato ground, all rented from the local landlord. Like even the poorest of Irish Protestants, the Whites considered themselves to be a step above the superstitious papists. In truth, however, the Protestants were every bit as given to portents ("freets"), faith healing, and the supernatural as the Catholics. John White Sr, like many of his fellows, spent hour after hour in a literal-minded reading of the Bible. Many nights he would hunch over the Scriptures and incline them on his lap so that the flickering light from the turf fire could illuminate the holy page. He would study in especial detail the prophetic books of the Old and New Testaments. Even during the summer months, when the days were long, he transferred a glowing piece of turf from his foundry to the cottage hearth so that he could fan a flame if the need to read God's holy word took him after nightfall. His first response to the news that the Catholics were doing something strange with turf and ashes was to open the Book of Revelation and ponder the section describing the signs of the end times. This he read to Martha who, being less religious than he and massively pregnant, smiled and sighed heavily. "John, dear man, the end time I await is the deliverance of healthy baby boy."

The Whites already had one son, John, named after his father. He had been born a year earlier and baptized by the rector of the Established (that is, Anglican) Church in the parish of Donegal on 8 May 1831. The Whites adopted the local Gaelic terminology and called their first born John Oge, meaning young-John, roughly the equivalent of today's "John Jr." Babies in rural Ireland were judged as much by their size as by their mental alertness, and in this respect John Oge was a prodigy. He was as fat as a summer stoat and the pride of his father's life. Sometimes John Sr would read aloud at night the section of the Old Testament that goes, "My love, you're as beautiful as Jerusalem, as lovely as the city of Tirzah, as breathtaking as those great cities." He called John Oge the apple of his eye, never realizing that he was borrowing the vocabulary of a Semitic love poem to a woman. The adoration of the beloved fit his sentiments exactly. "The best gift God could give us, Martha, would be another boy bairn, just like John Oge."

Martha White was an unusually optimistic woman, which was just as well, for childbearing in Ireland in this era was the greatest single danger to a woman's life. "I'm glad, John, that

I can bear another son. And, if it isn't a son, well, there will be more of them later on, so there will."

A severely practical man, John Sr knew what he must do as soon as Martha's labour began. The moment came in the small hours of the morning of the fifteenth of June. He hurried down the road to awaken an old widow who acted as midwife in Donegal town. That done, he stayed out of the way. By an unspoken rule, men were forbidden to be in the same room as a woman in parturition. John White Sr would have been more apt to break the commandment against murder than he would this fundamental law of the family. Some things were sacred. White retreated to his smithery and used a bellows to blow life into the embers on the raised blacksmith's hearth. He put on fresh turf and soon there was enough light for him to read The Song of Solomon. As the pained cries of his wife became more frequent, his thoughts strayed from the holy word. To keep himself occupied he took a piece of strap iron and placed it in the fire. When it was red hot, he bent it double over his anvil and began beating it into something, he was not sure what. He repeated this exercise several times until, between the bangs of his big hammer, he heard the small cry of a newborn baby. Then complete silence fell.

Moving slowly, as if afraid of breaking something, the blacksmith left his forge and went to the door of the family cottage. He held his breath. Hearing nothing, he proceeded cautiously across the threshold. By the light of the hearth, he could just make out the black form of the midwife. In her arms, wrapped in a large shawl, was the baby. Thank God, a son! He looked through the dark room at Martha. She was breathing regularly, in long, exhausted pulls.

The blacksmith entered the room boldly now and saw clearly that this was a great strong baby. "Let me take the lad from you," he said to the midwife. "There'll be yet another blacksmith in this family!" He took the infant into his massive hands.

"Sir..." The midwife said. "Sir..."

"A great lad entirely! Don't you agree?"

"Oh, yes, a great healthy child. Why, in two years, its strength will be that of a young bullock, no doubt. Only..."

"Only what, woman?"

"It's a girl child, sir."

White, startled, shook his head and held the new baby at arm's length to examine it. "Are you sure?"

"As sure as there's a God in heaven. I do know what I am about, sir," she added tartly.

"Well, woman, I'll just check."

The midwife inhaled audibly and from the straw-filled bed Martha White tried to say something. Her husband was about to break one of the taboos of Irish rural life. Men never dealt directly with the genitalia of children, even of newborn off-spring. Inside the mud cabins of the poorest peasantry, where the young frequently went naked until ages four or five, adult males were expected to stare past the generative portions of their children's anatomy. It was for mothers and elder daughters to deal with such things.

This was too important to White. He unwrapped the infant and held it to the light. "You're right, woman," he announced to the midwife. "This is a girl. No doubt about it at all." He swirled the baby back into the shawl and thrust her at the crone like a dissatisfied customer returning something to a shop-keeper.

"But look at the bairn again." The voice was Martha's, low and exhausted. "The child is special. Blessed. Don't you see the sign?"

The blacksmith made a move toward the child. Before touch-ing her he saw what his wife meant. It should have been obvi-ous. The caul! The girl had the caul! Plastered around the top and back of her head was a layer of amniotic membrane that had not been torn away in the birthing. Throughout Ireland, this was considered a sign of good luck.

"She'll never drown," the midwife declared.

"She'll have great good fortune!" Martha added from her bed.

"She'll have the gift of talking and will make people see the world her way."

There were a great many freets to pass on. John White knew most of them already, but he listened attentively. He was not a superstitious man, he told himself, yet he knew enough not to ignore good fortune. With plague sweeping the countryside and the suspicious activity of his papist neighbours, it was a relief to accept a little comfort. When the midwife had rattled off the last of her prophecies, he thanked her. He took the infant girl in his arms and looked at her with something akin to pride. Then, catching himself, he said gruffly, "Still and all, I'd rather it was a boy."

In County Donegal, however, the two adamantine rocks of everyday life – grinding poverty and endemic religious tension – remained unmovable. If anything, the cholera epidemic of 1832 made these matters worse.

In the 1830s, the town of Donegal had slightly more than eight hundred inhabitants and was a deceptively pleasant place to look at. With its row of sea-side businesses fronting on a wharf and a town square – shaped like a triangle and called

Historical Provinces of Ireland

"The Diamond" – with a wide road leading inland from its apex, the town linked sea communications with inland roads. The town of Donegal (located, as official documents noted, in the Parish of Donegal, in the Barony of Tyrhugh, in the County of Donegal, in the Province of Ulster), had been there in one form on another for at least a millennium. The name Dun-nan-Gall, the fortress of the foreigners, refers to its Vikings settlers, but the town as the Whites knew it had been shaped by the "plantation of Ulster." Early in the seventeenth century, the control wielded by the Gaelic chiefs of Ulster was finally broken and large parts of the north of Ireland were opened to settlement by Protestants from England and Scotland. In 1610 Donegal Castle, the last mansion of the great O'Donnell chiefs of the north, was granted to an English adventurer, Sir Basil Brooke. It remained in the family through the 1830s. Thus Donegal town became an ordered part of the Protestant plantation of Ulster. The town resembled a fortress, not physically but culturally. Donegal town was at the tip of the western salient of the Protestant north. It was the very end of a narrow Protestant peninsula in a Catholic sea.

The White's cottage-cum-foundry was only three-quarters of a mile west of the centre of town and the road was good. Armed with the excuse of needing a quarter pound of tea or some fresh-caught cheap herring, Martha White went daily to town. She did not move with the slow step of a countrywoman; even when she was carrying one of her increasingly robust children she walked confidently, her head up, looking at everything with undisguised curiosity. On her way she passed a number of churches and meetinghouses. Not only was there a handsome Church of Ireland edifice, built in 1824 and located just off the Diamond ("Our church," she told whatever uncomprehending infant child she held as they passed it), but also a thatched-roof Roman Catholic chapel ("shabby and that's as it should be"), a sub-fusc one-room Presbyterian meetinghouse, a Wesleyan hall, the Zion Chapel for one branch of Independents and, in converted houses, a chapel each for the Presbyterian Seceders and for another group of Independents ("I can scarcely keep them all apart").

Martha, ever optimistic, promised her husband that more bairns would come. An emotionally controlled man, the black-

smith said little, brooding about God's will. In the meantime
Martha raised John Oge and his sister, whom they had christened Eliza. The brother and sister were reared virtually as
twins. Each was strong. "Just look at the back on that lad," John
Sr would say. "And what about the girl?" was Martha's reply.
"She has a set of shoulders like a hill country teamster's already,"
adding quickly, "and the most lovely face." At that time Irish
boys and girls were not dressed differently until they were six
or seven years old. Before that age anything from a shift made
from an old shawl to pantaloons cut down from some adult's
garments served as everyday clothing. John Oge and Eliza
looked to all the world like identical twins, and acquaintances
of the family had a hard time telling them apart.

By the time John Oge and Eliza were four and three years
of age, respectively, they were able to accompany their mother
on her daily walks. A year later, they had become such great
walkers that she would take them on rambles through the town
and in the countryside.

In town they often saw some plump matron from Londonderry, or better still, from Scotland, visiting the town's sul-
pherous spa. "Och, look at that fine lady," Martha would note,
and they would watch the matron pick her way around the
town's numerous potholes and piles of manure. More often than
not, the visitor with the grand airs was not a real lady but the
cossetted wife of some merchant. To Martha and the children
it made no difference. These were creatures from the wide world
beyond Donegal and that in itself was fascinating.

The town harbour could not have been more interesting to
the trio if it had been a circus. To an outsider it was not much
of a place, for at low tide it turned into muddy slobland. But
fish, mussels, the detritus of seals, deal planks washed ashore
from passing ships, bottles and glass fishing buoys were for
sale on the wharf. Martha and the two children always made
a great show of examining everything, and now and then they
purchased a small item. Martha always tried to buy from a
Protestant. "Mother, why do we go with Mr Johnston, and not
to that man Duggan?" John Oge once asked. "Because he is
one of ours," was the reply. In Donegal town, even to a four-
year-old, that was explanation enough.

Half a dozen times a year a vessel of four hundred tons or

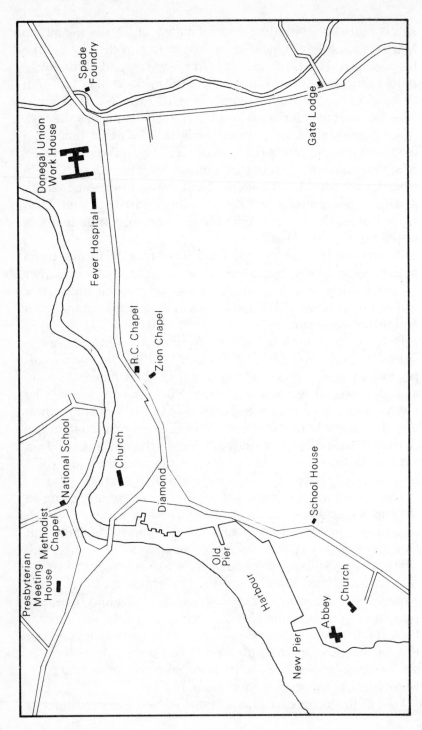

Vicinity of Donegal Town

more would be led into the harbour by the pilot boat. The town's new pier could take vessels up to fourteen feet in draught, but the business was tricky. The ship had to lie outside the harbour until just the right sort of westerly wind blew. Then she would attempt to thread her way in. The moment the wind shifted properly, half the town came out and watched. For young children, like the two Whites, these occasions provided lessons in geography, economics, and history, and allowed the family to hear of people who lived very differently than the Protestant working class of Donegal town. Standing close to their mother in a line of observers, Eliza and John Oge soaked up information from the moment the vessel's name and registration became visible – "Ah, she's a Bristol boat, she is, but registered to a Liverpool firm," a pipe-smoking observer would note, "I wager she's been to Amerikay and back." As the vessel was unloaded, heavy items being swung ashore by block and tackle, and lighter ones carried on the shoulders of seamen and local labourers garnering a day's stevedoring wages, the nature and origin of each drew analysis. Weighty arguments were carried on by loungers who themselves had hardly twopence in their pockets but knew a surprising amount about the intricacies of sea trade. The most exotic of all cargoes was human, and this was an export business. In the spring and early summer of the year it was common for half a dozen or more locals, sometimes two or three full families, to board the vessels. Amidst great keening from those left behind, they would begin a voyage to Belfast or Liverpool, where they would take another ship across the Atlantic, to the Canadas, or, less often, to the United States. The emigrants were so determined that in the late spring of 1836, when a ship from Liverpool filled with emigrants was too large to enter Donegal harbour safely, twelve families arranged to be ferried out to her while she anchored off shore. She was a slave ship, taken over when British vessels were banned from the slave trade, who, with only a change in name, now took the Irish to North America.

"Mother, please, why if going on those ships makes everyone cry so much… why do they do it?" Eliza asked.

"Sometimes, little love, because they have to" was all that Martha could say.

Tiny as the world of the White family was – in all 23 thousand

acres of the parish of Donegal, there were fewer than six thousand persons – the world that Eliza and John Oge saw was a
great deal larger than that of most Irish children of the time.
Martha White introduced the "twin-ones" (a term she and John
Sr began to use when the children were four and five) to the
rich past of the area as well as to the commercial bustle of the
present. One of Martha's favourite walks with Eliza and John
Oge took them by two prominent landmarks. The first of these,
in Donegal town itself, was the ruined but still imposing castle
of the last of the O'Donnells. Although the roof was gone and
the walls were crumbling, one was still awed by the grand hall,
arched and imperious, and by the upstairs banqueting hall
flanked by Gothic windows. Two sculptured chimney pieces
spoke of a level of wealth and craftmanship no longer seen in
Donegal. Next Martha would take the children a mile or so
south of town where they entered the grounds of a ruined abbey.
A derelict church and an abandoned graveyard were nearby.
One of Ireland's most important historical documents, the
Annals of Donegal (more commonly known as the Annals of
the Four Masters) was composed here in the 1630s. Most Protestants avoided the castle and the abbey: the first was a reminder
of the era of Gaelic sovereignty before the plantation of Ulster,
and the abbey, of course, had its roots in the pre-Reformation
era. Martha ignored these historical complications: instead, she
told her children tales of chivalry of the kind that circulated as
folklore in many parts of the British Isles and which Sir Walter
Scott eventually collected, embroidered and parlayed into a
fortune.

Martha White was unusual among rural people in that she
taught her children that the countryside was something beautiful. Almost all those nineteenth-century songs about Erin's
Green Fields were produced by urban exiles; for those living
in the countryside, the scenery is where you work, not something to look at. This was the era when, elsewhere, the romantic
idea of the sublime and the beautiful was gaining sway. When,
on fine days, Martha took Eliza and John Oge to the top of a
green hill, she talked to them of the surrounding beauty not
in poet's English but in a vocabulary full of Lallan's words that
came from her ancestral home in the Scottish lowlands.

To the locals, the rambles of Martha and the twin-ones became a regular feature of the landscape. The incumbent of the Established Church, a large red-faced man given equally to the principles of short-preached sermons and long-laid port, referred to their walks as the "rogation of the three Magi" and he laughed loudly at his joke.

Children are great disarmers of suspicion, so when they encountered rural Catholics outside of Donegal town, Martha and her little ones were treated courteously, even though it was well known that John White was a strong anti-papist. By most standards the Whites were themselves poor, but the bulk of the Donegal Catholic peasantry was so horrifically pauperized that Martha felt positively wealthy in comparison. Take the matter of shoes. It was a source of great pride to Martha that she and the twin-ones always wore shoes, not just when they were going to church or on fair days. And their shoes matched. Outside of Donegal town, in summer, fully nine out of every ten adults they encountered were barefooted. And although Martha made all her children's clothes and some of her own garments, she did so from store-bought cloth. The country people made their own cloth, either from coarse linen (flax was then grown in the area) or from home-fulled flannel. The Donegal women mostly wore grey dresses with dark shawls that had long fringes and, occasionally, gorse-dyed decorations. Grey clothing predominated in the area in the first half of the nineteenth century, for the knowledge of bright dyestuffs used in earlier centuries died with the retainers of the old Gaelic chiefs. Most of the men the White trio met wore shapeless trousers tied at the waist with a rope. They would sport up to half a dozen waistcoats under a dark-coloured jacket. So many layers covered the trunk of the average rural male that it was impossible to tell if he weighed seven stone or fourteen. For the most part these Catholic tenant farmers spoke Irish as their only language, but near the town many of them had acquired some English. "It's the Irish we speak among ourselves," one cottager told Martha. "But we have enough Scotch to speak till yourself."

Sometimes a countrywoman would invite Martha and the twin-ones into her cottage. Almost half of the Catholic small farmers of County Donegal lived in tiny one-room cottages.

Usually these had a smoke hole instead of a chimney and often they were without windows. The remaining population lived mostly in two-room cottages along with their livestock. A half-screen and a depression in the floor permitting animal urine to run outside demarcated the human side from the animal. John Oge and Eliza loved to visit these cottages. Not only could they watch mice play in the thatch, but they could observe the inevitable pig rooting about the house. If the sow had recently farrowed, there would be a delightful litter of piglets piling one on top of another as they suckled from their snoring mother. Martha White did not look down upon those forced to keep livestock in their cottages, but she was grateful her family was above such poverty.

Most Catholic peasants could not afford tea. The most common drink was a beverage called kilty made from barley, oatmeal, yeast and water. This was fermented slightly to form a near-beer of no potency and little taste. Neither Eliza nor John Oge could be made to drink it. Sometimes a countrywoman would give the White children a cup of buttermilk or of watered skim milk. To the small cottier that drink was a great luxury, and Martha would make certain that the twin-ones expressed their gratitude.

On one occasion they were asked to join a cottager family at its chief (and probably only) meal of the day. This took place at about two o'clock in the afternoon. Like the White family, cottagers ate masses of potatoes. In this particular household, the family table consisted of the front door, which was simply taken off its leather hinges and placed across four large creels used either for storage or for carrying things to market. The only other furniture was two low stools and some short fir logs for sitting. The family members took hot roasted potatoes from a rush bowl, peeled them and took turns dipping them into salt water. This was done without the aid of cutlery. The salted pratties were all that the family consumed, save a shared mug of kilty. John Oge and Eliza were quick on the uptake. Even though they used cutlery at home they followed their hosts' example and ate with great enthusiasm. When later that day they tried to do the same thing at their own evening meal, their father told them sharply to stop acting like a brace of heathen savages.

When Eliza and John Oge were, respectively, rising five and six, Martha White at last became pregnant again. "Thank the Lord!" John Sr proclaimed. "He hath heard the prayers of his servant." Martha took to singing around the house. John Oge and Eliza tried to share in the happiness, but it was difficult, for really it was their parents' pleasure, not theirs, and besides, weren't there children enough in the house?

This third child was an easy birth, a healthy boy, and John Sr was delighted. Holding the new bairn close to his heart, he did a jig around the cottage and for good measure went next door to his smithery, where he danced several times around the forge, as if offering the child up to the god of the foundry.

Both parents doted on the new arrival and the twin-ones were thrown more and more onto each other for companionship. Frequently they took rambles on their own. Sometimes they did things that their mother never would have permitted, such as sneaking into the Catholic chapel to see if it was true that nuns were held captive inside. But they felt keenly the loss of their wonted guide. Often they would sit at some familiar spot where they had spent time with Martha and would try to tell one another what she might have said.

Less than a year later a fourth child was born, and again it was male. Now there were two sets of White children, the twin-ones and two infant boys. Martha had her hands full. Too young to understand the demands on their mother, the twin-ones resented the new arrivals and felt betrayed by her. When they learned that mother was yet again with child they were angry and cast down. John Sr, who noticed their moping, quoted them scores of Bible verses by way of encouragement. He particularly liked the one that began "Let not your hearts be troubled..." and failed to see why it did not buck them up.

This time Martha's labour lasted eighteen painful hours. Dursing that time John Oge and Eliza stayed with their father in the smithery. The two infant boys were handed over to neighbours. John Sr prayed, paced, read the Bible and at intervals tried to do some metal work. The twin-ones hardly moved. They sat unblinking on low stools, watching their father.

Presently by midwife cried, "Come quickly!" and their father disappeared next door. It was to be several years before they were told fully what had happened: The baby had been lodged upside down and had come forth at appalling cost. Martha suffered a prolapse, her insides exposed. In excruciating pain, she fell into a delirium from which she was delivered by a death that was sudden and merciful.

The infant survived, but he was cruelly misshapen. His head had not cleared the canal properly and the force needed to pull him free left his cranium permanently misaligned, a rude cylinder atop a backward sloping forehead.

In later years John White Sr told his children the whole story of their mother's death and of the birth of their youngest brother. He ascribed everything to God's will, struggling to put a brave face on the event and using a phrase that engraved itself upon Eliza's mind. "Well, anyroad, it was the Almighty's decision and sure it's a great blessing the bairn was a lad."

2

Mumming

Martha White had been an unusual person – buoyant in hard times, happy with her lot in life and perpetually curious. She rejected the dogma of her time, espoused by Protestants and Catholics alike, that children were natural embodiments of sin. Instead she treated her children as friends and as fundamentally decent human beings. On this she was at odds with John White Sr, who had a decided belief in the doctrine of original sin. Martha's personality was so strong however that her warmth carried the day. "Sure, John, how could the good Lord put evil into the heart of every young one, the way the Church says?"

Similarly, Martha White had not entirely accepted the sub-ordination demanded of Irish women of the time. She ate with the family and spoke for herself when she felt like it. So it was only after her mother's death that Eliza McCormack White learned what the traditional role of the Irish woman was in the artisan and labouring classes. Her father hired a Mrs Crawford, a mid-fiftyish widow, to cook, clean and supervise the house garden. She lived only three rods down the road. She would arrive every morning, poke the ashes until the fire revived and then spend the day preparing food, sweeping, digging manure into the garden and trying to keep the younger children clean and the twin-ones out of trouble. She said little except to gaunch, and was quick to give the back of her hand to any child who got in her way. Each day looked to her to be her last, for she was cave chested and continually snuffled. She wiped her nose so often that the black shawl she used for that purpose had a long silver streak on it as though it were dyed. At day's end, she would hirple back to her cottage, her passing marked by a diminuendo in the rasping cough that emanated from her person all day long.

From Mrs Crawford Eliza was expected to learn the duties of an Irish woman. She came to dislike them as much as she disliked her teacher. Eliza was unusually strong for a girl and this turned out to be a disadvantage, for Mrs Crawford gave her the hardest physical work to do. First thing in the morning, she was expected to take oaken pails two hundred yards to a fresh-running brook and fetch the water for the day's potato boiling. Then, after completing several small tasks, she was frequently set to querning grain. The querns consisted of two smooth, elliptically shaped stones weighing perhaps fifteen pounds each. One of these was placed on a piece of old cloth that covered a bit of ground and handfuls of grain were placed on top of it. The other stone was then moved over the surface of the lower one, grinding the grain into coarse flour. This was done while kneeling and Eliza's arms and shoulders would soon burn with fatigue. Finally the flour would be gathered up in the cloth and Mrs Crawford would make bread. "Why don't boys have to do this?" Eliza asked the older woman. Her reply was unsatisfactory: "This is the way of the world little girl."

Naturally broadbacked and strong, Eliza was made more fit by demanding exercise. "I can do anything you can do, John Oge!" she boasted and he had to admit that she was right. Anything included besting him in a rough game where they took turns hitting each other as hard as they could on the arm until one of them could no longer stand the pain. Even the winner's arm would be black and blue for days.

When out of parental view, Eliza and John Oge would some-times practise "party fighting." At that time in County Donegal there was bound to be a fight between gangs of men at every fair and on every market day. Sometimes gangs were comprised of males from a single family, at other times of men from a certain townland or parish. The worst fights were between Catholics and Protestants. Cudgels and leaded blackthorn sticks were the most common weapons. John Oge and Eliza made their own set of three-quarter-size cudgels and kept them hid-den under the dung heap at the back of the cottage. With their father busy at his smithery and Mrs Crawford at the town market, they would pull them out, climb over the high wall that protected the gentry desmene from the tenant holdings and there, hidden from sight, stage their mock battles. They took turns being "the papish" and "the prod." They became dextrous in the basic moves – the thrust, parry, body blow, and head smash – and as long as their tempers stayed cool it was a good match and no great danger to their health. At times, however, John Oge would taunt Eliza. "Sure and you're only a wee pau-deen of a girl," at which she would ignite. She would lay into John Oge swiftly and with such fury that he would end up on the ground, dazed. Many times did John Oge resolve never to set her off like that again, and many times was that resolve broken and reforged.

Like most Irish people, the White family not only ate great quantities of potatoes, or praties, as they were called, they also grew them themselves. Potato growing involved much heavy labour and its tasks were shared by the entire family. Each household had its own division of labour. Where the "holding" was large enough to support an entire family, the man of the household did the heaviest work and everyone else assisted. In many households, however, the man was often away working as a "spalpeen," or migrant, labourer in Scotland or England. Then the women and children of the house had to do everything themselves. John White's foundry kept him fully occupied, so Mrs Crawford, Eliza and John Oge planted and harvested three-quarters of an acre of potatoes by themselves.

The amount of sheer brute labour the three of them performed was prodigious. The technique they used involved making "lazy beds" – anything but a lazy way to farm. These were raised ridges composed of sod, dirt and manure. The three workers began by slicing up their small plot in late February on days when there was no frost on the ground, and they kept at this thankless task for two or three hours a day until May. Planting the tubers involved yet more digging. Then the sets had to be covered with loose earth and more manure. Every minute of this job was arduous: there was no way that it could be turned into fun – especially with Mrs Crawford in command. In August and September the team dug out the crop of potatoes with a three-pronged fork. Since John White Sr was a blacksmith Eliza and John Oge each had their own digging fork. They filled basket after basket with new potatoes and took them to a "bing," a shallow pit where they were stored for the winter. Eliza hated potato growing even more than other household tasks. She did not fancy a future for herself that involved such an endless cycle of unrewarding labour. The dread of it led to the most important decision of her life. She decided to talk to her father about the future, and she would be clear about what she wanted.

Thus Eliza stood before her father one December evening when he was damping down his hearth for the night. She chose her moment carefully so that they would be alone.

"Father, I wish to be a blacksmith," she declared in a quiet voice.

John White's first instinct was to laugh – a girl saying that she wanted to learn the foundry trade was like the local rector deciding to become pope! But Eliza's countenance had that preternatural seriousness that one sees now and then in the faces of children. Eliza stood with her hands at her side, a tiny soldier before her commandant.

"Father, I am as strong as John Oge, and he is a year older than me. And I am quick and I work hard and I put in more potatoes and dig even faster than Mrs Crawford, and I..."

"And you are my darling daughter and you would not mind working every day with your grouchy old father." The blacksmith smiled, touched. Intrigued. He had reached the point that many small craftsmen reach – he had more work to do than he could handle by himself, but not enough to hire another man.

"I've always planned on taking John Oge into the craft," he said, almost without hesitation.

"Please, father, think of taking us both in. The two of us would become a full man to you."

The blacksmith reflected. "Well, not a full man, Eliza, maybe half a man." He sat down on a stool near the hearth. His heavy cowhide apron bloused out from him like a medieval breastplate.

"And then you could do what you said you always wanted to do." This was Eliza's best card, the one she had saved to play at just the right moment. "You could set up a spade foundry, like you said, and only make goods for cash money."

That was a shrewd hit. John White did not like being a general blacksmith, getting kicked by bad-tempered horses and being cheated by people who never paid or who brought a dozen eggs as payment for a long day's work. He could see it in his mind's eye: a nicely painted sign over his door, White's Spade Foundry, and farmers and jobbers coming from miles around to buy the best spades in all of Donegal, nay, all of Ulster. Trained as he was to take the Bible seriously, these thoughts put him on guard at once. Could this be the voice of Temptation? Was his own daughter bringing him a message from the Evil One? Was the sin of Pride even now ensnaring him?

"Eliza, what you say makes great sense. But it would be unnatural for the daughter of the house to learn a man's trade. The Bible says that the people of Sodom and Gomorrah were destroyed because men did not act like men, or women as women. Do you not see that, girl?"

Eliza nodded silently. She was close to tears. A lifetime of digging praties, carrying water, grinding flour, making bread stretched out in front of her. She brushed back a strand of hair from her face. She would not cry. She would *not* cry – she had to speak, or all would be lost. "Father," she faltered.

"Yes?" It came to her: fight fire with fire.

"Doesn't the Bible say that God is king of everything? The sky, the heavens? The angels? Everything?"

"Certainly."

"And the Bible says that on earth we should render to the king what is his due?"

"Yes. I've read that passage to you: 'Render unto Caesar what is Caesar's.'"

"And our King, the King of England and Ireland is the head of our land and is Christ's vicar on earth?"

"I have told you that many times." The blacksmith was pleased that his daughter had taken his spiritual lessons to heart, but he was puzzled about where the conversation was leading.

"Well, the king gave a pension to Maggie Dunbar, and therefore it must be right sometimes for women to do men's jobs."

A swift and cunning twist. Maggie Dunbar, who lived in a small cottage just off the old pier of Donegal town, was a local legend. She had served three years as a hand on an oceangoing vessel and for that King William IV had granted her a pension of ten pounds a year, a small fortune. The blacksmith was stunned by Eliza's argument. He needed time to think. "Go away, child. I shall tell you my decision later."

Eliza left the smithery with a gravity worthy of a Roman senator. She had a chance, she knew, but only a chance. If she could have held her breath all evening she would have done so.

Later that evening John Sr strode into the kitchen. "Eliza, John Oge, I have made up my mind." He drew a long clay pipe from his pocket and lighted it. "It seems best to me that two things happen." *Oh no! He's giving John Oge the blacksmithing trade and sentencing me to be a draught mare all my days!* "The first is that you both go to school and that you go together. You are near eight years, John Oge, and Eliza is rising seven, and it is time you learned the ciphering and the reading." *That is good news, but what about learning the trade?* "And, I think that our smithery here should become improved. It should become…" *Oh thank you God! He's going to say the right thing!* "the White Spade Foundry, and you two shall learn the trade when you are not at the schooling. Does that suit you now?"

Eliza could only hug her father in speechless gratitude. She had seen the walls of Jerusalem, and it was a goodly city.

Thus, the twin-ones began their apprenticeship. Their days were long, but it did not matter, especially not to Eliza. Each weekday morning either John Oge or Eliza was the "knocker-up" and had to rise at about 6 and get the other one up. Then together they would prepare the smithery for the day's manufacture. They alternated the job of knocker-up week by week. The task was hard because there was no timepiece in the family. The only way of telling time was to listen for the distant hourly chimes that sounded from the clock tower of the town hall. This was one of Donegal town's sources of civic pride, installed upon the completion of the new courthouse in 1833. The country people were so unacquainted with clocks that it was not unusual to find a knot of them on market day standing around the courthouse looking up at the timepiece and waiting for the hourly peal.

Being knocker-up for the week meant that one apprentice slept lightly, for the worst sin of all was to oversleep and thus lose one or two hours of work in the foundry. In deep winter waking required an immense act of the will. Once the twin-ones were awake, one of them stirred the ashes on the cottage hearth and put on some turfs to get the fire ready for cooking. Then they stumbled outside, half asleep, and entered the smithery. During nine months of the year the smithery was dark early in the morning and all the two helpers had to guide them was the glow of the banked forge fire. Once inside the smithery, one of them worked the bellows to bring the fire back to life, while the other carefully swept away the bank ashes from the top of the fire. The sweeper then used turf and lumps of sea coal to feed the growing blaze. These jobs required more skill than one might think. Working the bellows too hard blew out the precious embers, in which case John Sr had to be called to start a new fire. The bellows were heavy and it was all that either John Oge or Eliza could do to work them for more than a minute without needing a rest. It would take more than half an hour before the fire was burning safely. Next they would awaken their father and then one of them would walk up the road and knock on Mrs Crawford's door. With any luck, the three youngest children would sleep until she arrived. John Oge and Eliza would eat a bit of boiled potato dipped in salt and dress themselves for school.

For John Oge, getting dressed was of little moment. He just put on a pair of school cords, that is, clean store-made corduroy trousers, and a cut-down jacket inherited from his father. For

Eliza, though, school required a major personal transformation. She had to dress like a girl in a shapeless two-layer grey gown, the inner part of which included a long-sleeved blouse. The outer part was sleeveless. To keep warm in cold weather she carried a large shawl. From a distance she would have resembled a small, stout, strongly built matron. Eliza did not mind making the transition to female clothing, but at first it was hard for her to remember that she was expected to act differently when she was dressed as a girl. She could not throw rocks or balance on stone walls the way she would have done if she were wearing her trousers and jacket.

John Oge picked up on the unspoken set of social laws quickly, and he began to treat Eliza differently according to her dress. On occasion he would even carry her books.

There was nothing in Donegal town that could be deemed systematic elementary education. There were two charity schools and two day schools conducted for private profit. For no other reason than that the missioner came around and promised to put the twin-ones in the same class, John White enrolled his children in one of the charity schools run by a red-hot Protestant Bible society. The group running the school was the London Hibernian Society. Its principles were as follows:

> The great body of the Irish wander like sheep, that have no faithful shepherd to lead them. Legendary tales, pilgrimages, penances, superstitions, offerings, priestly domination, the notorious habit of reconciling sanctimonious accents and attitudes with abandoned practices, and all that shocks and disgusts in the mummery of the mass house, cannot fail to fix in mournful sentiment in the heart of every enlightened and pious observer... The hope, therefore, that the Irish will ever be a tranquil and loyal people and still more that piety and virtue will flourish among them, must be built on the anticipated reduction of popery.

Everyday Eliza and John Oge were drilled in the ABCs, they chanted their addition tables and heard screeds about the horrors of the Romish heresy. Exercises in Catholic bashing became increasingly intense as the year went along. Sometimes the

Protestant missioner became so excited that he flailed about with the willow switch that doubled as pointer and instrument of discipline, by accident striking children in the front seats. It was a blessing that the school day was short, only three and a half hours, and that the twin-ones could be home with their father by the time the courthouse clock struck one o'clock in the afternoon.

Upon arrival at home one of them went straight to the bellows while the other was allowed to get a bite to eat. "A blacksmith never leaves his fire," was one of their father's pet phrases. Once he started working in the morning he stayed in the smithery, eating while standing up between jobs. To watch John White Sr at work was to observe a man totally absorbed in his craft. He would hold a piece of metal with a set of tongs, keeping it steady in the clearest, hottest part of the fire. He stared and waited for just the right moment to start hammering, and he was forever telling one child or the other to sprinkle a little water on the fire, then to work the bellows a bit more. He worried constantly about the quality of his coal, sometimes thinking it was too fine and so needed more clinker, other times that it had too much dirt and would need the clinkers removed. Finally the rectangular piece of metal that he was working would be the right temperature and he would beckon whichever child was free to bring him his hammer. Then he would shape the piece into a loy or a spade.

Throughout Great Britain, and in the Belfast region of Ireland, spades and loys were being stamped out by large, hydraulically tripped hammers. But John White did a better job and made more money his way. To the modern eye one spade looks pretty much like another, but in nineteenth century Ireland there were hundreds of combinations of shape, handle type and foot rest. These all depended on what the farmer intended to do with the implement – plant potatoes, cut turf, set hedging – and they also varied to accommodate the height, weight, arm strength and personal preferences of the individual farmer. John White made a loy or a spade to fit each farmer in the same way that good tailor makes a suit to fit his customer. "Give people what they want and you'll never be poor," he told his two apprentices. Avoiding poverty was his own highest ambition: he never made any suggestion about how to become rich.

For Eliza and John Oge the best moment in the manufacture of a spade was the very last. One of them was sent out to select three or four well-seasoned handles. These were stored in the same midden where the twin-ones had once kept their small cudgels. Their father tested each one and finally selected the right one to attach to the blade. He heated a piece of metal about six inches square until it was red hot. Then welded it to the blade by using his hammer. Wielding tongs and hammer with great dexterity he next turned the sides of this piece inward until they joined, thus forming a sleeve to take the handle. This was quick work, and magical, but then came the drama. The selected handle was shoved into the sleeve and quickly, to prevent it from burning, the now-completed implement was thrust into a barrel of water. It made a demonic hiss upon hitting the water. For the sheer sensation of it John White liked to withdraw the steaming spade and submerge it again and again. "Will we ever be able to do that, Father?" Eliza wanted to know. "Someday you will be able to do everything," he assured her.

After less than a year in school, the twin-ones' education took a turn. The missioner for the London Hibernian Society lost his grip. John Oge and Eliza watched with a mixture of fear and fascination as each day he grew more agitated, redder in the face and more uncontrolled in his flailing with the willow stick. He talked about the damnable superstitions, the hideous errors and the perversions of thought that existed in the very bowels of Romanism. Some of his stories about the way priests and bishops kept women chained in convents were grotesquely interesting, but much of what he said did not make sense. He had developed a complicated theory that the number 666 (the code for the Antichrist) was the number representing the Protestant bishop of Londonderry.

"Are there mad things in this world for a reason, Father?" Eliza asked one night.

John White thought she was referring to the extraordinary number of mad dogs that roamed the Irish countryside. "God has a purpose for everything," he replied.

"But what should we do with them, when we encounter one?"

"Well, don't be afraid, either of you." The blacksmith knew that children often heard their elders talking about feral cats or wild dogs that descended into a cottage at night through the smoke hole and devoured every morsel they could find. If discovered, they bit and clawed ferociously. "If you have a graip handy" – he nodded in the direction of a three-pronged potato fork, "– then stick it into the beast."

"Even a mad human?"

The blacksmith roared with laughter. "Heavens, no! If you did that every time you meet a mad one, we'd have no travellers left!" Behind his amusement was the sad fact that the number of demented or starving persons who tramped the roads of Ireland was large and growing. "Sure, all the poor creatures do is grin and wave a bit and look round and talk strange, and chew on things and hurt no one."

"It's the chewing on things that the master does at the school," John Oge pointed out.

"Does he now?"

"Most often when he talks about the pope of Rome and the Antichrist, he puts his willow stick in his mouth and gnashes away at it. It's the only way he can find words."

"They say that Finn McCool, the Scotch giant, obtained wisdom by biting on his thumb, so maybe that's what your master is doing."

"No. We think he is mad," Eliza said. "And we are frighted, and do not want to go back there."

John White visited the Hibernian missioner the next day. He soon concluded that the man was no more able to teach than were the sad raveners of the countryside. With no ceremony, he told the missioner that he was removing his children from the school and that he wanted the few pence back that he had put into fees and the book fund. The master was not so far lost to reality that he could ignore a blacksmith's massive forearms. He pushed a handful of coppers into White's hand. "Go, go, go," he babbled. As the twin-ones and their father went out the door the missioner began scourging himself on the arms and legs with his willow switch in an attempt to drive away the demons inhabiting him.

Good fortune came from this. Their father found the twin-ones a place in a charity school supported by Mrs John Hamilton, the wife of the only resident gentleman in the parish. By present-day standards, the children's new school was run with severe discipline – any infraction of a score of rules, or even a bad attitude, earned strokes on the hand with a metal-edged measuring stick – but, paradoxically, its curriculum was wonderfully free form. The mistress in charge was a Miss Babcock, about thirty, from Carrickfergus, County Antrim, where her parents were middling merchants. She was the first middle-class woman with whom most of the pupils were closely acquainted, and for the girls, Eliza included, she was a model to be imitated. Eliza took to tossing her head impetuously when vexed, just as Miss Babcock did, and like her mistress would drum her fingers when impatient. John Oge teased her about this.

Because the mistress had only to please her patron, Mrs Hamilton, the children's lessons were eccentric, but their education admirable. Miss Babcock did not much believe in numbers. Calculations of profit, she said, were for the venal of this earth, and her patroness agreed. Instead of ciphering, the school taught reading, reading and more reading. When the children were not reading something themselves, Miss Babcock was reading something to them. She was partial to those of the ancient classics that emphasized the virtues of loyalty and trust. The children were made to memorize Greek and Latin tags, so that although they knew neither language, they could throw out an appropriate quotation as if they had been taught at home by the finest of private tutors. The school was intended to provide only three years of schooling, but, because of the unusual curriculum, by the end of her second year Eliza was reading books reserved for the fifth standard in government schools. John Oge did less well, but then he was slightly better than Eliza at blacksmithing.

In the first half of the nineteenth century, reading expanded horizons in the same way that sailing ships changed the limits and boundaries of the known world. Eliza read voraciously. She still loved being an apprentice to her father, but now in the evening she bent over the cottage fire and read whatever item of print she was able to put her hands on. John Oge was not so keen, so they divided their labour: Eliza would read some-thing and pass on the gist of it to her brother, who was quite content to ruminate on what he was told. In exchange, he kept the younger boys from interrupting their sister.

If the books that circulated in County Donegal, tattered and without their covers, had been collected, one would have been struck by how unimproving most of them were. In addition to the Bible and the pamphlets of various Protestant proselytizing societies, one ran accross such as volumes *The History of the Seven Champions of Christendom*, Ovid's *Art of Love* and a work of the fisticuffs champion, Mendoza, the *New System of Boxing*.

As a word-hungry ten-year-old, Eliza's favourite book was a battered copy of *A General History of the Robberies and Murders of the Most Notorious Pyrates*. When she read parts of it aloud to John Oge, even her father listened intently. This volume, first published under the name of Captain Charles Johnson in 1724, had gone through several printings. In fact, it was by one of the greatest journalists of the English language, Daniel Defoe. Most of its tales were gripping and factually accurate. For some-one like Eliza, living in a seaside town and familiar with the details of sailing ships and harbour life, the volume was not history but an evocation of possibility.

There were two tales in Defoe's masterpiece that Eliza read aloud several times to her family, "The Life of Mary Read" and "The Life of Anne Bonny." These warrant reflection. Both Mary Read and Anne Bonny were raised as boys, both were sexually attractive to men, both had bad luck with their men, both turned to pirating, and though they dressed and acted like men, both eventually bore children.

Eliza's edition of the book included two engravings by Dutch artists. One of these showed Mary Read in trousers, sword in hand, battle ax at her waist, blouse open wide enough to reveal small, feminine breasts. Anne Bonny was more stylish. In addi-tion to her trousers and small ax she wore a rakish hat over her long curls. Her arm was extended as she aimed a pistol and her shirtwaist was open so that her breasts were plainly visible. When Eliza looked at these engravings, especially the one of Anne Bonny, she felt a strange sensation in her body. Her heart palpitated, and she flushed and had to look away in order to catch her breath.

Mary Read

At about the same time, Eliza came across a volume by two female writers whose work had an androgynous quality that echoed the world view, if not the violence, of Defoe's female pirates. Miss Babcock, the schoolmistress, loaned Eliza *The Little Prisoner, or, Passion and Patience; and Amendment, or Charles Grant and His Sister,* put out by the London firm of Dean in 1828. The story itself is of no real consequence, but the way the authors reject conventions of male strength and female passivity is noteworthy. In this book the male figures become effective only to the extent they are feminized, and the females are the stronger and more sensible of the sexes. In the copy that Eliza was lent, there was no indication of author save a coy statement on the title page, "By the author of *Hugh Latimer* and *Disobedience.*" The two authors were Susanna Strickland and one of her sisters, Elizabeth. Susanna would continue writing along the same lines after she married a man named Moodie and moved to the Canadas.

Indeed, another of Eliza's favourite books, *The Backwoods of Canada,* was by a third Strickland sister, Catherine, but because she wrote under her married name, Catherine Parr Traill, the family connection went unnoticed. This volume, published in 1836 as part of a series, the Library of Entertaining Knowledge, was directed to the wives and daughters of emigrants of the higher class, so for Eliza it was as much a dream book as the tale of Gil Blas. While reading it, Eliza would pretend that she was Miss Babcock and that she owned several blouses with frilly fronts. She assimilated the earnest advice on how to overcome the scarcity of adequate servants in the Canadian backwoods. John Oge, when parts were read aloud to him, preferred the sections on clearing the land and on the array of tools required to take up farming in the New World.

"Father, do they use spades very much in Upper Canada?" John Oge said after Eliza had read a section on crop rotation.

John White Sr rarely answered a question quickly. He thought about this one for a time. Finally he pronounced, "But of course, lad. The spade is like a spoon: a man can't get through life without using it."

"Well, then, have you ever thought that we might take the White Spade Foundry to some place where life is easier ?" John Oge rarely carried a line of thought very far, but when he did it was worth hearing; Eliza listened closely.

"I haven't done that; nay, son, and that's God's truth." An uneasy silence followed. Then the blacksmith blurted out, "Och, lad, I told a lie, God forgive me. But aye, I have thought of crossing the ocean many times, so I have."

"Would we have money to do it, Father?"

"Oh, yes. We're not poor, you know." That sounded hollow. "I mean to say, thanks be to the great God, not like the poor wretches on yon corner. We have our wee mite."

By yon corner John White was referring to an edifice that had just been completed nearby, the Donegal Union Workhouse. It was an imposing structure, walled like a prison and divided into two sharply demarcated wings. Its construction had at first fascinated the locals, but in 1842, completed, it became a source of woe to the poor and a constant reminder to everyone else that a man could never rise far above the ruck. Unlike England, Ireland had never had a poor law – that is, a law to distribute the burden of caring for the poor. In the late 1830s high-principled, severe and naive English experts convinced the Dublin administration that the country required a poor law on the English pattern. This, they maintained, would be an infinite improvement over the existing situation where Irish poor were taken care of by Irish poor. Thus across Ireland a grid of "poor law unions" was established. The one serving Donegal town was instituted in November 1840. When the workhouse was completed, husbands and wives were separated from each other as a condition of receiving food and shelter. Many elderly couples never saw each other again. Infant children were allowed to remain with their mothers, but when they reached school age they were segregated and often lost contact with their families forever.

All this gnawed at John White. "Betimes I think we live in the land God gave to Cain," he said, staring into the fire. "Perhaps life like this is God's will; that's what I often think. But then I remember that Jehovah tested the chosen people before bringing them to the promised land."

"The promised land," Eliza murmured, and went back to reading about the backwoods of Canada.

ॐ

"An outing for the less fortunate" was the way Mrs Hamilton
described a party she gave for the children of her charity school
each year on All-Saints' Eve. "We will have them brought to
the estate by transport, and they shall have cakes and tea and
learn to act as if brought up to such graces." Thus she had
informed Miss Babcock, and for weeks before the event the
schoolmistress had prepped the children on how to hold a cup
and saucer, to take only one cake from the tray no matter how
much they were tempted to take a handful, to say thank-you
and to excuse themselves when it came time to leave. When
the big day finally arrived, every wheel-cart in town was hired
out to ferry the children to the estate. Even a few wheelless
slipes – two poles tied to a donkey with a seat lashed across
the poles, the ends of which trailed along the ground – were
pressed into service.

The Hamilton family seat had originally been about four miles
south of Donegal town, within a mile of the small desolate town
of Ballintra. The family mansion was called Brownhall. An
observer noted in 1800 that "dismall as the little town of Ballintra
is, more dismall and a great deal more gloomy, particularly on
the south and east, is the country which surrounds this mansion." The young John Hamilton, unable to bear such aesthetic
oppression, endeavoured to build one of Ireland's most unusual
estates. He took over an island of about six acres two miles
south of Donegal town and after stabilizing the shoreline built
an impressive mansion. It cost three thousand, five hundred
pounds and was completed in 1828. The entire island was land-
scaped, some of it as a rustic glade, the rest with fruit and
flowering trees. A small formal garden graced the main entrance
hall. Renamed St. Ernan's, the island estate combined magnif-
icent sea views with enviable privacy for its occupants.

The children had heard to this place, but few locals had ever
been permitted across the narrow isthmus that was the island's
entrance. Carts and slipes pulled up the isthmus and their
passengers debouched. The children stood about in complete
silence, afraid to talk or move until Miss Babcock formed them
into a single line and marched them across to the island. The

full panoply of the estate and its gardens made an impression upon Eliza that remained vivid for the rest of her life. She always described it in the same way. Having read recently a romantic history of the crusades against Islam, she used that vocabulary: "I thought that I was a Mussallim and that I had died and gone to paradise."

The rich have always been inhabitants of a different land than the poor, so Eliza's explaining how she felt in terms borrowed from an alien culture is not surprising. Nothing of any consequence occurred at the party, but the encounter with the other-world of the rich tied itself emotionally to another experience, and together these taught Eliza to build bridges from the world of reality to other, better lands.

This second event also was occasioned by the improving propensities of Mrs Hamilton and her lieutenant Miss Babcock. As Christmas approached Mrs Hamilton gave the schoolmistress three shillings, telling her to "buy some good chapbooks and do the Christmas rhyming properly this year." The rhymings were folk plays, sometimes called the Christmas mummery, and they were common throughout the British Isles during Advent. In the Protestant parts of Ulster there was a strong local variant, plays that reenacted not the Christmas story specifically but rather the death and revival cycles whose origins harkened back to the original Indo-European celebration of the winter solstice.

A typical play was something of a shambles. The presenter of a group of mummers, eight to fourteen in number, knocked at the door of a farmhouse or town lodging and, when granted admission, called forth the first two players, Prince George and the "Turkey champion." (This was Ulster dialect for *Turkish* champion.) Prince George and the Turkey champion were dressed in military gear. With swords in hand they fought until the latter was mortally wounded. Thereupon the Turkey champion's mother entered. She called a doctor, who would miraculously raise her son from death. The dramatic line ran wild after that. According to local tastes, there might be brief appearances by Cromwell, St Patrick and Beelzebub. This was all done in rhyme and the entire performance took from five to ten minutes. At the end everyone in the cast joined hands and sang a Christmas carol while the presenter collected a few coins from the host.

Mrs Hamilton did not approve of the rowdy, ad lib nature of these performances, nor of children cadging coins. Her idea was to replace the slapdash affair with a well-run, traditional version of the play, and she thought all gratuities should go to the support of her charity school. So from a bookseller in Derry Miss Babcock ordered half a dozen chapbooks of a mummers' play. These had been typeset in Belfast during the Napoleonic Wars and were nothing if not traditional. All the parts were defined carefully, and woodcuts illustrated how each player should be costumed. Miss Babcock found that casting, not costume, was the problem. In the traditional mummers' play (as in the formal theatre until comparatively recent times), all the parts were taken by males. This did not bother Miss Babcock – the girls could sew the costumes and the boys play the parts – but it upset Eliza McCormack White. She was polite but insistent.

"Please, ma'am, I wish to be the Mussalim, the Turkey champion." Miss Babcock said no. Next day Eliza returned to the subject. "Please, ma'am, I am not being bold. But I should be the Turkey champion from Turkeyland. I am just as good with a sword as any boy and I can act the dying champion better than any of them." Miss Babcock dismissed her. The following day, Eliza put the same case to the mistress, and this time Miss Babcock had her hold out her hand for five strokes of the measuring stick. Eliza repeated the request the next day. Miss Babcock realized that either she would have to give Eliza strokes every day or give in.

"All right, Eliza. Let us see how you die." The mistress used her measuring stick to wound Eliza as the knight would do in the mumming. Eliza slithered to the ground in a death rattle so convincing that it brought the pupils in the back of the room out of their seats.

So, dressed in the closest thing to Saracen armour and weaponry that Donegal town could produce, Eliza played a brief but triumphant season as the Turkey champion. "I'll cut you and slash you and then send you back to Turkey," she railed at Prince George. "And I'll have them mince you and bake you in an oven. And after I have done, I'll fight every champion in Christendom." It was generally agreed upon by all observers that the ensuing sword fight was the most energetic and realistic they had yet seen in mumming, and some of the audience had been watching these plays since the start of the Napoleonic Wars.

All too soon, Eliza's triumph was over. But in the twilight moments before she fell asleep, she would play her part over and over. She remembered every word of the play, every comment that various householders had made, and especially the words of the rector of Donegal who, when the mumming was put on in the large drawing room of the Glebe House, adjudged, "That young White girl is the best Turkey champion I have ever seen. Decidedly better than any lad."

Anne Bonny

3

Hard Roads

"Mrs Crawford, I need to talk to you." This was a suprise, for ever since Eliza had been permitted to join John Oge in a blacksmithing apprenticeship she and the older woman had kept a cool distance from each other. Mrs Crawford did not approve of girls who mitched off their rightful woman's work, and for her part Eliza wanted nothing to do with a world of female drones. "If you could come outside, I would like to talk to you alone." Eliza's face indicated that she was troubled, and the older woman relented.

"Now, what is it you have on your tongue that can't be said inside?" They were in the potato garden and no one was near.

"Ma'am, I'm bleeding, and I don't know what to do about it."

Mrs Crawford understood immediately. "Och, and you so

young." In the last century, the onset of menses was about age fifteen. In places where food was scarce it was not unusual for puberty to be delayed until ages seventeen or eighteen. Eliza was just ten.

Though she resented Eliza's refusal to take up female occupations, Mrs Crawford reflected that what with the child's mother dead, it was up to her to teach Eliza some important things about life. Thus, she gave a decisive flap to her apron and said firmly, "You and I will have to find the herb woman."

Eliza had heard the term before but she had never set eyes on this elusive person. In Donegal the herb woman was a familiar figure to the women of the countryside, but she would have been virtually unknown to the male population except by way of a few vague references that men might occasionally hear from their wives. This crucial figure in the social fabric has gone almost totally unnoticed by historians of Ireland. An herb woman existed in every rural district. She roamed the fields collecting plants and shrubs to be used in medicines. She processed them herself and used them to heal women, girls of all ages, and infant boys. Some herb women were said to go so far as to use foxglove and deadly nightshade. Other practitioners would even set broken bones using plaster or assist at childbirth. In rural Donegal the herb woman did for young girls what the shaman did for boys of various Siberian and Amerindian tribes at the onset of puberty: she would conduct a ritual marking adulthood and explain to them what was happening to their bodies. The herb woman Mrs Crawford contacted for Eliza was a Catholic. Eliza commented on this right away. "Shush, little girl," Mrs Crawford retorted. "All the herb women and spae wives are Roman. It's just the way things are." This fact did not keep the wives and daughters of Protestant labourers and artisans from visiting herb women. Some bonds run deeper than the divisions of sectarianism.

With a touch of pride, Mrs Crawford told Eliza that the herb woman in question was "one of the old sort." This meant that she believed in the use of smoke holes. Smoke holes were rock-lined caverns often cut into a hillside and large enough to hold a full-grown adult. An adjoining smaller chamber would house a turf fire. In well-built smoke holes the heat alone would seep into the main cavern. In less well-constructed ones large amounts of smoke filtered in as well. The remains of these constructions are found in hundreds of places in the mountain districts of Ireland. The usual local explanation is that they were used to store illicit whiskey (a frequent secondary use) or that they were hiding places for Catholic priests in penal times (possible but improbable). Once abandoned, smoke holes would sometimes be used as chambers where old men soaked the rheumatism out of their bones. Their prime function, however, was half ritual, half medicinal, and limited to women. At important times in a woman's life – at menarche, before marriage or, forty days after a miscarriage or still birth – three or four women would set the smoke hole working, and the woman in need would voluntarily be imprisoned for several hours. This usually was done under the supervision of an herb woman. The head of the participant poked out of the cavern. The remainder of the opening was packed with boughs. This allowed smoke to filter out but kept most of the heat inside. If an herb woman was present, she placed aromatic and healing herbs in the cavern. The practice was a form of ritual purification. It was also a sensible method of cleansing the body and helping someone to relax.

Because of Irish inhibitions about adults viewing one another's naked bodies, Eliza went into the cavern wearing a heavy, full-length dress that she left on during the entire process. She entered the cavern without much enthusiasm, but after becoming accustomed to the heat she began to enjoy it. As she sweated away, the herb woman and her helpers, including Mrs Crawford, sat in a half-circle facing Eliza and told her things that a girl should know as her body grew into womanhood. Hours later she was finally taken out. Her attendants left a clean, dry shift and a shawl on the ground and moved a small distance away, making a point of looking away as she dressed. Light headed, Eliza had to sit on a large stone until the vapours cleared. This too was part of the process: anyone who went through this cleansing was supposed to feel different in mind as well as in body.

The ritual at the smoke hole ratified a limited but important alliance between Eliza and Mrs Crawford. Although Eliza stuck steadfastly to her blacksmith's apprenticeship and refused to accept final responsibility for many of the traditional female household tasks, she and the older woman made a point of having a chat each day. Sometimes it was over a cup of tea; at other times Eliza walked Mrs Crawford back to her little cottage. In bits and pieces, Mrs Crawford continued Eliza's education in female secrets. Most of these were medical, for in the Irish household healing was delegated to women. Thus Eliza learned the cure for scrofula: a potato was cut into nine pieces, wrapped into a bundle and thrown over the left shoulder of the sufferer. Boils were treated by digging up the roots of orange lilies ("a good Protestant cure, this," Mrs Crawford noted) and boiling them in water until the roots were liquefied. The sufferer fasted overnight and ate two teaspoons of the jelly at hourly intervals until cured. Ringworm was cured by burning the waste material from scutched flax and rubbing it around the offending patch. Women in labour were given wasted barley. This later became the recognized medicine Ergot of Rye. The whooping cough could be cured by ferret's milk. Half the female medical secrets were white magic, half were sound medical practice.

This female knowledge Eliza did not share with her brother, but he seemed unbothered by this. John Oge was developing a rocklike placidity that was different from their father's Bible-browed seriousness. This permitted John Oge and Eliza to continue to work side by side without adolescent bickering. In contrast to Eliza, John Oge slid into puberty with an accepting bemusement. One day he noticed some black hairs growing out of his groin. He thought this was interesting, but nothing to worry about. He had heard that this happened. From a distance, Eliza and John Oge were still the twin-ones. In their mid-teens they reached their full height of about five foot nine. Each had dark hair and aquiline features. John Oge's face was a bit fuller than his sister's. For a girl, Eliza had broad shoulders. Her breasts were not prominent, and seeing her and John Oge in the foundry, dressed similarly, one had to look carefully to be sure which one was which.

Each day they worked alongside their father. Though never one to show much emotion, John White was happy to have his children with him. The younger boys were coming along fine, but it was the twin-ones he now treasured. They had progressed far in their training and were permitted to do every job save the final one of setting the handle of the loy or spade into its socket. Working together, Eliza and John Oge could beat the molten ingots of pig-iron into the requisite shape. They had good artisans' hands and, for their age, strong forearms. Heavy daily exercise had seen to that.

One of the great rewards of the successful progress of their apprenticeship was that the twin-ones were allowed to join their father as he made journeys, two or three times a year, to buy materials or deliver finished goods. These trips covered no more than thirty or forty Irish miles, but they were as enthralling to the young apprentices as if they had been circumnavigations of the globe.

The first such trip had occurred in August 1842, when Eliza was ten and John Oge eleven. This journey assumed the shape of a triangle, the first leg of which ran for a few miles along the seashore south of Donegal town. The second leg turned south and headed easterly over the mountains to Lough Erne. John White Sr rented a donkey and a two-wheeled cart from a local drover, and this he filled with spades for farmers living along the lough's banks. Mrs Crawford prepared a hamper of praties, hard bread, cheese and some salt fish for the journey. The three travellers each had a change of clothes. These, and some blankets for sleeping, were wrapped tightly and kept dry in a piece of old canvas that had floated ashore on the sea coast and been hawked at the town market.

The distance to lower Lough Erne was only ten miles as the crow flies, but the track was twisted and rutted and in places it rose five hundred feet above sea level. Then it ran through a lunar landscape devoid of any vegetation more than six inches high and which, even in midsummer, was brown and purple rather than green. In those days before the Great Famine even this unpromising landscape was populated. At furlong intervals along the road there were tiny cottages, usually made of mud, each the benchmark of yet another family trying to scratch a living out of bog and rock.

After delivering the load of loys and spades to a jobber at Pettigoe, John White led his little troop due north. This was the part of the trip that the twin-ones were excited about. On the way to a small forest plantation of mountain ash and hill oak, it led past Lough Derg.

Lough Derg was one of the focal points of popular Catholicism in Ulster, much to the embarrassment of church authorities. The lough had an island called St. Patrick's Purgatory, two chapels, a range of cabins and various stone configurations around which pilgrims moved on their knees. The full devotion consisted of a nine-day fast broken only by oatmeal and water once a day. For at least one night the pilgrim was expected to sleep on one of the rock formations known as the saint's bed. All this was well known not only to Catholics but also to the Protestants of Donegal, not least because William Carleton, the premier Irish novelist of the century, described the place in "The Lough Derg Pilgrim," his first published piece. This appeared in 1828 in an evangelical Anglican periodical called *The Christian Examiner and Church of Ireland Magazine*. Copies of that issue were carefully preserved by Donegal Protestants. Eliza had been loaned a copy by Mrs Crawford and had read the story aloud to the family.

As Protestants, the White trio had no intention of going to the holy island, but they were covertly excited by the thought of the place. Their excitement was heightened by the numbers of people on the same path from Pettigoe to Lough Derg. Save the Whites, all seemed to be pilgrims. Most were barefoot and some repeated prayers and devotions as they trudged along. This day was one of the saints' days most favoured by Ulster Catholics, the Feast of the Assumption of the Blessed Virgin Mary. Instead of staying the night at the ferry station, where most of the pilgrims rested before being rowed to the island early in the morning to start their devotions, the Whites pressed further up the lough to the place they would purchase their staves. That night, looking out towards the saint's island, they saw what John White always afterward called a sign. Instead of the various flickering fires of encamped pilgrims, they watched a line of light. At first it was broken but gradually it grew in strength and became a snake of fire. One of the hovels on the island that housed pilgrims had caught fire and the flames were jumping from the thatch of one building to another. The night was calm and the flames reflected off the surface of the lake. Next morning as news of the catastrophe spread through the neighbourhood, John White Sr added his own opinion. "This is a judgment on those who maintain heathen practices and hold up false gods. Let us each take heed," he said, looking sternly at his helpers.

For Eliza the main effect of all this was to awaken a curiosity about the difference was between "us and the papishes." It occupied her and her father on the arduous westward part of their journey, the final leg across the mountains north of Lough Derg. John Oge listened contentedly; he would as soon talk of blacksmithing, but if religion was what his father and sister were interested in, he did not mind. Thus began a series of intermittent tutorials that lasted three or four years in which John White tried to explain the differences between Protestantism and Catholicism to his daughter. He talked about the views the papishes and the Reformed Church had of the scriptures, of the antiBiblical authority claimed by the bishop of Rome (he could not bring himself to say the word *pope*) and of the graven images he said the Catholics worshiped, like Philistines bowing down before their heathen idols. But these were not the things that most interested Eliza. She wanted to know how Protestants and Catholics acted differently in everyday life, and how they thought about everyday things. In these concerns Eliza was not unusual; all of Irish society shared that preoccupation. After all, when two groups are as similar as Irish Catholics and Irish Protestants, it is only natural that they spend a lot of time explaining to themselves just how different they really are.

"Take the matter of colours," John White pointed out one evening.

"Colours?"

"Yes, to be sure." The blacksmith waited portentously. These sessions of explaining Protestant-Catholic differences in mores usually took a question-and-answer form. He liked to be drawn out.

"Which colours are Protestant and which are Catholic?" Eliza already knew the answer, but the explanation was bound to be of interest.

"Our first colour is orange. You know from your lesson books that this is because King William of Orange saved us from the popish tyranny of King James."

"Are you an Orangeman, father?" Eliza asked. She knew that he was. It was the one thing she could not get him to discuss.

"We don't talk about that, Eliza, now that the government has made the Orange lodge illegal." He softened. "Some day, dear child, I will tell you all about it. For the moment stick to your first question: What is the other Protestant colour?"

"Blue, of course."

"Correct. As in 'True Blue,' when someone is trustworthy and faithful to the cause. Blue is the official colour of Ireland – though heaven knows we don't see much of it these days, now that we're part of the Union of Great Britain and Ireland. Still, that's why a true Protestant will be seen with orange and blue ribbons; that's reminding us that William of Orange protected us from Popery and saved the kingdom of Ireland." This lore imprinted itself on Eliza, and in her later life in Canada, she was one of the few people to understand fully why the Tory Party adopted and maintained blue as its official colour – because the backbone of the Conservative party was composed of True Blue Irish Protestants.

"And the Papishes favour the colour green", her father continued. "Not all of them, mind you. Some go for black. But when the troubles come, when there is a real party fight, you'll find most of your heathen with shamrock-green ribbons on their sleeves or trailing from their cobeens."

"Are those really important, Father, those differences in colours?"

"In truth, yes, lass. Things like colours make all the difference in the world." That was his final judgement.

Another night he opened a discussion with, "And, then, take history." He was still in his leather blacksmith's apron and he gave it a smack to assure that he had his helpers' attention. It was as effective as if he had banged a gavel. "Everything the Papishes think was a defeat – Aughrim, Derry, the Boyne – we say was a victory. That means they think history works differently than we know it does."

The puzzled look on the faces of Eliza and John Oge told him he was being too vague, so he started again. "Do you mind that anchor in the harbour?"

John Oge made one of his rare contributions. "The huge one, the one that's covered with mud except only when the tide is way out? The one no boat or winch can raise up?"

His father nodded. "Now, that anchor came from a French ship sailed by French atheists and republicans in 1798. The vessel came to the harbour after a French general named Humbert tried to raise the Papishes of Connaught and Ulster against their rightful king. The Papishes and the republicans! A rum bunch, that. Of course they got nowhere. The great man-of-war tried to pull into Donegal harbour to take off some retreating French troops, or no, maybe it was to land new ones; but anyroad, the Frenchies sailed so badly that they grounded on the mud-flats and could get off only by cutting away that massive anchor."

"But what do the Papishes think about it?"

"Och, they have ballads about the sad day that Donegal town was not freed, and they say the day will come when this country will be all theirs and when all 'hereticks' – that's us, children – will be swinging on a gibbet."

Everyday Irish Protestants and Catholics had a remarkable knowledge of Ireland's history; it was not the facts about which they disagreed so much as what the facts meant. John White Sr knew a great deal about what had happened during that seismic episode in Irish history, the 1798 Rising. He knew about events in the west of Ireland and about what happened in Antrim and Wexford as well. Both Protestant and Catholic versions of the uprising agreed that many of the Protestants of County Antrim had been in favour of revolution, of throwing off the crown, and of forming some sort of radical democracy. In local Celtic mythology the failure of the Antrim rising was a tragedy. To John White and his fellow Donegal Protestants, the Antrim rising was a joke, something to be ridiculed. The blacksmith had a party-piece that he could be cajoled into performing at a *ceilidh* or at some other homely gathering. In broad lowlands Scots he would recite "Donegore Hill" by the County Antrim weaver-poet, James Orr. This piece told of the cowardice of the Antrim Presbyterians who started out to be revolutionaries. They were not very stern stuff to begin with:

> Some melted lead – some saw'd deal-boards –
> Some hade, like hens, in byre-neuks.

But many of them went off wearing cockades of green. Along the way they thought better of it, and individuals began to slip off, usually under the guise of having to urinate:

> Some letting on their burn to make,
> The rear-guard, goadin', hasten'd

The blacksmith, forgetting his usual self-restraint, loved to describe how even those who made it to the battle site soon broke and ran:

> The camp's brak up. Owre braes, an' bogs,
> The patriots seek their sections;
> Arms, ammunition, bread-bags, brogues,
> Lye skail'd in a' directions.

It was a long poem, fourteen stanzas, and when the blacksmith was done everyone clapped hands and asked him to repeat two or three favourite verses. Eliza learned the poem by heart, and John Oge stirred himself enough to commit three or four of the best stanzas to memory.

John White had an Orange friend in Ballintra, a great man for the books, and from him he borrowed two histories of 1798 to help his children understand why they and the Papishes could never be at peace. One of these was written by a ranking Orangeman, Sir Richard Musgrave. *Memoirs of the Different Rebellions in Ireland, from the Arrival of the English* was nothing less than a two-volume chronicle of Catholic perfidy from earliest times onward. The other was George Taylor's *History of the Rise, Progress, Cruelties, and Suppression of the Rebellion in the County of Wexford in the Year 1798*, and it was explicit and exploitive in its depiction of violence. Both books had the cruel intoxicating power that hate literature shares with great art – the ability to stir the passions. Two episodes in these volumes were so deftly presented that upon first reading, they gave Eliza a physical sensation half of nausea, half of sexual excitement. On a second reading, her feelings gave way to a resolve never to surrender to the Popish savages, not an inch. One episode concerned the events on Wexford town bridge in 1798, the other described the atrocities at Scullabogue barn. In the former instance Catholic rebels, temporarily in control of Wexford, took to tossing unarmed noncombatants about on upraised pikes for the sheer joy of watching them suffer. In the latter, 184 Protestant men, women and children were burned alive in a barn, the charnal carnival being a source of great merriment for their Catholic captors. These reports were true, but in presenting them out of context, and as part of a Catholic conspiracy rather than as isolated incidents of a civil war in which neither side had control of its lunatic elements, the Musgrave and Taylor works, like the great body of hate literature that poisons Irish history, helped build up that hard xylem of animosity that seems so permanently impervious to gentling.

Once a year John White Sr made a journey to the wild northwest coast of Donegal. Three times John Oge and Eliza made the journey with him, and each time they were more amazed at what they saw. This was the world of Gweedore, and it was as exotic to visitors from the towns of Ireland as the Pacific islands were to contemporary English travellers. The area was beautiful, undeniably, but more strange than beautiful. Gweedore was the name of a seaside hamlet and also of a district that ran from the coast to barren mountains over 14 hundred feet high just south of the Bloody Foreland. The lowland community was packed together like sheep in a fold – over four hundred people per square mile – and every inch of ground was cultivated. It was a place of great poverty. After one particularly stormy winter, a contemporary observer reported that many of the people had only one meal a day and that there was so little food for the cattle and sheep that the beasts were dying of starvation. Some of the farms were so impoverished that their owners cultivated them with only a rake as an implement, spades being too expensive. "This is the way all Irish people lived before British laws and the Protestant religion lifted them up," the blacksmith told his children.

Gweedore was indeed the last great outpost of the Celtic system of land ownership. Even as the Whites visited it the system was crumbling. The people lived together in a great sprawling village rather than on individual farmsteads, and each day they walked out to their holdings. Until recently they had operated on the ancient system – land was a communal rather than an individual trust. Outside the villages it was divided into "rigs," long strips, of which each farmer had a dozen or more scattered throughout the neighbourhood. With this system – usually called rundale by scholars – quarrels were frequent and improving farming methods was virtually impossible, for any such changes required communal consent. The land on the hillside, too rugged for cultivation, was held in common, and everyone had a specific number of cattle or sheep that could be pastured there. Many of the locals had two houses: they spent the summer in the mountains with their animals and the winter on the seaside below.

John White cannot be blamed for failing to see the awesome integrity of these arrangements. This was a social and economic arrangement that had survived since before the time of Christ. All he saw was manifest poverty. Therefore he taught Eliza and John Oge to associate Roman Catholicism first with poverty and then with a stubborn refusal to make changes that would directly improve the community's standard of living. "These people would rather be poor than change their ways," he told the twin-ones. "That's because they are the slaves of Rome, and once a man is a slave he never thinks for himself."

Gweedore, however, was changing fast, and change was why the three Whites were there. In 1838 Lord George Hill had bought about thirty square miles of this hostile land and set about improving it. The people were so poor that the previous landlord had not even bothered to collect rents. Seriously committed to improving both the lot of the people and his own rent roll, Hill rearranged everything on his estates. The wee parcels of land were rezoned so that farms had consolidated holdings. With less success, Lord George tried to break up the clusters of houses. Most inhabitants resisted moving to their new land-holdings. Still, a certain prosperity began. In 1842 an inn was put up at Lord George's order, part of his plan to introduce outside commerce to the area. "You can see what a bit of honest labour and sound vision can do," the blacksmith adjudged. Eliza and John Oge were dazzled by the prospect of staying in a hotel for the first time in their lives.

Eliza and John Oge first saw Gweedore in 1843. Recently it had been opened to the wider world by road. So rare were strangers that the local inhabitants upon hearing the approach of visitors would stand outside their cottages and gravely salute the passersby with the same mixture of solemnity and fascination they would have accorded an ecclesiastical procession. John White Sr was only delivering loys but the mere appearance of these goods excited great comment.

"These folk are different from us," the blacksmith told the twin-ones as they passed a cottage where the father, mother and six children lined up to watch them pass.

"Father!" John Oge whispered. "Can't they hear you?"

John White saluted the man of the house by raising two fingers to his forehead. The man took off his knit cap and bobbed slightly, as if he were meeting royalty. "Oh, no fear. They can hear all right, but they only speak Erse. That's why I have to deal with that rascal Duggan. He speaks God's English."

The rascal Duggan was a wholesaler of illicit spirits and one of the sorts of people that Lord George Hill was trying to drive out of business by introducing commercial farming onto the estate. Gweedore, like many of Donegal's mountain communities, had a poteen industry. This was less a matter of choice than of necessity. The Gweedore folk made high-quality whiskey the traditional way, using malted barley. In many areas malted barley was being replaced by raw grain, or worse, by potato liquor. For many of the people in Gweedore, the whiskey trade was the only way for them to lay their hands on a little cash. Some grew barley and sold it to illicit distillers. Others grew their own grain and did their own distilling. In either case, all but the largest traffickers sold their product to a cadger, a professional middleman such as Duggan. From the Donegal mountains a network of cadgers moved the drink on to publicans in the small towns and, eventually, as far away as Belfast and Dublin. From the viewpoint of Donegal's small farmers this system was more than satisfactory; they received a lot more money for grain sold in the form of whiskey, not in the husk, and whiskey was much easier to transport to market than an equivalent amount of grain. Whiskey was money.

This explains why John White and the twin-ones followed Duggan up a small track into the mountains. He acted as middleman in a double sense: he was a translator – the connection between the English-speaking outside world and the Irish-speaking rundale world of Gweedore – and he also exchanged the poor farmer's resources (whiskey) for the goods that they desired (in this case, well-made loys). Up into the hills the three Whites and Duggan went, the path twisting and doubling back so that it seemed as if they made no progress. The children who came out of their cottages to stare at the travellers were for the most part sickly and stunted. Sometimes one of them found voice to ask, in Irish, for an ort. The cottages were the filthiest Eliza had ever seen. In most cases, the garbage heap and cesspile were right beside the door, and in defiance of good sense, these were often on the high side of the doorway so that when it rained heavily the effluent would wend its way into the cottage. No wonder the largest prize in Lord George Hill's improvement scheme was for the neatest and cleanest new cottage. That prize, three pounds, was a fortune in Gweedore.

All the time they climbed Duggan made conversation. He guffawed heartily at his own jokes about Father Matthew and the temperance crusade and about excise police. John White pretended to be amused, but he found the man repugnant. Finally they arrived at a small hut that originally had been used as a summer shelter by shepherds but now seemed abandoned. This was Duggan's storehouse. He was proud of it. "Why, a gauger would never know that there's 300 pounds of the finest whiskey inside, all ready for the drinking."

An aged man, a live-in guard, appeared from inside the hut. He smiled, revealing his only tooth. "Let's unload these loys," Duggan said to the old man. As each one was taken off, the old one muttered something to himself. Each implement had been constructed to the requirements of a specific farmer, and the watchman knew by heart which loy belonged to what farmer.

With the unloading completed, Duggan said, "We'll need your strong backs on this next part. Those are forty-gallon casks we'll be loading, and to drop one would be a tragedy." They loaded the whiskey carefully and began the long trip down the track. John Oge and Eliza were both nervous, but Eliza was better at keeping silence. So it was John Oge who said, "Father, how will we get these casks back home without being seen? Those firkins are fat as hogs and about as easy to spot!"

Duggan laughed. "You'll see how it's done, lad. You'll see!"

When they hit level ground Duggan had them pull off the track, and there, behind a hedge, by several bundles of thatching reeds. These were of a particularly hardy sort, harvested in the shallows of the Clady River and much favoured by well-off town dwellers. "We'll just build a few sheaves of these around your treasure. Then you can drive right into the rector's own stable yard and no one will suspect what you have on board."

He was right. When John White and the twin-ones returned to Donegal town they drove right into the stables of the town's only hotel. The blacksmith went inside and a few minutes later White, three lads and the new owner of the hostelry emerged from of a side door. The owner, a stranger in town, had tried to drive a hard bargain with John White, but the blacksmith seemed pleased enough. The lads quickly took the containers off the wagon and stored them in the basement of the inn. They left the thatching rushes. This job done, the innkeeper motioned for White and the twin-ones to come into what today would be called the public bar. He threw the blacksmith a small cloth bag that clinked. "Count it," he instructed, but the blacksmith just smiled and said he knew the amount was right.

"And now, Mr White, we'll sample what you've brought me." He handed glasses all around. This was the twin-ones' first experience with drinking; they both agreed it had merit. The part Eliza liked best was riding the rest of the way home in the cart, sitting next to her father and listening to the usually quiet man humming an old tune and intermittently quoting a bit of Robert Burns. He had three one-gallon jugs of poteen behind him. These had been hidden beneath the bottom sheaves of rushes.

Eliza was made bold by the drink. "Father, wasn't it wrong to trade with the keeper?"

"No. I did what the Bible tells us to do."

"Oh?"

"You remember what we did before we reached the village?"

"Yes. You used a syphon to fill both of those jugs with whiskey. And then you filled up the big firkins with water."

"The finest, purest water, I'll bid you to say." The blacksmith was laughing. Then he made the only joke that Eliza ever heard come out of his mouth. "So, you see, that new innkeeper... Like the Bible says, 'He was a stranger, and I took him in.'"

ठ&

In the spring of 1844 the patron of the twin-ones' school, Mrs John Hamilton, took a chest complaint and had to be sent to Italy to improve her respiration. Sun and salty air were prescribed. She died under the Mediterranean sun six months later and her charity school was discontinued at the end of the school year. John Oge ended his schooling at that point. Eliza switched to a local "national school" and attended it until she was fourteen. The Irish national schools were a remarkable set of institutions in that they brought mass popular education to the Irish people from the 1830s onward, a full four decades before the same thing was achieved in England and Scotland. There were some advantages, it seems, to being a backward colony.

The national schools were distinguished by far and away the best set of school texts available in the English-speaking world. The series took children from their ABCs to the equivalent of today's secondary school education – if the pupils stayed on long enough. Eliza had already done so much reading in Miss Babcock's emporium that the national school's literary curriculum was easy. What she learned now were the practical subjects and mathematics that had been neglected in the other school. She learned mental arithmetic, a skill that served her well throughout her life. As an extra subject she took Italian bookkeeping – that is, keeping double-entry financial records, a technique only recently invented. "It is always good to know the ways of commerce," the teacher told Eliza one day, and Eliza, thinking back on some of her father's mercantile methods, reflected that the best ways were not always found in books.

Eliza's new school was a female national school; a short way down the road was the male national school. Eliza liked the all-girl environment. Her father bought her two new outfits, adult ones, and if she did not look quite as formidable as the school mistress in them, she looked imposing nevertheless. Because she had progressed beyond the literary curriculum, Eliza was frequently put in charge of teaching the youngest children their ABCs and drilling them on addition and subtraction. In a severe black dress, with a shawl over her broad shoulders, this tall young lady was someone the little ones took seriously. This was the first time that Eliza had wielded power in a female role, and she loved it. For a while she thought of becoming a schoolmistress, but she learned that the money needed for training was more than her father could afford.

One of the best things the national school did was to put Eliza in touch with the official culture of the British empire. Irish national schoolbooks were not Irish in any narrow sense; they embodied the general beliefs of the governing class of the British Isles. The books were so well conceived and cheaply produced that in the middle of the last century most English working-class children were learning to read from Irish schoolbooks – and, paradoxically, were picking up British middle-class attitudes in the process. The same thing happened throughout much of the empire. The second to last year that Eliza was in school, 1845, an energetic Canadian named Egerton Ryerson was visiting Dublin to learn about the Irish national system. So impressed was he with its texts that when he returned to Canada West, where he was superintendent of public education, he virtually compelled the books to be used in the province's elementary schools. Thus when Eliza eventually fetched up in central Canada, she found that the official culture of the school system was exactly that which she had imbibed at Donegal town's female national school.

In early summer 1846, the day Eliza finished her formal schooling, her father did an uncharacteristic thing after the evening meal. He told everyone to be still, he had something to say. "Tomorrow, I'll be knocker-up. I shall rise early and build the forge fire perfectly."

Neither of the twin-ones asked why, but they were burning with curiosity.

"And tomorrow, you, John Oge, and you, Eliza, will be the smiths. I'll tend you, and each of you will make a spade. From the very beginning to the end, right through to attaching the stave to the metal. Everything." This was John White's equivalent of the *Meisterwerk*, the creation of a well-crafted tool as the last step of an apprenticeship. He was serious about the test, and the twin-ones knew he would be more demanding in checking the quality of their work than if he were not their father.

Neither of them slept well that night. They heard the courthouse clock strike each hour, and at six they heard their father rise. It was all they could do to stay still and feign sleep until he returned from the forge to wake them up.

Eliza would remember this as the single most exhausting day of her life. She worked for four hours making a spade for herself, and when done assisted John Oge as he made his. Their father worked the bellows but otherwise did not raise a finger to help them. The physical work was arduous, but Eliza had worked with heavy hammers, tongs and similar tools for several years and her muscles were well formed. The exhaustion was not physical; it was in knowing that each stroke, each beat, was being assessed by her father's sharp and critical eye. When finally she shaped the collar, inserted the spade handle and plunged the completed instrument into the barrel of cold water, the hiss and spit of this final step was a chorus of approving angels. She knew she had done a good job and she wanted to sing, to dance. Instead, she looked up at her father and they smiled broadly at each other, fellow members in the select company of the competent.

When John Oge had produced his test piece, more quickly than Eliza but perfectly nonetheless, their father told them they should have a half holiday. This was a phrase he had read in an English newspaper, and he had to explain to the twin-ones what it meant. He gave them each a shilling and told them to enjoy themselves. In his gruff way, he was happier than they had ever seen him.

"Oh yes," he threw out just as they set out for the shops in town. "While you're about it, you two should plan your journey." Without giving an explanation, he turned back to his forge.

What John White had in mind for the twin-ones was his own version of what recently qualified roundsmen or journeymen did in many trades on the continent and in some places in the British Isles. They went on a journey around the countryside working for one master craftsman after another until they had learned enough and saved enough money to set up shop for themselves. White's thoughts were less grandiose: he hoped that the twin-ones would spend a few months working their way around Ulster and central Ireland and then return to work with him at the White Spade Foundry.

The summer of 1846 was one of the most bewildering times in the history of Ireland. To be in the Irish countryside as summer changed to cruel autumn was to see compressed in a few weeks many of the emotions and tragedies that compass human experience. The potato harvest of 1845 had been a partial failure: Antrim, Armagh, parts of Kerry, Kildare and Wicklow suffered. In places fairly near to Donegal town, in Counties Tyrone and Monaghan, potatoes harvested in good shape turned to a rotting, stinking mass within a few days. The 1845 potato failure was by no means universal, but the blight's leprous spots horribly disfigured the national countenance. Everyone lived in fear of what would happen in the summer and autumn of 1846.

Eliza and John Oge's original plan was to work their way down through Fermanagh and into Monaghan, then up to Armagh, Belfast and, by way of the city of Londonderry, back to Donegal – a large circle they thought would take them six to eight months. Their father gave them the names of Protestant blacksmiths en route, and they felt sure of shelter and at least a little work at each stop. They dressed alike, in the multiple waistcoats, homespun trousers and dark jacket that was the preferred uniform of the Irish labourer. Each carried a bag with basic tools, a leather apron, a few personal items, hard bread and harder cheese. Eliza wore a knit cobbeen and John Oge a tattered hat that had once belonged to a cattle drover. To all the world, they were two sturdy lads on the road looking for work.

From their very first day they recognized that the world had gone awry. They spent the first night in a large granary outside Ballyshannon, a day's walk south of Donegal town. The owner was one of the new breed of County Donegal farmers growing grain for market rather than for distillation. Since their father had sold the man farming implements the twin-ones assumed that he would readily agree to give them shelter in the granary. They were surprised when at first he said no. Then, thinking better, he told them they could sleep in the granary, but that they had to help keep watch. There was a watchman in the granary hired to stop the thieving of grain by hungry wanderers from locales where potato crops had failed.

The next day the twin-ones went to the twice-yearly hiring fair in Ballyshannon. They had no intention of signing on with an employer; they knew from experience that it was fascinating to watch the farm labourers and the farmers who needed their help negotiate a wage. These hiring fairs always had something of a slave market tinge to them. Employers felt no compunction about coming up to a man and asking to see his hands, or asking him to pull up his sleeves to show his forearms. Sometimes they would tell him to stand straight so that the breadth of his shoulders could be gauged. In good times the labourer could afford to be rude to a farmer who had a reputation for treating servants badly or who paid below the going rate. Now, though, the Ballyshannon fair was bulging with labourers of all sorts, many of them in such a wretched condition that one could not imagine their doing a day's work, much less six months' hard labouring. Worse yet, only a few farmers came to town to do the hiring. Instead of adopting their usual posture of feigned indifference to the farmers' appraising eyes, the labourers jostled each other and tried to call themselves to the attention of their potential employers.

"I can plow – both with horse and oxen," one claimed.

"Never been sick in twelve years..."

"I've a wife and four childer away home, and would work hard as the devil himself..."

"Faith, I'll work for only food and lodgings."

Seeing these decent men bob up and down with the manic desperation of fleas on a graddle for a few shillings and their daily bread made the twin-ones turn away, sickened at heart.

John Oge and Eliza proceeded by stages into Tyrone and Monaghan, but there was now no joy in their journey. What struck them most was that people were digging up all their new potatoes in early August. The twin-ones stayed overnight with a widow cottager who was so excited about unearthing her first new potatoes that she ate several of them raw – the form usually reserved for feeding pigs. Despite her extreme poverty the widow was the soul of hospitality and only accepted a ha'penny from each of them, and that after considerable argument. They convinced her that their payment was a luck penny.

All over Ireland, tenant farmers laboured with the frenetic energy of worker ants. They unearthed their potatoes as quickly as possible, held a feast and then, as fast as they could, buried their harvest underground, all the while praying that the blight would pass them by.

But this time, 1846, it spared no one.

Eliza and John Oge were staying in the outbuildings of a Protestant blacksmith in the hills of Monaghan near Clones when they heard a remarkable keening. It came from a nearby cottage. There the cottier had dug up his clamp of new potatoes in order to check that they were saving properly, and instead of his hard first potatoes he found a black mass. His wife raised the lament usually reserved for the death of a human being. The same terrible discovery occurred repeatedly all over Ireland.

Now that the harvest was a failure, the twin-ones decided to return home. Peasant farmers no longer had any money to support blacksmiths or other rural tradesmen. Suddenly, the roads were filled with an army of paupers, dirty, desperate and lice infested. Though they felt great pain for these people, Eliza and John Oge tried to avoid them as much as possible, for they carried disease. Despite their best efforts they were brought cheek to jowl with the beggars and paupers on several occasions. The same hospitality that led a cottager to permit the twin-ones to lodge under his roof meant that later arrivals were admitted as well. Being ill-clothed, the paupers rolled close to any other human being to keep warm in the night.

On their path home, the twin-ones frequently encountered individuals, pairs or sometimes whole families who had what was called road fever. This was not a single disease – the term covered typhus, relapsing fever, diptheria – but to the sufferers such scientific distinction was meaningless. In their starving condition they were almost certain to die, whichever malady attacked them.

The final leg of the journey home took the twin-ones over the same mountain road from Lough Derg to Donegal town that they had once taken with their father. There were many more pilgrims at the lough than previously, but now their fervour was increased by desperation. Throughout Ireland a massive religious revival was beginning, rooted in the nation-wide perception that the Almighty was punishing the people for some great spiritual sin.

As they trudged over the mountains towards Donegal town, John Oge's pace became slower. He felt lightheaded. Eliza noticed that his face was slightly swollen. She did not tell him this, but quietly took his travelling sack so he could move along without burden. By the time they reached their home town John Oge could hardly move. They had to stop several times in each mile to rest. Now he seemed to be wearing a mask of red- and blue-veined blotches. Typhus rickettsie was attacking his blood vessels. The attacks were most severe in the small blood vessels found in the skin and in the brain. The disease, transmitted by lice, had been contracted from one of the paupers with whom the twin-ones had shared a cottier's hearth on their way home.

When the blacksmith saw Eliza and John Oge dragging themselves toward the entrance of his foundry, he ran forward and picked up his son as if he were no heavier than a bundle of whins. He carried him into the cottage and placed him on the bed with such gentleness that it seemed to Eliza that a feather could have fallen to the ticking harder than John Oge's body.

The young man was soon lost in a fitful sleep, one moment burning with fever and the next overcome with chills. John White, still in his leather apron, never let go of John Oge's hand. When the chills returned, the blacksmith laid down and clasped his son to him, trying with his own prodigious strength to overcome the forces that fought to steal his treasure away from home and hearth.

Eliza was awed by this love. But she wanted to live. "Better one dead than all dead," she murmured. Decisively she turned and left the cottage. She went into the foundry and took off all her clothes and threw them and the traveling gear onto the hearth. They burned, but only partially, and she had to stir the fire and add more fuel before they were finally consumed. She threw some forge ashes and a cup of lye into the barrel of ice cold rain-water used to cool forgings, then she bathed herself.

She submerged herself several times in this frigid baptistry and only came out when her skin started to take on a bluish tinge from the cold. She wrapped herself in an old tarpaulin and, barefooted, went outside. Eliza stood on the threshold of the family cottage.

"Father! Better one dead than all dead."

No response.

"Father!!"

At last the blacksmith broke away from John Oge. He stood up and came outside. Eliza backed away, lest he touch her. But now his eyes were clear and he was ready to surrender to the hideous reality thrust upon him. John White went back inside the cottage, tenderly lifted his son and, without a word, walked down the road to where, not more than fifteen rods away, a row of large canvas tents had been erected alongside the Poor Law Union workhouse. This was the governmental fever hospital. Eliza followed about twenty paces behind. For John White, this furlong was the longest of his life and the cruelest. The hard-pressed attendant at the fever hospital directed him to put the patient on a cot and took down John Oge's names for the records. That is all that there was to it. The last they saw was John Oge's eyes, momentarily clear and accepting, as they had been all his life, of whatever fate ordained, now staring from a face so congested by disease that it was virtually black.

The blacksmith shuffled home. At Eliza's direction he burned his clothes and the ticking mattress that John Oge had lain on, then underwent the same caustic cold-water baptism that Eliza had earlier had. He did not speak, nor did Eliza. She worried that even these steps were too late for both of them.

John Oge was buried by the hospital authorities without ever being visited again by a member of his family. If any sufferer could have accepted the necessity of this, it was he.

As ever in times of trouble, John White Sr turned to the Bible for comfort, but little did it seem to provide. He took to spending his evenings in complete silence, staring into the fire.

Eliza tried to explain to herself what had happened, but her thoughts careened and tumbled as crazily as the rocks she had seen coming down the mountainside on one of those trips to

Gweedore with her father. One moment she was able to say aloud, "The twin-ones are dead," and the next aver that, no, never would that happen. John Oge was gone, but Eliza swore that as long as she lived the twin-ones would survive. Time seemed to harden her resolve.

4

Rites of Passage

"We're lifting," John White said suddenly. The words came from the depths of one of his coal-black silences. "We're lifting for Derry and then for some place far from this godforsaken country!" This was ten days after John Oge's death, and it was the first purposeful thing he had said since learning that his first child would be buried in a common grave alongside scores of other fever victims. When he heard that news, he had stopped tending the fire in his foundry and never lighted it again.

Eliza was relieved to hear her father sound decisive, although she did not immediately consider the magnitude of the decision he had just announced.

"Eliza, find me the book by that woman on the backwoods of Canada. It should be in your things somewhere."

"Would you like me to go to town and get the loan of other books for emigrants?"

"Do that. And from Mrs Crawford, the lend of those letters her cousin sent the family."

By the 1840s the flow of information back to Ireland from previous migrants was a rich stream. Thus when Irish people moved to the New World, it was with a shrewd idea of the wages to be earned, the cost of lodgings and the networks of Irishmen who could be counted on for help.

Eliza collected all the material she could, but her father did not take it in. He looked at the odd page, turned a few, found that he could remember nothing he had read and went back to staring into the cottage fire. Eliza, though, read every word avidly. "Do you wish me to tell you what it says here about Toronto?" she would ask.

"Do that." His orders were clear, but his voice was hollow. Whether or not he heard the details was irrelevant to him: they were going. That decision, seemed to have used up the blacksmith's remaining store of resolution.

"Father, you will have to make some arrangements to sell the foundry. Should I ask Mr Hamilton's agent to come by?"

"Do that." The blacksmith went back to staring. In a matter of a few days he had suddenly become old. He sat hunched, as if crippled by rheumatism, and when he walked his was the shambling gait of an old man.

Fortunately for the White family John Hamilton Esq was a forward-looking landlord who felt keenly the importance of keeping an enterprise such as the foundry in operation. He had his agent pay John White Sr £350 for the foundry and cottage and for the unexpired term of the lease. Tools were included in the sale so that a new tenant could start the business up again quickly. And so the Whites walked away from their livelihood with very little in their hands save three hundred and fifty pounds. However, this sum was a fortune compared to the money most Irish emigrants of the famine era carried away. From the Crawford family letters, Eliza had learned that one could buy a decent cleared farm, of maybe 200 acres, for that amount in central Canada. This idea seemed to appeal to her father.

There was no American wake for the Whites when they left

Donegal town. The ritualized outpouring of grief when someone left Ireland for the New World had been common in the
1830s, but now everyone knew that the emigrants were going
to a finer land, not into unhappy exile. What few tears there
were were often shed for those who stayed behind.

"I think we should give Mrs Crawford five sovereigns. That's
for all the years she has taken care of the house and the boys
since mother died." The family and its belongings were loaded
on a four-wheeled wagon that Eliza had hired for the journey
to Derry.

John White nodded. "Do that." Those were the last words he
uttered in Donegal town.

Emigrant ships did not ply the North Atlantic after the end of
summer in most years, but 1846 was different. The discomfort
and danger of autumn and winter crossings were set aside.
The misery of the Irish was so great, their desire to flee their
poisoned homeland so strong, that throughout autumn they
poured into ports where the great shipowners of Liverpool,
Bristol and Dublin sent their vessels to load human cargo.

The White family that rocked and jolted towards the city of
Londonderry was unusual only in being better off financially
than the average migrant household. Their minds, however,
like those of the abject poor, were set on getting out. John
White Sr slouched impassively on the jouncing wagon. Eliza
and the three boys jumped off when the potholes and ruts
became too severe. All three boys, aged seven, eight, and nine,
were dressed in new corduroy trousers and dark furze jackets.
Her hair cut short, Eliza, could have been either a young man
or a girl. The youngest boy, his head still misshapen in cruel
memory of his difficult birth, wore a cobbeen hat that he never
took off.

Since the end of the Napoleonic Wars in 1815 Derry, in the
far north of Ireland, had been a leading emigration port. Eliza
knew that, if ships were sailing, they would be sailing from
there. It was the best Irish port to sail from because it was the

only one whose ships still provided passengers with meat and molasses as well as potatoes, salt and fish. The practice of provisioning passengers had died out completely in other Irish ports, where the price of passage included only water and cooking fuel. All food had to be provided by the emigrants themselves.

Most of the vessels from Derry went to British North America, as had the ships from all Irish ports until the mid-1840s, when changes in the navigation laws made it cheaper for the Irish to go to the United States than the Canadas. Of the few ships in this earlier period that went to the United States, the majority went to Philadelphia, the city with the closest ties to Ulster. So when it came time to choose a vessel, the choice came down to one for Philadelphia or another headed for Montreal. The Philadelphia-bound vessel was leaving sooner, but John White had strong feelings about loyalty to the crown, so he chose the ship destined for British North America. For thirty pounds he obtained passage for himself and his family on the *Kingfisher*. Their accommodation was on a deck above the steerage level. There deal-wood partitions had been erected to provide semi-private rooms for families or small groups who did not wish to be crammed into the steerage with the bulk of the passengers. The White family was to travel across the Atlantic in an eight- by ten-foot room with narrow bunks. The blacksmith went to the booking office and put down his gold coins. The process of leaving Ireland was simple. This was the era before passports and visas: if one wanted to go, one simply paid passage and left. John White carefully pocketed the dockets containing the particulars of his family and of their possessions. For the first time since John Oge had died, he began to feel better.

At quayside Eliza asked to see the travel dockets. "Father, what is this?" she said after looking them over.

"Eh?"

"The dockets name you, the three boys, and John Oge!"

The blacksmith blinked, bewildered. He looked at the dockets. No denying what they said. "Well, there's no use changing it now. Means nothing anyway. We're a family and I've booked passage as such." He was confused and distressed by his mistake.

Eliza touched his arm reassuringly. "Perhaps it's for the best."

So, as John Oge White, Eliza boards the *Kingfisher* for Quebec and Montreal. No one challenges the erroneous dockets; the scene is one of great confusion. John White Sr, grown weary by the chaos of the world, cannot even watch. He retreats to the family's cubicle and sits on a bottom bunk, his elbows on his knees, his head in his hands. If the New World was to be a promised land, no one would ever have guessed it from his countenance.

Eliza and the three boys stay on deck. For the boys, unlike their father, the chaos is wonderful and promises a more exciting world and better future. The *Kingfisher*, a moderate-sized vessel of 550 tons, is scheduled to sail in two days, weather permitting. Navvies run up and down the two gangways carrying sides of salt pork, hampers of dried fish and sacks of dried peas and beans. The steerage passengers come on board, mostly in family groups. Some wear the determined air of young heroes going on a long march – "That one looks like Buck Whaley on his hike to Jerusalem," Eliza observes. Others look as if they are going to the gallows. At quayside there is a great pressing of hands and hugging, and once the emigrants are on board a lot of yelling between quay and ship. The steerage passengers are forbidden to get off the ship once they are on board. Previous captains lost several passengers who took their last nights on shore as an opportunity to drink and who subsequently had wandered away.

For the White children, the most interesting scene is the arrival of a group of nine well-dressed individuals led by a cocksure young man in his mid-twenties. The master of this party assesses the ship the way a person does a horse, looking at her lines to judge the conformation of the beast. These migrants to Canada are Irish gentry. Well off and poor alike have been ruined by the famine. If some of the gentry are leaving Ireland with more resources than tenant-farmers, their fall is perhaps the greater.

Eliza is particularly struck by the clothing of one of the gentry children. A boy of age four or five, he wears a dress, has on tiny balletlike slippers over white stockings and sports a floppy straw hat with a floral band. This is the first time that Eliza has encountered the practice, increasingly fashionable among a narrow hand of genteel families on both sides of the Atlantic, of dressing boys as girls until the age of six or seven. She is fascinated and slightly excited, feeling the same way she felt when she poured over the engravings and tales of the female pirates Anne Bonny and Mary Read.

"Will the gentlefolk stay on deck?" her youngest brother inquires, breaking Eliza's gaze.

"No, they have cabins of their own. In fact, the mate says they have two cabins on a separate deck. And they have their own china to eat off and their own white tablecloths and silver."

Large trunks of superior quality are being hoisted aboard by windlass. The gentry, fallen though they may be, are clearly not going to British America empty-handed.

"Will we ever be like them, do you think, Eliza?" The youngest one's query is more prescient than he can know: fascination with one's betters is a characteristic of the Old World. The determination to join them is a hallmark of the New.

"Faith, child, I don't know. But if we work hard, I'd say so." She pauses and puts her arms around the shoulders of her handicapped brother. "And sure if that doesn't work, there's always the chance of marrying a rich woman."

Twenty-four hours later, as if loath to keep the gentry waiting, the weather quickens and the passengers are ordered to make ready to sail. The vessel eases down the river, hoists sail and departs.

During the first ten days of the voyage the wind is fresh and steady, and Eliza and the three lads spend a lot of time on deck. Their father stays below. Eliza asks him if he feels ill and he says no, just a little weak. Several times each day the boys and Eliza walk to the stairwell that drops steeply into the hold and look down upon the steerage passengers. The Whites observe carefully the way the people below line up – always in the same order, family by family – for their twice-daily allowance of water and for use of the limited cooking facilities. About a third of the steerage passengers are Protestants, small farmers getting out before things get any worse. One can tell the passengers' religion by what they do before meals: Protestants say grace, either aloud or silently, Catholics bless themselves.

On the eleventh day out of port the wind changes and the vessel, which has been driving steadily forward, bobs irregularly and goes several points off course. The White children are natural seafarers and watch with shameless fascination as the steerage passengers become beastly ill in their confined space. Down below, bulkheads seem to be shifting, the deck tilting. One after another the passengers "shoot the cat," as the ship's crew calls it. The lower deck acquires a viscous veneer.

Eliza witnesses these events with a cold eye and then quotes James Orr's emigration poem, "The Passengers," to the youngsters. They particularly like the verse that describes such troubles as the ones they are seeing:

> An' some, wi monie a twin an' throe,
> Do something wad be nauceous
> To name this day.

The steerage passengers who hear this do not find it comforting. Nor these lines of Orr's:

> What sickness and sorrow, pervade my rude dwelling!
> A huge floating lazar-house, far, far at sea.

But if she is hard towards strangers, Eliza is deeply solicitous of her father's well-being. When she goes below she finds that he is lying down. No, he says, he is not seasick. But he is perspiring heavily and feels hot to the touch. He tries to joke. "Well, at least *you* won't drown in a stormy sea, girl," he says, reminding her that she was born with the caul.

With great effort, John White pulls himself upright and tells Eliza to bring him a small hide-covered chest in which he keeps his few treasures. He takes out a piece of parchment, sixteen inches by eleven, embossed with a seal and with orange and blue ribbons attached. Eliza wonders if her father will break his wonted silence concerning the Orange Order. The parchment is a certificate proclaiming, "Our Well-Beloved Brother,

John White, Is a Member of the True Society of United and Loyal Orangemen, Province of Ulster, County of Donegal." The blacksmith is very proud of this certificate. It shows that he was inducted under the "old system" that prevailed before the Order went underground. White tries to explain to Eliza what it all means, but he runs out of words and strength. Ceasing to speak, he hands her a buckrum-bound volume, *Annals and Defence of the Loyal Orange Institution of Ireland*. He catches his breath. "All the history and the meaning and the truth of the Order is in there," says, tapping the book. "And, Eliza, note the name of the writer of the book, Ogle R. Gowan. A more Loyal man never existed. And he is in Canada right now. Remember that, if you ever need help."

Two days later, the storm winds abate and turn into that rare and desirable force for transatlantic voyages, the brisk and steady easterly. The crew is happy and talks about a near-record crossing. The enthusiasm is contagious. Some of the steerage passengers begin to play music. A small band is formed – flute, fiddle, clarinet, a pair of cymbals – and an impromptu dance is held. The set is just done, when a pod of whales is spotted and everyone rushes on deck to watch the amazing sight.

John White does not improve. His fever is now continuous and he is constantly wet with perspiration. The first mate comes and examines him and says it is some sort of a fever, he is not sure what sort. As long as White stays in his cubicle there is no danger to the other passengers, the mate opines.

Now Eliza and the three boys enter the compartment only at intervals. They sleep in the passageway, leaning against the bulkhead, their knees drawn up under them. Eliza ministers to her father, but at his insistence she stays away from him as much as possible.

Precisely what physical malady John White Sr suffers is never known. Eliza believes then, and continues to believe all her life, that he is in the first stages of typhus and that he has caught the disease from his impulsive embrace of the suffering John Oge. But something else is also happening. Her father is simply giving up. The shoulders of the blacksmith can no longer carry the weight of such a world. His last act is to give Eliza all of the money he has left, slightly over 300 pounds. He tells her that she is in charge now, that for all intents and purposes she is the man of the family.

Man that is born of a woman hath but a short time to live, and is full of misery. He cometh up, and is cut down, like a flower; he fleeth as it were a shadow, and never continueth in one stay.

This is the moment Eliza loses her compass. The captain of the ship is reading the burial service. Without John Oge, without the great protecting forearms of her blacksmith father, there are no trustworthy landmarks, only the terrors of an unknown land and the knowledge that she is entering the New World in journeyman's clothes under her dead brother's name. No comfort that.

In the midst of life we are in death; of whom may we seek for succour, but of Thee, O Lord, who for our sins art justly displeased?

The next thing Eliza remembers clearly is the *Kingfisher's* approach to Grosse Isle, just below Quebec city. A flock of small birds joins the ship as it enters the St. Lawrence River and they fly about in the rigging, setting up a home for themselves. Are they emigrants too? Eliza wonders. Do they know who they are and where they are going? As the vessel moves up the St. Lawrence, where the broad land is increasingly broken by farmsteads, Eliza and the three boys stand on deck. Eliza is motionless for long periods of time. The boys, though bewildered, do not bother her. The first mate sights something at the water's edge and says it is a red man. Eliza sees the creature and wonders how the mate can tell its colour at such a distance.

Grosse Isle stands below Quebec like a sword before a warrior. No one passes into the New World without the approval of its governors. At one time the island was beautiful, covered with trees and shrubs right down to the water's edge. Now, however, it is barren and hostile. In 1832, at the time of the first great cholera epidemic, it was made into a quarantine station. Low white examination sheds and fever wards were imposed on the landscape. The eastern front of the island that greets newcomers is rocky and has a farmhouse or two on it. In the middle are the quarantine facilities. At the far western end is a high bluff where the telegraph facilities are arranged. The island is not covered with fever tents – as it will be scant months later, in the spring of 1847 – but it is frightening in its medicinal coldness.

Eliza and the boys are the only ones on the ship who are scrutinized by the island's health officials, for their father's death was the only one on the voyage. As they wait to be examined, an anxious Eliza cautions her brothers to address her as John. A kindly doctor examines their throats, takes their pulses and talks to them about what they intend to do. When he learns that Eliza has some money and that her father had been an Orangeman, he gives her two pieces of advice. "John, if I were you, I would keep my fortune a secret and in my shoes. And when you get to Montreal, ask at the British garrison where the Orange lodges in the city meet. When you find out, show them your father's certificate."

"Thank you sir," Eliza replies in a nervous, gruff voice.

"And now we'll see that you continue your journey." He completes a passed-quarantine certificate for "John White, young adult, male, foundryman, and three attendant male juveniles."

Thou knowest, Lord, the secrets of our hearts; shut not thy merciful ears to our prayer, but spare us... suffer us not, at our last hour, for any pains of death, to fall from thee.

The passengers are set on shore at Quebec city. For many who wish to settle in the United States, this is the jumping-off point. For most of the other passengers, it is a chance to walk on solid ground for two days, to investigate the New World in the flesh before transferring their belongings to a steamer bound for Montreal and Canada West. Eliza and the three boys watch everyone else disembark. It seems that they will be staying on board until the eldest lad draws Eliza from her revery and convinces her they should see the city.

On shore, her disorientation increases. The quay area is fairly quiet as this is the tag end of the sailing season. Soon, however, she and the boys are on a crowded throughfare. Immediately it becomes clear that the New World is indeed different. At the harbourside there are brown, black and yellow people, and many varieties of white. Some of the coloured people dress in garish foreign garb. Was this not *British* North America?

The quartet leaves this cosmopolitan bazaar and proceeds to the city centre. Here they encounter the captain of the *Kingfisher.* He remembers them from the burial service of their father and kindly invites them to a hotel. There the English-speaking landlord serves him an enormous tumber of cognac and gives him a pipe, about three feet in length, along with a paper of Virginian tobacco. Eliza is offered a pipe but wisely declines. The sea captain grows expansive and tells the Whites which places in Canada West would suit them best.

"There are piles of foundry work to be found in Toronto. Or Kingston, Belleville or Gananoque. Mark my words, young John, you will have no trouble finding a place, at least if you are as stout a worker as you look to be.

Eliza nods modestly.

Three large cognacs later, the captain suggests that they walk a bit to prevent his falling asleep. He offers to show them the summit of the city and the celebrated Plains of Abraham. Having sailed in and out of harbours all over the world, the captain is something of an authority on maritime redoubts. Quebec city, surrounded by water on three of its sides, presents an especially challenging topography for the military planner, he explains, and of course on the fourth side the city is open towards the plains. The walking tour proceeds amicably if, in the captain's case, slightly drunkenly, until they come upon a wooden sculpture about four and a half feet high, carved and painted red, white and black, with the name JAMES WOLFE incised on its wooden pedestal. A long crack runs down Wolfe's torso, the carving having been executed with unseasoned wood.

The captain becomes visibly upset. "By God! Will you look at that!"

"What is it, Captain?"

"It is intended to be a monument to a great man."

"You mean General Wolfe?" Eliza had read of this hero at the national school.

"Of course. But look at it!" The captain points in disgust. "*That,* a monument to a man who by his skill and valour annexed vast territory in the Canadas to the British empire!" He spits. "That is a pitiful tribute. If that is the gratitude of the people of Quebec, then hell roast them!!"

He continues to rant, but to Eliza his voice is transformed into the low monotone that had read the burial service.

O most powerful and glorious Lord God, at whose command the winds blow, and lift up the waves of the sea, and who stillest the rage thereof; We thy creatures, but miserable sinners, do in this our great distress cry unto thee for help: Save, Lord, or else we perish.

The steamboat trip from Quebec city to Montreal takes less than forty hours. During the daylight portions of the journey Eliza stands at the rail. She looks down at the water and worries that she is drowning. One part of her mind recalls that she was born with the caul and will never drown, another tells her that the weight is too much, that carrying the three boys through life will be impossible and that they will pull her below the surface. The two youngest lads stand at the rail with Eliza and hold her hands. They know something is happening. Around them, loud-voiced passengers comment with false expertise on the passing countryside. The soil, one braying English gentry voice says, is obviously inferior, the climate severe and, he adds loftily, the habitants are clearly not given to hard labour. Eliza does not hear him. Her mind is fixed on the fear of drowning.

When the boat docks in Montreal, she tells one of the mates that she will be back for the baggage and gives him six pence to care for it. The moment the gangway is down she rushes off the ship, pushing through the passengers. She must get to land, to keep from drowning. The three boys follow as best they can. Eliza heads away from the harbour and straight uphill to high ground. But instead of safe refuge she finds an alien hell. The streets for example: the habitants insist on erecting wooden steps from their front doors right into the street. Some streets are so narrow that these wooden projections almost block the way. The windows! Montrealers seem to be obsessed with security; everywhere Eliza turns there are private homes that resemble nothing so much as small-town gaols. She sees the heavy front doors made of sheet-iron, presumably designed as storm doors for winter, and recalls the iron-clad door at the back of the courthouse in Donegal town. And then there is the Montreal custom of covering most ground and first floor windows with wrought-iron grills.

In these canyons of limestone and iron Eliza begins to walk faster and faster and then she begins to run, every now and then casting a look around to see if she is being followed by her enemies. The only pursuers are her brothers. Finally she stops, gasping, and they catch up.

She slumps against a stone wall surmounted by heavy grill and takes stock. She is just opposite a church; that much is obvious. Then she notices that there are crosses and a bell tower: it is a Popish conventicle. Everything in Eliza's heritage tells her to hasten away, but she needs sanctuary. From her childhood reading she knows that churches are always islands in the harsh seas of life.

She and the lads softly creep into the church. It is dedicated to St. Mary, the Blessed Virgin. What they see is overpowering. The ceiling, high and arched, is divided into conic sections. Each section has a gilt moulding setting it off from its neighbours and each is filled with holy figures, saints, angels, dominions and powers painted in vivid colour – smalt, cinnabar, orpiment. The figures do not lie flat on the painted surface but seem to radiate from it. In the very centre is a large, vaulted circular space where a massive painting of the ascension of Jesus Christ reigns supreme. Such is the magic of the artists that as you continue to view the work, the Christ figure seems to rise higher towards heaven. Eliza takes hold of one of the rough pine pews. She stares, transfixed, for several minutes. She marshals her senses, turns and studies the massive altar, the more-than-life-sized statue of the Virgin that is set on a block of white marble, the four-foot long altar candles and a dozen statues of various saints. Finally, her gaze moves back to the ascension of Christ and fixes upon it until she believes that she is rising into the heavens to meet Him.

Lord into thy hand we commend this spirit.

This comes in a voice that only Eliza can hear. The voice's timbre and accent are those of the ship's captain reading her father's service. This is not something she remembers; she actually hears the words.

Lord into thy hand ... Lord into thy hand ...

This time the captain's voice opens a vista of clear consciousness amidst the tumble and terror of Eliza's mind. She recalls the advice that the quarantine doctor on Grosse Isle had given her: find the British garrison and the local Orangemen.

Discovering the British army garrison in Montreal is not hard. What is difficult for Eliza is guessing who the best person to speak to might be. First she thinks she will go up to one of the officers entering or leaving the barracks. Then she decides they look too formidable. This is a fortunate decision. The Orange lodges are now illegal in the British army. Officers know of course that Lodges still exist among the enlisted men and the noncommissioned officers, but they turn a blind eye. It is certain, however, that no officer will help a stranger find an Orangeman.

"Excuse me, sir." Eliza approaches a sentry patrolling slowly on foot in front of the barracks.

"Yes lad?" The soldier is glad of a chance to break his dull routine.

"Sir, I was told there would be someone here of help to some children from the old country who have no parents."

"Yes?" He frowns, puzzled.

"Children whose father was True Blue and who was an Orangem –"

"Say no more!" The sentry's voice is sharp. He looks around to see if anyone is within earshot. No one is near. "It's a very good thing you spoke to me and not to that papish scut on the back reach. He'd have had the town police arrest you for vagrancy just for the mentioning of Blue and Orange!"

"Then you can help?"

"Just say that a tip of the wink is as good as a nod to a dead horse."

Eliza nods. From earliest childhood she has heard proverbs. Country people quote them incessantly and often inappositely. Whatever the sentry means, he is a man of good will; Eliza listens carefully as he tells her that the sergeant major of the barracks is True Blue and will meet her and the wheens in a nearby tavern after sundown.

The tavern is a quiet place used by the military and not given over to rowdies. Eliza indicates with a gesture that her brothers are to stand quietly against the wall. She orders a hot whiskey for herself. She offers to buy a ball of malt for the barman, who accepts readily.

The sergeant major arrives. He is a figure out of the tales of empire – tall, square-shouldered, with a full set of sideburns and a robust mustache. His voice is surprisingly soft and he listens to Eliza's story gravely. Several times he looks over her shoulder to appraise the three lads; the youngest attracts special attention. He questions Eliza slowly and in a way that reassures her. Finally he takes a piece of paper from his tunic and hands it to her. "Son, this is a map that will show you and your brothers how to find some True Blue friends. The man is a Mr Burton, one of the founders of the first lodge of Orangemen in this benighted Papish stronghold. He is not a poor man, but he is tight with the money, so don't expect anything for free. But he will put you in the way of work and all that. And maybe schools for the lads. Be there tomorrow." He stands to leave. "And don't forget to take that parchment that your father left you – the one with his name on it and the seal and ribbons."

The Burtons live much higher up the hill on which Montreal sits, by the time the four Whites reach the place, they are tired and Eliza is lightheaded. For the first time since her father's death she allows herself some hope. *Lighten our darkness we beseech thee Oh Lord and by thy great mercy grant us...* Grant us what? Any boon, anything at all.

William Burton is a successful dry-goods merchant and his house resembles nothing so much as a small bank building. It is a Georgian structure, perfectly symmetrical, of smooth grey slabs of limestone. Even the trim is grey. Eliza pulls the bell sash, her brothers in line behind her. The two older ones and Eliza remove their caps. Eliza expects that a servant will open the door and has memorized a sentence asking for admittance to see the master or mistress of the establishment. Instead, Elizabeth Burton, a plump woman of sixty with a round smiling face, answers. She has been expecting them; the sergeant major called early that morning. Would they like a glass of chocolate before they go up to Mr Burton? This is the first time since the death of Martha White that Eliza has encountered a woman who is generous and optimistic. She trusts her immediately.

They meet Mr Burton in his library, at least that is what Mrs Burton calls it, though there are very few books in view. It is a walnut-paneled room with a grey ceiling and nearly dark, even in the middle of the day. A small brass coal-oil lamp casts a circle of light on a massive desk piled high with ledgers and sheets of accounting paper. Mr Burton greets Eliza formally and asks her to sit in a chair directly in front of the desk. The three lads perch on a leather chesterfield while Mrs Burton remains standing.

"You have a piece of parchment for me, do you not?"

Eliza hands it over. Burton takes off the ribbon, a faded rose band, and unrolls the document. He bends over it carefully, using his eye glasses as a magnifying glass. He is silent for more than a minute, then pronounces himself satisfied. "Yes, this is the genuine article."

Eliza says nothing. She stares unblinking at him.

"This John White was your father, was he not?"

"Yes sir."

'And you, young John White, are his eldest son and chief heir, are you not?"

Eliza hesitates. Everything spins for a moment, and she considers telling him the truth. The captain's voice threatens to interrupt her thoughts and to silence it she blurts out, "Yes sir, I am." The room seems to be warming considerably.

Mr Burton leans back in his chair and digs his thumbs into his waistcoat, expansively delivering his judgement. "My brother in the order – your recent acquaintance the sergeant major – formed a good impression of your character, young John White, and I must concur. You are straightforward and honest in your manner." He leans forward and puts his forearms on the desk. "It seems to me, young man, that as heir to your father you have one major responsibility to undertake."

"Please, sir?" Eliza is struggling to concentrate.

"That is, the care of your brothers until they are old enough to learn a trade and fend for themselves. Does this seem accurate to you?"

"Yes sir." Eliza is so overpowered by the situation that she would answer yes to anything. But Burton is right in any case:

the lads are the reason she is terrified of drowning.

"How much money did your father leave you? Tell me."

"Just under 300 pounds sir."

"Ah..." Mr Burton leans back and makes a steeple of his index fingers. He calculates. "Were Mrs Burton and I to have these children placed in good homes and schooled and apprenticed in decent trades, it would be a great load off your young shoulders, lad. Of course, it would not be without cost. But I calculate that it should involve only 75 pounds per lad. Two hundred twenty-five pounds total."

Eliza has two violently contradictory emotions, one of immense relief, the other of guilt as she remembers the Old Testament story of the evil brothers who sold their flesh and blood, Jacob, into bondage. She cannot speak. But Mr Burton is no longer addressing her. "Stand up, you three, and come forward."

Hesitatingly, the lads come toward Mr Burton's desk. Mrs Burton moves along with them to provide reassurance. As they come out of the shadows, the dry-goods merchant notices that the youngest still wears his knit cap. "You there! Take off that cobbeen and let me see what you look like!" Eliza jerks forward, interposing herself between Mr Burton and the lad, but the youngster has already obeyed.

"Oh merciful Lord!" Mrs Burton, ashamed of her reaction, claps her hand over her mouth. "Surely, you are one of God's children, anyway," she adds lamely.

"I see the problem," Burton notes dryly, staring at the pear-shaped, receding cranium. The sloping forehead has almost no hair and several red blotches: eczema or ringworm. "Put the cap back on, lad." Burton is somewhat discomfited. Even your unfortunate brother deserves schooling and entry into a trade. I shall stand by my offer."

Eliza is sitting on the forward edge of her chair. *We therefore commit his body to the deep...* She clenches her fists to keep the cacaphony from rending her. *...to be turned into corruption, looking for the resurrection of the body, when the sea shall give up her dead...* "Seeing, however, the particular problem with your youngest brother," *and the life of the world to come, through our Lord Jesus Christ,* "there undoubtedly and unavoidably will be additional expenses involved in entering him into an apprenticeship for a skilled trade" …*who at his coming shall change our vile body, that it may be like unto his glorious body "*… suggest that we plan 75 pounds for each of the older lads and 100 pounds for the youngest. For a total of two hundred and fifty pounds. Is that agreeable to you, John White?"

Eliza agrees in a loud voice, loud enough to cut through the other ethereal voice. This achieved, she hears the sea captain complete the Divine Service: *Whereby He is able to subdue all things to Himself.* Eliza knows now that she will not drown and, like a rescued mariner, far past exhaustion, but now safe, she lets herself slide down the vertiginous slope to soft, welcoming unconsciousness.

Part Two
New Dimensions

Eliza McCormack White appears in the public record in Canada in January 1847, and in a very curious way. She is the female Lothario mentioned in the following story, taken verbatim from the Brockville Record of 7 January of that year. No copies of the Hamilton Spectator, the paper in which the story first appeared exist.

A FEMALE LOTHARIO. The *Hamilton Spectator* says that a young servant girl of the name of Eliza McCormack, has been in the habit for some time past of assuming male attire, and in that disguise paying her court to the young girls of the city. Six of her pretended courtships have been with dress makers - and to three of them she had popped the question of marriage. She has assumed all manner of names and characters, sometimes a limb of the law, and sometimes she was a student of medicine a clerk in a dry goods store, and again, a gentleman of property arrived from Ireland, and hard up for a wife. She was discovered in her most recent adventure, while under the name of Crawford, paying her addresses to a young seamstress; this young girl was not so green as her pseudo lover had expected. She had her suspicions that *Mr.* Crawford was of the feminine gender and communicated them to a young man of her acquaintance. On the next meeting, the *gentleman* was pounced upon, and after a short scuffle "stood confessed, a maid" in all her charms. She was taken to the police office and locked up for the night. On Monday morning, she was liberated, as no person appeared against her. Miss McCormack is said to be the same person who figured in Galt a short time since, as a sick taylor.

5

I Blush to Remember

I stayed with the Burton family for a week and they were kind in every way. Mrs Burton had the servant girl make up a bed for me and there I remained, unconscious for two days. When finally I came to, Mr Burton was there, watching me. He was not as austere a man as he had at first seemed, and now I could imagine him a smiling grandfather. I was grateful that the Burtons' sense of decorum had kept them from removing my garments whilst I was unconscious, as that would have been most unsettling for everyone, not least myself.

I progressed from hot broth to eggs and soft toast and then to full meals of beef and potatoes. Never had I eaten so well. Mrs Burton declared cheerily that in no time at all I would be twice the stout lad I already was. Soon I was impatient to move about and see this house, then the world. The Burtons had a

servant girl of the habitant class who flirted with me in a libi-
dinious way, thinking me to be a young man. This was most
agreeable, allowing me an occasional glimpse of her smooth
bosoms, for she wore a lace bodice that was cut much deeper
in front than mere ventilation would require.

The shock of losing first my dear twin, John Oge, and then
my revered and beloved father had injured my mind and damp-
ened my spirits. Thus it was inexplicable that at the time, lying
in the Burtons' house, I felt strangely elated. Or, one might say,
giddy. There was animation in my heart and lightness in my
head. I giggled at things that no one else thought amusing.

Mr Burton, falling comfortably into his grandfatherly role,
took me around Montreal and showed me the sights he thought
most instructive for a young man about to begin his journey
in life. He was especially proud of the biggest building in the
city, the Bank of Montreal. "Any nation that makes its banks
bigger than its cathedrals must have a great future," he observed.
"There should be a statue of Mr Molson, its builder, in front of
the edifice." When he said this it was all I could do – for what
reason I do not know – to avoid an outburst of hysteria.

Another sight he thought instructive was the New Market
area. There, opposite the city's court-house and gaol, we beheld
what Mr Burton denominated a fortuitous architectural omen:
Nelson's monument. Did I notice how similar it was to Nelson's
pillar in central Dublin? I confessed never having been to Dublin. Well, he explained, it was a most striking resemblance,
indicating that the British empire was a single unity and that
this unity was the basis of all our future prosperity. The empire
was the future, not the republic to the south, as he called the
United States.

Were there, I asked, other pillars to Nelson elsewhere in the
British empire? He did not know, but thought it a good idea
that there be a plethora of these monuments and all of the same
design. In fact, he would write a letter to the War Office in
London suggesting that they issue standard plans for Nelson
pillars.

Several times Mr Burton inquired if I truly wished to continue
life as a foundryman. Each time I replied affirmatively.

"A well-mannered, clean-faced, intelligent lad such as you
could do well in the dry goods and mercantile line," he pointed

out. In an effort to interest me in this sort of employment he took me to one of his emporia, a high-class haberdashery and men's outfitter. He was very proud of this place for being genteel. His customers' accounts were posted to them only once a year, just as in the best shops in London.

The employment he proposed was far from the healthy, vigorous work I had known in Ireland. It would have been my task to stand near the front door and when a customer entered to bow and scrape and ascertain what his wishes were, then to take him to one of the senior staff who would bow and scrape and satisfy his wishes. I would open the door and bow as he left. After a few years of this I would work my way up to counter clerk and then senior counter clerk, perhaps even assistant manager. Mr Burton thought this was an infinitely attractive prospect for a young man and was disappointed that I did not see it as suiting my talent. I could not tell him that he was offering me a life of slow suffocation.

Since I expressed my firm determination to continue onward to Canada West and take up my trade there, Mr Burton kindly gave me a letter of introduction to the leading Orangeman in that province, Ogle R. Gowan, M.P. It was a name I had heard before. The gentleman in question was often in Montreal, Mr Burton said, but at present was in either Brockville or Toronto on business.

Too quickly the time came to take leave of my three young brothers. The parting was most touching, one of the few hours in this period of my life when I did not feel lightheaded. I gazed into the eyes of each before embracing him, and embraced with all the more feeling because I was at once sister, brother, father and mother. The youngest wore a newly knitted cobeen that Mrs Burton had provided. I wished them well and promised that we should meet frequently. This promise I intended to fulfill, but for the duration of my life I saw the two eldest no more than a score of times. The eldest eventually settled in the west of Canada and the second in the United States. I lost track of both of them. The youngest for a time lived in Madoc, Canada West, and was employed briefly in a foundry that I came to own.

That, tho', was the future. I left Montreal on a clear autumn day in 1846 with fifty pounds in my pocket and with as clear a conscience as ever I was likely to have.

The first part of my journey to Toronto took me to Ottawa, on one of the last passenger-carrying Durham boats. Despite the cool fall weather, it was an exhilarating choice. The Durham boats, unlike the steam vessels that replaced them, were propelled by hand. They were admirably adapted to the river – about forty feet long and six across, tapered at both ends – but they were certainly not luxurious. I paid for one of the small cabins on board. Most of the passengers, however, went ashore where we tied up at night and slept in small tents or on the open ground. The chief charm of this mode of travel was that it allowed one to learn the details of the countryside at close hand. The Durham boat was a pleasant, if slow, way to travel. The vessel was navigated by a French captain who spoke passable English and was propelled by four habitants. They worked extraordinarily hard, singing as they did. The chief boatman would start a song and the others would pick it up.

> *Dans mon chemin j'ai rencontré*
> *Deux cavaliers très bien montés*

And the rest of the crew sang a refrain:

> *À l'ombre d'un bois je m'en vais jouer,*
> *À l'ombre d'un bois je m'en vais jouer.*

One of my fellow passengers was a lady of a certain age who occupied the other tiny cabin on the vessel. She engaged me in conversation and seemed pleased with my manners and good looks. She told me that I had very fair skin and fine hair for a foundryman, which sent me into a fit of laughter. "Why, you're quite the little schoolboy, aren't you?" she said.

As the boat steamed slowly upstream it heartened me to watch the water ripple by and to have no fear of drowning. That terror was behind me forever. My companion and I talked for long periods. She said she was a Palatine and I inquired what that might be. She replied that her people were Protestants who had been driven out of the Germanies by the French Cath-

olics and had settled in Ireland, then moved to New York State
and finally to Canada West. She, like many of the Palatines,
had a keen interest in Methodism and for a time was the helpmeet of an itinerant preacher, a circuit rider, by whom she had
two children. This man took to having visions and tried to start
up a religion of his own, after which he went to the United
States and followed Joseph Smith and Brigham Young. Now he
was a Mormon and had acquired two more wives. He frequently
wrote to the Palatine lady importuning her to join him and his
new spouses. She refused. I laughed inappropriately at this
story, but she continued undeterred: she now had a nice man-
friend in Ottawa, an older man who took very good care of her
and her two children. There were, however, disadvantages to
being tied to a man who had lost his vigour.

Each evening the boat tied up and dinner was cooked ashore.
The second night of the journey we took shelter in a clearing
on the far side of a thick hickory boscage. The clearing was
perhaps forty yards from the boat. The habitant crewmen sang
some songs and prepared their bedrolls. As long as the night
was dry, they slept under the stars. Having eaten, my Palatine
friend and I took our way back to the boat.

"Do you know the song of your national poet, Thomas Moore,
about this river?" she asked.

"No," I replied.

"It goes like this:"

> Ottawai's tide: this trembling
> Shall see us float over thy surges soon.
> Saint of this green Isle! hear our prayers!
> Oh! grant us cool heavens and favouring airs!
> The rapids are near, and the day-light's past!

I offered my lady companion a hand to help her over the
gunwales. She accepted, but didn't let go her grasp once this
courtesy was accomplished. Clasping tightly, she pulled me
along the deck and into her small cabin. A three-quarter moon
provided enough light to permit our passage without stum-
bling.

"You have very smooth hands," she noted, sitting me next to
her on the narrow berth.

I explained that I had not practised my trade for some time and that... that... She interrupted by placing my hand on the bodice of her dress. When I made no move, she opened the dress and shoved my hand inside.

"So smooth. Yes, so smooth," she whispered.

I became faint and at the same time had the desire to giggle hysterically. This passed and I felt my heart beat like a hydraulic hammer in a forge mill. My companion peeled her dress down with a dexterity and celerity I found amazing and in an instant she was bare to the waist. Having never examined a member of our superior sex, I was overwhelmed and felt a rushing in my head like the sound of a thousand winds. The Palatine instructed me how to move my fingers, to lightly twirl them around her nipples. "So smooth! So smooth! were her only words. Then she stood up and I found my mouth at one of her breasts and her hands running rapidly through my hair. The low cuddy that serves as a cabin on Durham boats prevented my lady companion from standing fully erect, but that was no matter. She bent over me, lowing indistinguishable words as I suckled.

Soon I was at a loss for breath, and at a loss to know what was expected of me next. Fortunately, my companion took a half-step backwards and reached down and took one of my hands. This she pulled under her skirts. I had examined my own private parts and I knew where things were. But the way they felt on someone else came as a complete surprise. Everything was more moist and slippery than I expected. The Palatine lady hitched her legs apart and used her hand to guide me in two or three manoeuvers that otherwise I wouldn't have known.

After a short time, no more than half a minute, her knees buckled slightly and she stopped breathing for a moment. Then she shook her head like a sleepwalker suddenly awakening, removed my hands from her body and, recovering herself, gave me a kiss on the cheek. "Ah, dear boy, you know one way to make a lady happy. Be off with you now!"

I went reluctantly to my own small cabin and thought of her and also of John Oge for a long time before falling asleep. I was seized of a comfort that I might yet live his life and manhood for him. And often since that day I have thought of my sweet

Palatine, always finding reason to be thankful for the encounter.

In candour, I must admit that my first and subsequent experiences with members of the male sex were not nearly so satisfactory.

In Bytown, the old name of Ottawa, I transferred my belongings to the *Britannia,* a steamboat that was on a run to Kingston. My lightheadedness had abated somewhat, but there remained moments when, for no reason that I could apprehend, I would start giggling and would have to take out my handkerchief and cover my mouth.

This embarrassing condition manifested itself even at the most tragic of times. To wit: as the *Britannia* entered the first lock of the Rideau Canal a wee Irish bairn, the child of newly arrived immigrants, no more than ten or eleven years of age, passed me with a cup of tea in her hand. She had just been to the galley, where the cook had kindly given her tea with a large dollop of maple syrup, and she was very happy. She skipped perilously near the rail of the vessel at precisely the wrong moment, for the boat bumped the side of the lock and lurched sharply. This catapulted her overboard. Like most Irish children, she could not swim, and the blue-black waters immediately swallowed her up.

I knew I must do something, but was rendered impotent by that strange surge of hysteria such as had lately afflicted me. Some other passenger raised the alarm and the cook came crashing forward, ready to dive in. Incapable of uttering even a single word, I pointed to where the child had disappeared, and to his great credit the cook instantly plunged in. He emerged with no result. After gulping air, he went down again. Again no result. Other crew members joined him, but it was a full quarter of an hour before the girl was dragged from the water. All efforts to restore her breathing failed. The captain of the *Britannia,* a Mr Henshaw, insisted that we not journey forward until the child was buried. This was accomplished the next day, to the wailing accompaniment of her bereft parents.

The cook who had acted with such instinctive heroism was not a prepossessing man, but his manner lent itself to mutual conversation. His name was Wilson Benson and he was an Ulsterman, born in Belfast, about twenty-five years of age. Originally he had been a weaver, he said, but times in the old country were harsh and in 1841 he emigrated. He lived in Kingston and in the winter season had employ as a night-watchman. In his spare time during the day he bought and sold small goods. He had scores of "tips" to give me, and I listened attentively. Kingston, Canada West, was a rich city, he said, with several foundries. The place was not as wealthy as it had been, but a good broad-backed lad such as I could certainly do well there. He made me an offer to stay with his family at a rented house in the Stewartsville section of the city while I sought employ. Readily, I accepted.

'What Mr Benson had not told me was that his family was not with him, tho' the house gave evidence of his being a married man, as he claimed. After we arrived at his domicile, he made a list of foundries and smithing establishments in Kingston and passed these to me along with a hot, strong whiskey punch. He inquired if my arms were as strong as they looked, and I permitted him to examine them. With the second pint of whiskey punch he ceased to call me a good stout lad and began to refer to me as a darling boy. No matter, thought I. And when Mr Benson suggested that I retire for the night on a settle bed that he had made up near the wood stove, I acquiesced and was soon in a deep sleep.

I awoke to find him in bed with me. He had manoeuvered me onto my stomach and removed my lower garments. The moment I came awake he was trying to insert between my buttocks something that felt like a dowel. In an attempt to dislodge him, I bucked up. This gave him an opportunity to strengthen his grasp on me by putting his hands around the front of my lower body. He did so and then froze.

I was undone.

"*Mr* John White is it, my lass?"

Frightened, I begged him to say nothing to anyone. By the light of the stove I saw him smile. He uttered a proverb familiar to every small trader and animal drover the world over. "You'll have to trade me a horse for a horse."

What he meant he quickly made clear: he would have his way with me as a man has with a woman – in turn, my secret would be safe.

"Just once?" I wasn't so frightened as to stop bargaining.

"Just once."

And so it was that I discovered the feeling that comes to a woman with a man. It was neither painful nor pleasant, simply joyless. It left me feeling cold and blank inside.

I left Wilson Benson's house with his list of foundries and smitheries in my pocket and the full intention of seeking work. But, still having nearly 40 pounds in my pocket – or, more accurately, in my shoe – I elected to see the borough of Kingston. It was a handsome place and yet it had the air of an abandoned monument. This, I learned, was because many of its buildings had been constructed during that brief moment when the city was the capital of the Canadas. Two years before, the capital had moved. It now was Montreal. So Kingston was full of large edifices that were half empty or were being used for some temporary purpose, such as storage.

The borough had its attractions. It was very Irish and very Orange. One heard the same accents, only little modified by the Atlantic crossing, as in Londonderry: brisk, sharp voices given equally to sly irony and to billingsgate.

Finding a place to lodge was no problem: I had the pick of a score of reasonably priced establishments. I chose to lodge on the top floor of the Grimason House, on the upper part of Princess Street. The proprietress, who ran a tavern and a hostelry under the same roof, was a native of the north of Ireland and had been in British North America for less than a decade. She allowed me to work off half of my lodgings by serving the odd hour in the tavern, lifting kegs and being a jack-of-all-trades. Her husband, an Ulsterman, had died recently. Mrs Grimason never mentioned her widowhood without taking a handkerchief from her sleeve and dabbing her eyes. This she could do even while serving a pint of ale to a customer. As befitted a widow, she wore black.

Mrs Grimason sometimes drank a good deal of the house ale herself, and when in her cups she would start to cry and blather in memory of her husband. "Oh, thank the dear God for the kindness of Mr Macdonald," she would say, rocking back and forth and drawing her black shawl tightly around her shoulders.

After witnessing this performance two or three times, I ventured the next day to inquire who Mr Macdonald might be. "Och, you silly laddie, everyone knows who he is! He is the coming star in the heavens." It turned out that the man was a Kingston lawyer who now sat as a member of Parliament for the city. A few years previously, the late Mr Grimason had bought land on Princess Street from Mr Macdonald under a contract that required regular payments. When Mr Grimason became ill Macdonald did not press for payment, and he was even more lenient after the Ulsterman's death. He did not ask the widow for any payment. Instead, he became a silent partner in the Grimason House, where he drank deeply and occasionally carried on discreet liaisons in its upper chambers.

Mrs Grimason talked of Mr Macdonald reverently. "*He* sits always at that table," she informed me many times, pointing to a corner of the tavern. "*He* prefers clear honey to sugar in his hot whiskey in the winter." Would I ever meet this demigod? "Och, laddie, it's a great shame, but he has to spend ever-so-much time in Montreal on parliamentary business." Her round face bespoke a tragedy of epic proportions. "And then he is to go to New York for Christmas. His wife is ill, poor dear, and has spent a year in Georgia. In Savannah. They will be reunited." This prospect did not seem to cheer Mrs Grimason greatly. "But just you wait, my lad," she said, brightening. "Mr Macdonald and his good friend, the M.P. for Leeds, Mr Gowan, will be in this very room before the New Year is long past."

That was the third time I had heard the name of Gowan.

Kingston, being a garrison town, supported a lively professional theatre – melodramas and singing reviews were the staple. It was the theatre that brought on some of my most unsettling spates of laughter and led, eventually, to my humiliating experience in a public court of law.

The Theatre Royal at the corner of Queen and Montreal streets was a two-storey frame building painted a dull beige with chocolate-brown trim around the windows. It was the first playhouse I had ever entered and, tho' doubtless common by the standards of the world, to me it was a royal pleasure dome. The first night I attended I arrived early, so as to purchase one of the cheapest seats. I was helped to my seat by a young lady in a black skirt and white blouse who seemed to me to be the height of cultivation. Although from where I sat I could see only half the stage, it mattered not. Merely to watch the officers and their ladies arrive, to see the good burghers of Kingston, portly, well fed, escorting their powdered and manicured wives, was an enthralling entertainment. The first play that ever I saw was *The French Spy* and one of the most beautiful women in the world, the great Miss Chapman, played the lead. The next night I returned and purchased a seat on the main floor, centre. And every night thereafter, whatever was on the bill, I returned. Undeniably, the stage is a form of magic that draws many individuals, espcially the young. But it was something more that brought me. I felt an identity with the actors and actresses, with everyone on stage, for they, like me, were dressing in costume and thereby taking on a deeper, more passionate, more real self.

One of the players to pass through Kingston was Mr Leonard, billed as the best Irish comedian living, and perhaps he was. He acted in two delightful one-hour comedies, *The Irish Tutor* and *The Irish Attorney*. In one of these, quite by accident, he set off a chain of events in my life. In *The Irish Tutor*, he pointed his sword at a villainous imposter and exclaimed, "Though you wear all the costumes of the Turkey champion and his tribe, you shall never fool me or dupe my own true love." It was a silly speech, to be sure, but it put me in mind of the fine times I had had as a youth performing the Turkey champion in mummer's dramas. The future possibilities that this memory suggested set me to laughing, and I was grateful that the play was a farce so that my reaction was not noticed.

Next day, still lightheaded, but now pulled forward by a seductive vision that I did not wish to control, I took 20 pounds, half of my remaining funds, and visited several clothing emporia. I acquired the habiliments of a young lawyer, a tailor, a chemist-shop assistant, and two or three other occupations. I hurried back to my room in the Grimason House and impatiently tried on one costume after another. Then, more deliberately, I practised the gestures and postures of each sort of person in front of a mirror. To perfect my roles, I spent some hours in the tavern below watching and listening to men of various trades. So intent was I that Mrs Grimason asked me if I were in training to be a police witness.

Far from it. Armed with my observations and a schedule of the stage-coach lines that traversed Canada West, I was ready for the intoxicating weeks that would be, though not the happiest, certainly the most exciting of my life.

In the six weeks before Christmas I paid court to, and gained tangible affection from, no fewer than eight young ladies in four different cities. This I accomplished without detection. That I can remember in detail the dress of each darling, the way each acted as I had my first encounter with her face or her hair or her body, and that I could recall, were I so minded, the details of every stage-coach I took, of its schedule and whether it had leather or canvas curtains, whether it was set on steel springs or on heavy hide straps, bespeak my escape from the blackening unconsciousness that had afflicted me since my father's death at sea. I know the boot each of the darling girls wore, whether it was affixed with button hooks or with eye slits, whether she wore a chemise or a mere shirtwaist, and what she said as I told her she was lovely and put my lips to hers. All this serves to establish that I was not mad, only intoxicated. These weeks of pleasure and excitement did indeed purge my mind of the disease that had plagued it since the deaths of my brother, John Oge, and my beloved father.

Surely I did no harm. For these shop girls, dressmakers and mill workers, to be courted by a landed gentleman from Ireland or by a budding young lawyer could only raise them in the esteem of their fellows.

That is why I cannot fathom the narrow-mindedness of a vixen seamstress named Catherine Delpnic Oleander Wilcox – four names mind you! and for a mere seamstress – and her misbegotten thug of a male friend who apprehended me in Hamilton, Canada West, on Boxing Day 1846. I was taking the air in Hamilton's main square, walking through the snow-laden trees, when out from a small copse sprang a mangy scoundrel, a terrier of a fellow with ginger hair and squint eyes, ranting and raving and calling me unnatural and saying that I had defiled his heart's treasure. He beat at me with his fists, yelling all the while. It was an embarrassing spectacle. Later I learned the seamstress had teased him along and finally told him about me, a gentleman suitor. How he discovered I was not a male is beyond me; I can only assume that he spied on me and that I gave myself away in some small gesture. But for my surprise I could easily have knocked him down. Instead, he managed to land his blows and wrestle me to the ground. Just as I was getting back up and preparing to dispatch the ruffian a constable arrived in the company of the seamstress. I was charged with being a public nuisance. At least I had recovered my wits enough to realize that this was one occasion where my lost name might prove its worth. It is a sign of the low character of the harpy seamstress and her terrier that neither of them appeared against me in magistrate's court. In the end, Eliza McCormack was discharged unconditionally and both she and John White were immensely relieved.

6

Prospecting

"Good afternoon, young lady." (My brush with the law had been harrowing enough to make me wear skirts.)

I was staring into the window of a tea shop on King Street, Toronto, and I was cold and hungry. January of 1847 was warm by Canadian standards, but this only meant that the snow turned to muddy glaur and the moisture soaked all the more quickly through the soles of my shoes. Since being discharged from the Hamilton court I had worn dresses and a short jacket, more stylish than practical, for it did not prevent the damp wind from chilling my back. A satchel held all my worldly goods. This morning I had left my lodgings on Dundas Street, my money completely spent.

"Good afternoon, young lady," I heard again. It was the loud voice of a man used to addressing crowds. I turned, rather startled, from my contemplation of the sticky buns, creams and pastries inside the shop. The gentleman raised his hat and bowed slightly. "You seem very taken with the comestables inside the establishment." He was in his mid-forties and wore an unusually long frock coat and a cravat of uncommon design: a white neckstock with a small bow tie over it. "Would you consider it excessively forward of me if I were to ask you to join me for something to eat?"

I did not consider it forward at all.

The gentleman watched with a faint smile as I devoured a plate of scones and several tarts. Had I been less hungry I might have noticed that he was equally interested in the black bodice of my dress.

"You are Irish." It was more of a statement than an inquiry. I nodded. "And I think, from the fact that you do not bless yourself before eating, that you are not one of the Romish Irish." Another nod. "That's good. All to the good. For I am a man of God, though at present I serve Him in the field of governmental service." He did not explain this arrangement with the Almighty, and I accepted it as some sort of oracular utterance. "And you attended the national school of your homeland, did you not?"

"Yes."

"Excellent. I shall want my assistant to interview you some time. But excuse my manners. I speak selfishly of my own business. Tell me something of your fortunes and of your interests in life."

I was surprised to find myself telling him in long if edited detail of my troubles. Details poured forth of the famine, John Oge's death, Father's tragic illness. I cried softly and the gentleman patted my arm paternally. "And you have no place to live at present. No money?" I shook my head. "Then I shall loan you a small sum and recommend you to the keeper of a little inn that I know."

I did not object. I had an idea of what might be expected of me, but better dishonoured than starved, I calculated.

Which is why I was surprised that once the gentlemen had steered me to a small hotel and seen me registered, he formally shook my hand, gave me 2 pounds in coins and said, "My assistant will call on you in a day or two. Good day, young lady." Then he turned and was gone.

ঌ

I had made the right choice in selecting Toronto as the place
to reorientate my life. Surely it was the easiest large city for me
to understand. That is because, next to Kingston, it had the
largest Irish population in Canada. More than one-third of its
people had been born in Ireland, and best yet, most of the Irish
were practising Protestants not papists. At the time of my arrival, fourteen of the twenty-four city councillors were Irish immigrants and Protestants. The Orange Order had more staunch
brethren in the city than any political party. Although I had to
learn the layout of my new home, the culture was not very
different from that with which I had grown up in Ireland. A
good choice.

The Classon Hotel, where I had been given lodgings, was
nothing if not discreet. It was one building down from the corner
of Yonge and Wellington streets, where the Bank of British
North America was located. This bank, praised as one of the
most decorous and tasteful monuments to the city's mercantile
advancement, influenced the entire neighbourhood, including
the Classon hostelry. The owner was never seen by the inmates,
although members of the staff steadfastly claimed to have
glimpsed him on occasion. The barman, an Irishman named
Nelson Stewart who only rarely used his own name, oversaw
the daily management. He introduced himself to me with a
deep bow and a sweep of his arm. "I am, madame, your Faithful
Retainer," he said, and that was the name he went by. He managed the hostelry, which contained a dozen well-appointed
rooms, from a paneled barroom that was dark but spotless.
Most Canadian taverns gave drinkers little privacy; the Classon
provided separate drinking enclosures in the fashion of the
newest flash saloons in Great Britain. In each enclosure a table
and seats accommodated no more than four occupants. The
Faithful Retainer presided over this scene from a centrally
located bar, the inside of which was raised nearly a foot so that
he could always be looking down on his customers.

When, early that evening, I hesitantly entered the barroom,
it was nearly empty and I wondered how such a slow business
could prosper. The Retainer repeated his deep bow and offered

me a whiskey punch. "Don't look so fearful, young lady!" he said as he poured the liquor out.

I smiled wanly.

"You look as if you were afraid to be dempstered on a derrick, dearie."

I was puzzled.

"Hung on a gallows!" The Faithful Retainer smiled. "Why, once you've been lodged in this establishment for a week, you'll be as much at home as a gad yang on the Yangtse."

Doubtfully, I agreed. The Faithful Retainer had a strange way of speaking, but he might also have some advice for me about seeking employment. I asked him.

"Well, little lady, I would not be in too much haste or you will be going through the chapter house without taking a wicket." He seemed pleased by my frown. "I mean, if you're out looking too hard for employment, you might miss the opportunities that come your way here."

The first of these offered itself two days later when someone pounded on my door. I opened it and a weedy man in his late twenties blinked at me.

"I am John George Hodgins" he said, as if surprised I had not recognized him.

"Oh?"

"I am expected. Mr Ryerson sent me."

"Who is he?"

The Reverend Mr Egerton Ryerson is superintendent of education for Canada West. You met him two days ago. I am his assistant."

I asked Mr Hodgins inside. He had a thin face and a long set of ginger-coloured sidelocks, which along with his quick black eyes made him look like a weasel. He removed his coat and after carefully folding it lengthwise, placed it across the room's only armchair so that I had to sit down on the bed.

"I was born in Ireland," Mr Hodgins said in an awkward attempt to place me at ease. "And though I have lived here since childhood, last year the Reverend Mr Ryerson sent me to Trinity College, Dublin, to learn the latest methods of training teachers. The Irish are quite the most advanced in the field, you know." I did not, but that hardly mattered. "And, since in Canada West we have taken up not only the teaching methods but also the

Irish school books – wonderful books at a bargain price, I must say! – Superintendent Ryerson wants me to ask you a few questions about how the books were used in your own school as a child." He took out a foolscap pad from his satchel and sat down on the bed next to me.

"Tell me what you recall of the First Book of Lessons."

"How much of the Bible story did you learn from the schoolbooks?"

"What was the last book from the National School that you studied?"

As he went down his list of queries his hand rested on my knee and gradually moved up my thigh. Having resigned myself to this prospective transaction two days earlier with the weasel's employer, I let this one happen.

"Did any of the books confuse you?" he said, and without wasting a breath, "Where are the hooks on this dress?" He did his business quickly, in true Musteladian fashion, and for that I was glad. Then he buttoned himself up, carefully placed his notes in his satchel and slicked back his hair with both palms.

"I'm sure Mr Ryerson will find the notes on our little eclogue most helpful in improving our Irish-bought schoolbooks." Beast, I thought. "By the way, Mr Ryerson wants me to extend to you a further loan of 2 pounds. He hopes to be able to call on you in person soon." With that, the man put on his hat. "Oh yes – I shall give a small *douceur* to the barman below. Good day, miss."

As the weasel's footfalls disappeared down the stairway. I took a sudden loathing to my room, scooped up my coat and resolved to get out of this place. Barreling down the stairs, I bumped into the Faithful Retainer.

"You look a bit browned off," he observed. "You need some fresh air. But first have a bit of a mumble-warmer with me." He meant a hot whiskey. The Retainer, for all his strange talk, was a sympathetic and worldly-wise man. "Sure, it's hard for us folks from the old country to adjust here in Amerikay. I mean, the good times are gone over Borough Hill with Jackson's pig, and it's like finding a hare in a hen's nest for one of us to discover a good way of making a living."

"My feelings exactly," I said, smiling despite myself.

He led me down to the bar, where as he talked, he began

polishing a little circle of the walnut bar as if trying to wear a hole in it. "The way I see it, someone like you has to go carefully over the bricks. I mean, it wouldn't do, would it, to be falling in with gutter-prowlers and jack-bungers?"

I conceded his point.

"So, it seems to me that the best way for you to floor the odds is to think of yourself for the nonce as a prospector. I mean, opportunity walks in here, like flies to a horse's bottom. And the Classon is as safe as Balmoral Castle. Maybe more so." He concluded, "You take your walk now and think about that."

And so I did. The day was sunny and again unseasonably warm, a false spring. I jingled the forty shillings that the weasel Hodgins had given me; they were heavy in my purse. I felt rich and hailed a hansom, telling the driver to take me on a tour of the city so that I could ascertain its prospects. This I did with hauteur, like a grand dame in a play.

The tour started unpromisingly. Just off Yonge Street, along the north side of Bloor, was the Potter's Field where two exhausted grave diggers were breaking up the thawing earth with pickaxes. The hansom driver made a joke that I affected not to hear. "Most distressing," I said, and gave a dowager's sniff.

The cabbie took me to the tollgate on Yonge, north of Bloor, and for a time I watched farmers coming in from the country, reluctantly paying their ransom to pass. Not much there. "Take me past the cottages of the substantial citizens," I commanded, and the driver happily pointed out Ridout's wooded bush, where a bull was tethered in the mud and snow, Sheriff Jarvis's properties and the "cottages" of the wealthy families, whose names I pretended to know but actually memorized on the spot. Prospects looked better here. Toronto might be half bush still but some people had money, no question.

On reaching Queen's Street, I ordered the driver to let me down, as I wished to do some shopping. I tipped him excessively. As he drove off, hat raised and looking back at me in acknowledgement of the tip, his ponies and cab disappeared into an unfinished drain that had been left unmarked by the improving city fathers. "Silly man," I commented to a pedestrian who had witnessed this spectacle.

A nearby milliner's shop attracted my notice. I went through the door and changed roles – no longer a grand dame but a flighty young thing looking for a cute bonnet.

"Oh my, such a wonderful selection you have here," I said to the assistant, "it is so hard to make up one's mind. Goodness, this year's colours are excessively mauvish, aren't they?"

The assistant was no more than seventeen, a fragile, dove-skinned girl, a piece of fine porcelain that needed the gentlest of handling. I selected a hat at last and she promised that the mauve ribbons would be replaced. Could madame call back in three days' time when the work would be done? I left the shop convinced that not all of Toronto's prospects were financial.

Before returning to the Classon I stopped in a book shop and browsed for more than an hour. Here I was serious and said almost nothing to the clerk. If I were going to improve myself, I should fill the empty hours with books. I bought a novel by Maria Edgeworth and a guide to the business establishments of Toronto, and picked up the prospectus for a promising new literary periodical, the *Victoria Magazine*.

"You've been to the mountain to view the promised land," the Faithful Retainer observed when I returned to the hotel. "You must have concluded that if you stayed in this place, you'd never walk penniless in Mark Lane. I'll send the old herb woman around. She'll teach you how to avoid all sorts of things. Especially providing another archdeacon for the church," he chuckled.

I had entered the most exclusive echelon of the world's oldest profession, and this quite by accident and good fortune. It was extremely remunerative. I never entertained more than three or at most four times a week, and I garnered the most outrageous sums – 2 to 5 pounds – on each occasion. The work was not enjoyable, but Our Lord teaches us that because of Eve's sin in the garden, we must all labour amidst the thorns and the pricks. The elusive Mr Classon ran a hotel of the highest quality, and I was the only lady of accomplishment situated in it. For the most part its clients were substantial citizens, married men, who brought their mistresses to its private precincts. The barman remained protective towards me. Whatever its debits, my life was infinitely to be preferred to that of the poor wretches back in Ireland, filthy, starving and infected.

The debits, of course, were the men. The least offensive was the Reverend Mr Ryerson. He called on me twice a month, on average, when he was not travelling in the countryside and or in Europe on business. Each of his visits followed the same pattern. He would have the Faithful Retainer accompany him to my room, as if he were being shown it for the first time. The Retainer would knock, and when I opened the door he would introduce me to Mr Ryerson. Each time there had to be a formal introduction. After taking off his coat, Mr Ryerson would suggest that I be seated on the bed. Meanwhile he took a seat on the overstuffed chair and, exhaling heavily, uttered this sentence: "Many people have asked me to describe to them the course whereby I became a Methodist minister and a lifelong servant of God…"

The question worried him greatly, else why would he have brought it up so frequently? This prelude was followed by a narrative of some part of his life. "I was born on the twenty-fourth of March 1803 in the township of Charlotteville, near the village of Victoria, in the London district, now the county of Norfolk," was how he commenced our first meeting, and it took me a minute or two before I realized that I was not expected to make any reply, only to listen. "My father devoted himself exclusively to agriculture, and I learned to do all kinds of farm work… At the age of fourteen I had the opportunity of attending a course of instruction in the use of English language, given by two professors, one an Englishman and the other an American who taught nothing but English grammar." This, I thought, explained why he spoke the way he did. "But the person to whom I am principally indebted for any studious habits, mental energy or even capacity of decision is my mother, who poured religious instruction into my child's mind and infused it in my heart by her prayers and tears."

He spoke of his mother with much emotion, which made me think that now we would get down to business. "When I was very small, under six years of age," he continued, "having done something naughty, my mother took me into her bedroom and told me how bad and wicked I was and what pain it caused her." Now we were close to the moment of truth. I expected him to move to the bed. But he only kept talking. "My mother kneeled down, clasped me to her bosom and prayed for me. Her tears, falling upon my head, seemed to penetrate to my very heart." He went silent for a time. "This was my first religious impression. And, now, let us pray." He fell to his knees and with his head resting on the chair delivered a five-minute extempore prayer, following which he stood up, put on his coat and gave me a "loan" of 2 pounds. Always it was a loan. Then, with a grave face and formal bow, he took his leave.

The curious thing about Mr Ryerson's narrations in that he never repeated himself. Invariably he asked the same opening question, about how it came to be that he was a lifelong servant of God, and then carried on in those long and perfect sentences without reference to anything he had said at our previous sessions. Had I taken up the role of amanuensis, I would have been able to publish a chronicle of one of Canada's most singular and powerful individuals. Beneath his formality, he was not an unkind man. Once he asked the date of my birth, and on his visit nearest to that day he gave me a subscription to the *Victoria Magazine* that I had been interested in.

In the early days of this arrangement with Mr Ryerson I described his behaviour to the Faithful Retainer, for I was genuinely puzzled, tho' far from aggrieved, by his failure to consort with me physically. "Dear Eliza," the Retainer explained in his most worldly fashion, "to some men congress of the body is only the loose change on the table of life."

Meanwhile the weasel Hodgins kept knocking on my door and pretending that he was visiting at the behest of "the reverend superintendent." He always had a series of education questions, that he claimed, Mr Ryerson wished answered. He was not a man of substance, and he usually left me money in small coins.

Tho' I never positively enjoyed the physical aspect of congress with a male, there was one gentleman with whom I formed a temporary mutual bond. He was another Irishman, slightly shorter than average, with greying red hair and the aggressive mien of a pug dog. The first time I extended my services to him he was more intent on getting value for his money than on talking. Eventually, however, he started to chat. I asked him his name, for I have found that most gentlemen will readily give it, and that once the cloak of anonymity is withdrawn they are much better companions. "Ogle Gowan," he replied. I was dumbfounded, for it was a name I knew. My father had denominated him the truest Orangeman in all of British North America, and I had heard the name on several subsequent occasions. In my surprise I started to cry, the encounter having put me in mind of my beloved father, and presently I found myself blurting out the story of my family. He listened with great compassion. From my trunk of personal belongings I retrieved Father's Orange certificate, which he read with intense concentration. "No Orangeman's family is ever alone, so long as a single True Blue Orangeman has a loyal heart in him," he said and promised to help me, but exactly how he was not sure. He had just lost his seat in Parliament, and his newspaper in Brockville was losing money.

It was at this period in my life that my heart forever ceased to resist the pulls that nature exerted upon it. I began taking out young girls again, and wearing men's clothes when I did this. The Necessity within me was doubtlessly physical in origin – I had learned from my gentleman visitors that bodily needs do indeed exist – but the pageantry of it, the theatre, the being an actress and outside my own life for a while, that was a Necessity as well. I was very careful, for I did not wish to spend another night in gaol. My hair, which I had allowed to grow long, now was cropped short, and even in the Classon I wore mannish if not quite male clothes. The Faithful Retainer, when he first saw me attired this way, suggested that I was about to set up shop on Goodwin Sands, by which he meant that I might be shipwrecked when my gentleman callers saw me. In truth, the effect on them was quite the opposite.

The first time Mr Gowan saw me in my new clothes, he did not recognize me. "Where is Miss McCormack?" he asked the

Faithful Retainer, who replied that I was the person seated in a corner of the bar. That amused me and excited Mr Gowan considerably.

As is the case with most gentlemen, he needed to talk as much as he needed physical release. He had enemies all around him, he said, in Brockville, in Parliament, in Kingston, in the cabinet, in the Roman Catholic Church and even within the Orange Order. The list was long and the details of his run-ins extensive and frequently lurid. As a labour of love, but also to repair his financial position, he was engaged in a three-volume history of the order. On occasion, after finishing with me, he would turn to this topic and trace the story of the order from County Armagh in 1795 to his founding of the Canadian branch in 1830 and thence to the present. Every battle, every argument, every Roman Catholic atrocity he declaimed in an outraged voice. He talked fast. Sometimes he would mention all of the important Canadian politicians who were Orangemen and say that someday there would be no Republicans and no "Yankoos" in British North America, only True Blue Tories. Mr Gowan was very hard to stop once he got started.

Our acquaintance grew into a sort of friendship – I began to call him Ogle – and from this alliance I learned something about myself that I had never known before. This was that, just as many of my gentlemen callers needed someone to confide in, so did I. With great hesitation, I decided to reveal my secret life to Ogle. I cannot say why, but my usual direct manner of speech deserted me in my confession, and when I spoke it was with the coyness of those frail feminine creatures whose favours I pursued.

Alas, my secret made him uneasy, and as he was an instinctive and perpetual pontificator, it was inevitable that eventually he would tell me how to straighten out my life. "Unless you stop being both a man and a woman," he declared one day, "sooner or later this good city will burn you crisper than St. James's Cathedral." Fire was on Ogle's mind. It was mid-April 1849, and less than a week before central Toronto had burned. Ten to fifteen acres in the city were leveled, including the city market and the Anglican cathedral. Gowan had come to Toronto specially to see the carnage. "You won't get any place in this world unless you act, dress and think like a man."

Ogle's advice, like his opinions, was part shrewd insight, part self-interest, and probably part prejudice. That did not mean his advice was wrong. A year before, for example, he had warned me against my fellow Irish emigrants. "Stay away from the famine Irish," he had said. "They give us Irish a bad name. We give the honest Protestants help through the order, but the mass of helots are beyond redemption. Let them seep into the United States where the damned Republicans can take care of them!" It was harsh advice, but not unrealistic.

"I have a plan," he continued. "It all hinges on whether or not you can convince everyone – not merely harebrained shop-Janes – that you're a sturdy young man."

I knew I could convince anyone.

"We have to do a test," he said.

This explains how Ogle Gowan, former member of Parliament, founder of the Orange Order in Canada, Brockville newspaper proprietor, came to be sitting on a stage-coach alongside John White, artisan. We were headed for Kingston where Ogle was to attend a meeting with some politicians before going home to Brockville. We were the only passengers inside the coach; two young lads rode half-fare on the roof. To pass the bone-shuddering miles I took to asking Ogle what he, as an experienced politician, thought of various men in Canadian public life. It being my rule to practice absolute discretion in my professional life, I acted as if their names were chosen randomly, though in fact the men I mentioned all were customers. What about Superintendent Ryerson? Ogle pronounced him a Methodistical humbug the size of the Colossus of Rhodes. And George Brown (owner of *The Globe* and one of my most generous and secretive visitors)? "A national disgrace. The one man in British North America who deserves a public lapidation." I did not know the word. "I would stone the rogue to death!" Ogle explained. Trying to take the edge off his malice with humour, he added, "And I might even do that to the Jehu who is driving this coach. He seems to think we are in a chariot race." What about Schuyler Shibley? He was a small-time politician in a big-time way in the Kingston region and the one customer who had come close to violence with me. "A pig's bastard," was Ogle's curt assessment. And what did he think of John A. Macdonald, the M.P. for Kingston? "A coming young man. I have given him some good advice. You'll meet him, in fact. That is part of your test."

I looked forward to seeing Kingston again. When I said this to an ostler at a rest stop he responded, "Well and good for you, my man. But you're Irish, that's clear, and there're lots of your countrymen who never made it through that city." About fourteen hundred Irish immigrants had died of typhus in Kingston in 1847.

Eventually, the coach jolted into Kingston and started up Princess Street. "Where are we going?" I asked Ogle.

"To the Grimason, of course. You said you'd been there."

I started to worry. "What do I tell the owner, Mrs Grimason? What have I been doing since I saw her last? How have I been employed?"

Gowan laughed. "That, Mr John White, is another part of your test! I'm certain you'll be convincing."

Desperately I searched through the possibilities and fastened on the best source of information about the world of men's work – the endless tales of the Faithful Retainer.

Ogle and I reached the Grimason House and the proprietress greeted us warmly. "Mr Gowan, the esteemed publisher! And his friend, our former guest Mr John White! You must have a welcoming glass and won't Mr Macdonald be pleased to see you, Mr Gowan, and..." By the time these effusions were over I had my story straight and was able to spout out endless details about being a stevedore, a storeroom clerk and four or five other things, my narrative replete with the Faithful Retainer's distended demotic expressions.

Ogle listened admiringly.

"And what do you plan to do for future employment?" the proprietress wanted to know. Mrs Grimason leaned close to me and I was afraid she would discover that I was too clear of face, too soft of body, to be a man.

"John here is a ready lad, and I plan to find him work," Ogle said, taking Mrs Grimason by the arm and firmly leading her towards the taproom. "Now, what about some of your famous whiskey. Not the watered stuff, the real Mackay!"

The proprietress clucked happily and did as she was bid. Ogle and I had been served when she began flying around the room like a wild turkey in a cage. "Mr Macdonald is here! Oh, what a pleasure to see him! And, yes, it is a fine day, sir!" And on and on. No zealot ever worshiped his god with more enthusiasm than Mrs Grimason her John A. Macdonald.

Mr Macdonald was both pleased and slightly embarrassed. When Ogle introduced me to him, he clasped my hand firmly. "Another Tory voter, if I know my friend Ogle. Welcome!"

"And the son of a late Orangeman, my friend." This was important. In 1841, at Ogle's insistence, Macdonald had joined the Orange Order. "Mr White here is soon to join the order himself." This was a surprise to me. I adopted a mien of resolute modesty, hoping it was appropriate.

For a time Macdonald and Gowan traded stories, while Mrs Grimason kept us steadily supplied with the house's best whiskey. I watched Macdonald with fascination. He told stories brilliantly, in a we're-all-men-of-the-world-sort of way. He had a distinct manner of engaging in small talk: he made a point of asking the opinions of those he sat with, he frequently looked his listeners in the eye, and he flattered them. The only disquieting thing about him was a habit of sniffing the end of his fingers, particularly noticeable because his coat was cut an inch or two too short for his long arms. When he wanted to his listeners' especial attention, he would lean forward and drop his voice to a near whisper. His listeners were compelled to draw their heads down toward him, and there they huddled, a cabal.

"Now, Gowan," he said softly, drawing his clique around him, "we must plan how to stop this annexationist movement." The movement, to bring British North America into the fold of the United States, was largely business-driven, in the wake of the repeal of the British Corn Laws. But it was something no Loyalist, no Orangeman, would contemplate. Some English-speaking politicians saw annexation as a way to outflank the French. "Have you seen that even Sir Allan MacNab says we ought to consider annexation? He says we should fight French licentiousness by seeking an alliance with a kindred race."

Ogle snorted derisively. "Race of Yankee thieves and rebels!"

"True, Gowan. But we must plan."

I listened with some difficulty, on account of the whiskey, as the two men worked out a scheme for a body – "Call it the British North American League," Gowan suggested, "that would fight the annexationists." I managed to nod at appropriate intervals. The room started to spin and I refused any more of the ardent spirits Mrs Grimason brought round, but the two men kept drinking and scheming. God, don't let me be sick! I prayed.

Just when I felt I could hold my ground no longer, I realized that Mr Macdonald and Ogle were standing up shaking hands. I put my palms on the table and pushed myself to my feet. Macdonald, still apparently as sober as when he arrived, took my hand warmly. "It was a great pleasure to meet you, Mr White. It's rare these days to find young men who listen intelligently rather than barging into other people's conversations." Mr Macdonald would have flattered the town clock if he thought it had a vote. "I look forward to greeting you in the future as a Brother Orangeman. Till then..." And he was off, with Mrs Grimason bowing him to the door as if he were the grand vizier of some fabled Arab land.

I plunked down, beginning to perspire. Ogle was a little unsteady himself and he too sat. He leaned forward and in a conspiratorial tone gave his judgment. "Well, Mr John White, you showed me you can keep in character even when you have drink-taken. And you gained the acceptance of one of the shrewdest young men in all of the Canadas."

Then he stood back up, lurched and caught himself. "Tomorrow I'll expound to you my entire plan."

7

Hard Graft

I took up Ogle Gowan's plan readily because my life no longer
fit me. Lives are like clothes, I think. Tho' for a time a soul can
wear a suit of clothes that pinches, or flaps loosely, sooner or
later the fit must needs be tailored. Gowan knew that my life
no longer fit me. And, being Ogle Gowan, he knew that there
were things I could do that would benefit him.

It was late in the year 1849 that the plan began to mature.
When I told the Faithful Retainer that I would be leaving Toronto
without providing a forwarding address, he said, "You're a great
and game lady and I know that you'll never lose the shine-rag."
He meant that I would always be lucky.

The only awkward aspect of my leaving the Classon concerned the Reverend Superintendent Ryerson, who upon being
told of my prospective departure demanded repayment of all

his two-pound loans. From a notebook in the pocket of his frock coat he calculated the amount at nearly two hundred pounds. When I enquired which firm might be the most suitable publisher for my narrative of his life, he suggested that the loans be considered a gift. I felt a certain amount of guilt over this conclusion to our business, for as I have said he had not used me in the manner of my other patrons. However I was saving for the future.

Mr Gowan's plan was that I should establish my character as an honest, hard-working young man in the neighbourhood of Belleville. He had friends among the Orangemen in that area and would get me started. He would also recommend to one of the local lodges that I, being a strong Protestant from the old country, be admitted to brotherhood. This plan suited me; I assumed that after a few months working for various farmers, my skills in working metal would become well-known and I could set up as a blacksmith or foundryman.

What Ogle Gowan wanted in return was some information. He needed reports on a man he called the Pope and another, the Pope's Bow-wow. The Pope was George Benjamin, who in 1846 had succeeded Gowan after the latter's resignation of the Grand Mastership of the Loyal Orange Institution of British North America. Ogle had taken a great dislike to this gentleman, a substantial burgher of the modest city of Belleville. His second bête noire was a Belleville journalist – Gowan seemed to dislike all of his fellow journalists – Mackenzie Bowell. An Orangeman and close associate of George Benjamin, he owned Belleville's chief newspaper, the *Intelligencer*.

I was to write to Ogle at monthly intervals or less if necessary. In particular I was to watch for anything in the order that did not seem quite right, and to read Mr Bowell's paper in search of "intelligence," whatever that was.

I looked forward to this new role, but as things turned out my monthly reports were not as useful to Mr Gowan as he wished; in part that was because he made enemies so quickly that one would have needed an entire army of observers to watch them all.

Still, I received benefits. Finally I established a place and an identity for myself. I met the woman who eventually became my darling wife and the mother of my children. And

I joined the Orange Order, which made my political career
possible.

I was initiated as a member of the Loyal Orange Lodge, Number
1101, in Roslin, a small town in the northeast corner of Thurlow
township, about fifteen miles from Belleville. The town had
only fifty inhabitants. The lodge was located in the rear half of
the establishment of one Mrs Livingston, a widow who was
a storekeeper, a milliner and a gossip, and extremely anti-
Catholic. She was tactfully absent for the evening. All the male
Protestant shopkeepers and merchants of Roslin were present:
George Mowatt, the postmaster and general storekeeper; William Martin, who owned the local inn; Charles Hudson, blacksmith; Lowrey McNellis, cabinet-maker; and about twenty
farmers and three or four farm labourers from the surrounding
area. The hinterland of Roslin, though mostly Protestant,
housed a strong minority of Irish Catholics. The contrast
between the farmers, with their massive gnarled hands and
weather-beaten faces, and the merchants, plump and sleek as
cats fed on cream, was marked. One of the purpose of the order
is to keep Protestants of all sorts together so that we do not
split the rich from the poor.

Orange master: Brother, whom do you introduce?

Introducer: John White, a worthy friend.

Master: What do you carry in your hand?

Introducer: The word of God.

Master: Do you reverence that word?

Introducer: We do.

Master: What is the other book?

Introducer: The constitution and law of the Orange Association.

Master: (addressing me): Friend, do you, of your own free will,
desire to be admitted into our Loyal Association?

Candidate: I do.

Master: Kneel down.

I knelt down at a table, the brethren now standing, while one of the group read scripture over me: "O Lord God of our Fathers, are not thou God in heaven... so that none is able to withstand thee?" More scripture, and then the master bade me to stand. Then I took an oath almost identical to the one Father had taken in Ireland many long years before:

Candidate: I, John White, do solemnly and voluntarily swear that I will be faithful and bear true allegiance to Her Majesty Queen Victoria (... Father would have sworn fealty to George III,) and to Her lawful heirs and successors in the sovereignty of Great Britain and Ireland and of the Provinces, Dependencies of the said Kingdom (I wonder who wrote this oath?) so long as She or They shall maintain the Protestant Religion and the Laws of this country (that's the heart of the matter, isn't it?) that I will be true and faithful to every Brother Orangeman in all just actions, not wrong him, nor know him to be wronged or injured. (I was wrong. *That* is the heart of the matter) I swear that I will ever hold sacred the name of our Glorious Deliverer, King William the Third, Prince of Orange; in grateful remembrance of whom I solemnly promise to celebrate his victory over James on the 12th of July in every year. I swear that I am not, nor ever will be, a Roman Catholic or Papist (too true!) nor will I marry a Roman Catholic or Papist (marry?... me?) nor educate my children nor suffer them to be educated in the Roman Catholic faith (a wife and two or three daughters would be lovely, and no, I wouldn't bring the bairns up as papishes) so help me God.

Master: Therefore, I, the Master of Loyal Orange Lodge Number 1101, welcome you, John White, into our fellowship and in token thereof pass on to you our signs and passwords.

These secrets disappointed me, as holy mysteries often do when unveiled. The passwords consisted of a set of three questions – What givest us the Lord? What gavest King William to our land? What seek we for our people? – the answer to all three of which was the same: Oh, Lord, give Peace! But, disappointed or not, in joining the order I had made one of the smartest moves a Protestant immigrant could in Canada. I had joined a semisecret society through whose membership rolls, according to some estimates, passed one-quarter of the adult Protestant male population. The usefulness of the order to a new settler could not be overestimated. It immediately identified me as a person of the right sort, a member of the English Canadian Protestant majority, and a trustworthy one.

During my first ten months in the Belleville area I was a chore boy for various farmers, all of them Orangemen. None were ogres, but their lives were hard and so, perforce, was mine. I came to be more grateful than ever for the long hours I had spent at my father's forge, for, besides craftsmanship, those hours had taught me how to lose myself in my tasks. Instead of fighting hard labour, one must swim in it.

The soil in Canada is far superior to Ireland's. Here in an open field farmers can grow vegetables that would grow at home only in a hotframe. Potatoes are planted here; a horsedrawn drill replaces most of the worst labour, and the varieties grown are far superior.

There was at that time a great shortage of hired hands, for every immigrant wanted to own his own farm. Wages were high. I received nine or ten shillings a week plus lodgings, and sometimes the odd garment was passed my way as well. Mind you, for an Irishman the winter climate came as a great blow. I have seen cold that freezes the cup and saucer together at breakfast time. In summer, we worked from daylight to sunset harvesting hay and grain, often under a scorching sun.

The farmers I worked for were impressed that I read the newspapers so carefully. Ogle Gowan had given me a small sum for their purchase, but mostly I obtained them gratis after others had finished with them. The farmers said I was a lad of parts and would soon have land of my own. One Scottish farmer, a Galloway man, lent me Smith's *Wealth of Nations* and Watt's *Logic,* and I though I could not make much of them and he could not explain them to me, he said the reading of them would do me a power of good, just as when a person reads a part of the Bible he does not understand.

The farmers and their wives were respectable people, and I never had any difficulties concerning my private person. They bathed rarely, and out of modesty kept themselves well covered.

Even during the hot summer haying, when we would start work before breakfast, swing the scythes and haul the rakes until midday dinner and then, after a short rest, work until sundown, with only one break for water, we worked with our shirts buttoned to the neck. Often we wore scarves to prevent chaff from getting into our clothes.

Thus was I able to maintain my male identity. I came close, however, to being unmasked after taking a job in a bush lumber camp in the winter of 1850–51. That was a mistake, and I should have known it. I was so taken with the idea of learning a new set of skills that when a gang boss came through in November to put together a crew for a small camp in the Tweed area, I signed on. Farm work was mostly done for the season, and lumbering promised some money and a bit of adventure. The crew was not a large one, some twenty men from farms around Belleville, sons of farmers who did not wish to stay at home all winter and watch the snow fall and be talked at by their parents. Most of them were as green as I. When we arrived at the camp, a low building of hewn, unsquared logs chinked with mud and moss, the crew made a great scramble for the beds. I ended up in the corner, far from the fire that burned in the centre of the building. The draughts could get at me from both sides of the badly chinked cabin. I slept uncomfortably, for the beds were just frames with brush or hay on them. Thank heavens everybody kept their clothes on, it was so cold.

Next day I was given a five-pound axe, heavy by any standard, especially for a novice, and was sent with a crew to clear logging roads. The area we worked had been badly cut over years before, and there were lots of dead logs lying across the road. Our job was to cut them into moveable lengths and then use cant hooks to roll them out of the way.

Saturday nights there was always a party, or a sports, as the crew called it. We had a good fiddle player with us and we danced. Half of us wore hats, playing girls. That was as droll a situation as ever I had been in.

After the fiddler tired we played games, none of them very gentle. A great favourite was kick-ass. The name describes the games. One man sat on a chair in a corner and held his hat upside down on his knees. A victim was selected to bend down and put his face deep into the hat so that he could not see who was behind him. Then people would take turns spanking him as hard as they could. He had to stay there until he guessed the person giving him a wallop. I may have had a bit more padding on my posterior than most of my fellow workers, but even so nothing stings so much as a whack from the leather-tough hand of a lumberjack.

The other game the crew enjoyed was pull-the-stick. It nearly undid me. Someone said it was an esquimaux game, and it could have been. Two players would sit opposite one another on the floor, legs straight out, soles of the feet touching. They both grabbed one end of a short, stout stick and pulled. The game was to pull your opponent off the floor. Because I was a green lad, they played a trick on me. I entered into a contest with a strong fellow who slowly pulled me off the floor, while, without my knowing it, one of the veterans put a tub of icy water behind me. When the fellow suddenly let go I tumbled back into that freezing vat. Everyone laughed uproariously. I had to be a good sport and laugh too, when in fact I was terrified. "Well, go and put on some dry drawers, lad," the foreman ordered, giving me a good-natured clap on the back. "Right," said I, thinking fast. I went over to my bed and grabbed a dry pair of long johns and a set of corduroy trousers from my bedroll and made as if to put them on. "My god," I said, "that cold water sure makes a man want to piss!" and I hopped from one leg to another as if my bladder were pressing. The men laughed as I hurried outside, ostensibly to relieve myself in the snow. No one was about, so fast as I could I ducked around the corner of the cabin, peeled off my wet garments and put on the dry ones. When I got back inside the men were well into another game.

That was too close. I realized that as long as I performed heavy manual labour, I ran the risk of falling through a half-frozen stream or injuring myself in some other way that would betray me. Therefore when, two weeks later, the cook flew into a rage on account of something his assistant did and fired him, I told the foreman that I had some cooking experience and he made me the new assistant. As it turned out experience was not necessary, for my chief task was to keep the wood for cooking piled high. Our method of preparing food was very primitive. For a base we used a raised platform made of notched logs, filled with sand and set right in the middle of our cabin. Smoke escaped through a hole in the roof. We did two sorts of cooking. In the sand around the open fire we buried crocks of beans, bread pans and containers of salt meat; these cooked very slowly. And right over the fire, from a huge metal tripod, we hung a large pot for soups and oatmeal. A small crane held a five-gallon can of water always ready for tea or coffee – both of which we made so black that the liquid could have been used for ink.

During the long slack periods as a cook's assistant I kept up my reading of newspapers, which we received a week or two late. When the loggers came in from the bush at night the cook and I served them on tin plates, using ladles the size of horse bowls. The men pushed and shoved and there was always the danger that a fight might break out. I discovered that I had a knack for calming men down by shouting out jokes or mimicking the troublemakers. My antics were so well-received that even the offenders laughed. The day the newspapers came up from town, I stood on a big block of wood while the men ate and read them choice items from the press.

When camp broke up early in March I was sad to lose the camaraderie. As time went on I saw many of the lads here and there, and when I ran for political office several years later some signed on as faithful assistants.

Belleville was a proud little town and well it should have been: it had a number of wooden sidewalks. Visitors, asked how they liked Belleville, always got a second question: "And what do you think of our sidewalks?" Back from the bush camp, I liked them just fine. With a portion of my winter's pay I bought a new suit and calf-high leather boots in the style made famous by the Duke of Wellington and strolled happily down the main street of Belleville, taking in the afternoon sunshine free of mud.

I entered the office on the *Intelligencer*, on business for Mr Gowan. It was a two-storey frame box with a false front covered in peeling white paint. Through a large window you could see the work going on inside. I had decided to make the acquaintance of the editor and coproprietor, Mackenzie Bowell. The *Intelligencer*, a weekly, employed a printer and an office boy. Most of the writing was done by Bowell. The printer was nowhere in sight: the day before had been publication day, and no doubt he was exercising the immemorial right of his trade to get blind drunk before starting on the next week's edition. As I stopped in, the office boy scurried out on an errand. The remaining occupant of the office was a solidly built man about six feet in height, no more than thirty years of age, but with the mien of someone twice that age. He inquired the purpose of my visit like a schoolmaster examining a pupil.

"My name is John White," I stammered, "and I come only to make the honour of your acquaintance."

"Oh?" the man said curiously.

"I'm a brother Orangeman."

He seemed to relent a bit and began to introduce himself, then stopped short and demanded the answer to the three questions of the pass ritual, to which I replied, each time, "Oh Lord, send peace." Only then did he put out his hand and say, "Well, you are welcome. I'm Mackenzie Bowell. Come and have a seat." He probably expected to be touched for money, for one duty of serious Orangemen was to help their immigrant brothers find jobs and places of settlement.

He asked me where I came from and what my background was. I satisfied him that I was of solid Ulster stock, had good Orange lineage, knew an honest trade and was willing to work. After some minutes, perhaps because I did not appeal to him for money, and had repeated my desire only to make his acquaintance, he invited me down the street for an early pint of beer. "This office can shift for itself," he said, and slapped me across the back.

As Mr Bowell was shutting the door a large man in a well-made suit came in. He had a heavy walking stick that he carried like a club.

"What can I do for you, Sheriff? Print another notice of land going under the hammer for back taxes?"

The big man nodded. Despite his imposing presence he had sad eyes and seemed unable to speak. Silently he handed over a piece of paper with the notice scrawled on it.

"This is an Irish friend of mine, John White. Sheriff Moodie, Dunbar Moodie."

The sheriff bowed gravely. "Honoured to meet you sir," he said, and turned to leave.

"Aren't you the Mr Moodie who edited the *Victoria Magazine?*" I asked.

He turned back around. "Indeed I am, but of course Mrs Moodie did all of the hard work."

"I must tell you, that was my favourite reading and I am sorry it didn't continue."

"So was Mrs Moodie," the sheriff said morosely. "You must meet her some time and tell her that."

Mr Bowell and I made their way to a small tavern. "Sheriff Moodie is one of Britain's gifts to our civilization," Bowell said, his eyes twinkling. "I'm surprised he didn't ask you how you liked our sidewalks."

Once inside the taproom, Bowell carried on a soliloquy about the town of Belleville and its inhabitants. He spoke about local politics: Hasting County had just been created out of the old Victoria District, and every cheese factory owner, general store merchant and small-time land speculator saw himself as a great politician. At present "good old George Benjamin," the founder and former owner of the *Intelligencer,* was trying to unseat the new county's first elected warden and entertained visions of becoming a member of Parliament. Considering that Benjamin was also head of the Orange Order in British North America, said Mr Bowell, this was a "noble task." I could not tell if he was serious.

Mackenzie Bowell puzzled me, but I liked him. To this day I cannot figure out why the man had power over people or explain how he eventually came to be prime minister of the dominion of Canada. Perhaps it was because he was a hard, concrete-minded man melding the style of the old country with convictions about how things should develop in the new. As he talked on I realized that he was absolutely serious about matters of principle and ironic, almost sarcastic, about everything else. He seemed earnestly committed to the principles of Protestantism, empire and family, and at the same time willing to take the piss out of anybody who took up pose. While he did not like people with their hand in the till, he accepted their actions as the way of the world; what he could not bear was procurers who pretended to be choirboys.

What he spoke, actually, was immigrant. Among those of us from the British Isles and our offspring, irony is not just a mode of speech, it is a test of membership and intelligence. If someone makes a joke, the right response is not to smile but to remain deadpan, going along with it. Only the eyes are allowed to laugh. To show in this way that one understands is to pass a test – as important an exercise as getting the Orangemen's pass ritual right.

I listened, fascinated now, as Mr Bowell described his origins. Born in England, he had been brought to Canada at age nine. Then his mother had died. "That's one reason I took to you, John," he said. "You've had real problems, as have I." His schooling had been cut short. "Thank God Mr Benjamin took me into the *Intelligencer* office. That was my schoolroom and my university." He shook his head, as if in wonder at fortune's turns, and stroked his beard.

He had a full set of whiskers, which at first I thought looked strange on such a young man, but I was getting used to it. Perhaps I'll have to acquire facial hair, or at least long sidelocks, I thought. I knew some theatrical outfitters in Toronto who could fix that up easily enough.

"There's just one piece of advice I'd give you, John, and that's to be married at the first right opportunity."

"I don't have any prospects at present," I said.

"The moment will come, mark my words. I married at an early age, twenty-four, and Miss Moore – she's Mrs Bowell now – is the light of my life. Think about it, man."

With that, he announced that he had to get back to his office. We would meet again, he hoped.

As we approached the office my foot went through a rotted piece of boarding. "Very nice sidewalks here in Belleville," I noted.

"Yes, John, the very finest!" Mr Bowell swung into his office with a straight face, but his eyes were twinkling once again.

એ

I called in on Mackenzie Bowell at intervals of a month or so, and each time I was received most cordially. We hit it off well. On one occasion he invited me to be a guest brother at his Belleville Lodge, L0L 274. In my company he talked freely and with complete honesty. And that is why I began to cheat on the reports I sent to Ogle Gowan. Mr Bowell was becoming a real friend, and betraying his trust was not in my line. For a time I fended off Gowan by sending him innocuous items about the newspaperman.

Meantime I made a reasonable living doing strenuous work. During the summer and autumn of 1851 I earned good wages harvesting hay, corn and small grains in a ten-mile arc around Belleville. I thought some of going back to the lumber camp for winter, but then a conversation I had with Mac Bowell (that is what his friends called him, and I now counted myself as one), made me think: Why not use my smithing skills over the winter, going from farm to farm mending things for cash, food and lodgings? It would be a smart way to learn about the area. I hoped to buy a farm or business soon, and idle conversation often provides the best information. So I purchased a supply of threaded rods, various-sized metal straps and small bars, oddments that could be bent into almost any shape and a soldering iron for mending small items such as tea kettles and pans. I found, to my disappointment, that other craftsmen had been through Thurlow township in the fall; the pickings were thin.

To the east, tho', no craftsman had been for years. Tyendinaga township was Indian – at least the front land on the Bay of Quinte and the first four or five concessions inland – and no one reckoned that the Indians would pay for work. They could not have been more wrong. Not only did they have loads of work, but the Mohawks were the straightest, most trustworthy people I ever met. Some of them served me later with a loyalty as true as blood itself.

As far as I could see, they were to be preferred to the Catholics. The Mohawks were a proud people, and all the Six Nations maintained a fierce loyalty to the queen. In fact, the Tyendinaga Mohawks had formed two Orange lodges. But their loyalty was special, in that they viewed themselves not as subjects of Her Majesty but as her allies. They had been settled on various lands in the Canadas through a treaty signed by two equals, the British and themselves. Whatever their reasoning, they were as True Blue as anyone in the country. "Too bad they can't vote," Mac Bowell said to me one time, "for surely they'd vote Tory!"

For a miller in Shannonville, Richard Lazier, I fixed a broken sprocket and did some repacking of the gearing on his mill works. Lazier was a patriarchal figure – he had been a captain of volunteers in 1837–38, and the government rewarded him with a lifetime plum, the collectorship of customs for Shannonville. Thus he walked around town with his thumbs in his waistcoat pockets most of the time. Satisfied with the job I had done, he took me down to the council house to introduce me to members of the Tyendinaga band who might have some work.

The half-dozen council members interrogated me, and not entirely amicably. "What sort of an Irishman are you?" one asked. I did not get the exact meaning of his question. "Are you Popish or loyal?" This was important to the Tyendinaga. "Are you Methodistical?" No I was not, I replied; I had belonged to the Church of England and Ireland since birth. That was the right answer though I never fully understood their thinking about religion. Perhaps, without really being Christians, they adhered to the Church of England because the Queen was the head of it. That, for them, took care of the matter. Not long previously they had rebuilt Christ Church in Tyendinaga. The dedication brass declared: "To the glory of God our Saviour, The Remnant of the Tribe of Kan-Ye-Ake-Haka, in token of their preservation by the divine mercy through Jesus Christ, in the sixth year of Our Mother Queen Victoria." The band possessed a communion set presented to them by Queen Anne.

During the winter of 1851–52 I moved from one Mohawk family to another. Sometimes I lived in good-sized frame houses, sometimes in log dwellings, but however simple the surroundings, my hosts always made certain that I lived as well or better than they – which is something I cannot say for the farmers I chore-boyed for.

The Mohawks would have made fine Ulster Protestants; they were very dry in their manner of speech. One evening a man asked me why white people could not be like the Mohawk, all of one mind. I argued that I knew of two band members who were Roman Catholics. He acknowledged this, but added, "Still, brother, you must admit – you white men murdered the Saviour. If he had come among us, I think we should have treated him better."

The local Church of England clergyman was a drunk, but they did not mind. He was also well known for abusing his wife when in his cups, and not just with words. One of my Indian friends met him at the door of the church on Sunday and asked how could be abuse his family and then preach such a good sermon. "Did I preach a good sermon?" "You did, sir," my friend replied. "Well, then, follow the light, and let the lantern go to the Devil." That mixture of dryness and realism commanded respect among the Tyendinaga.

During the early spring of 1852 the Methodist missionaries came out in great numbers, like flies generating in the early spring sun. They had much on their minds, and it was hard to tell if they were more worried about the disposition of the clergy reserves or the iniquity of drinking among the Mohawk. Whatever it was, they upset the band elders, and some of the rebellious younger men and women of the tribe took to Methodism.

At one of the Methodist revivals held in the school near the council house, I laid eyes on Mr Ryerson for the last time in my life. As superintendent of education he was supposed to be a full-time employee of the government, not the Methodist connexion, but when he travelled about the province on school inspection tours he mixed in a good deal of circuit riding. The schoolhouse was packed, for three preachers had been advertised, and the meeting promised to last all night. Before they began, Mr Ryerson was introduced as a celebrated educationalist and guest of honour. He arose and began one of the autobiographical soliloquies I knew so well. "Many people have asked me to describe the course whereby I became superintendent of education and a lifetime servant of the public good..." He went into some detail, and also talked about his most recent tour of the educational establishments of Europe.

After about three-quarters of an hour the crowd grew a bit restless – they had come to hear some hellfire and damnation preaching, not the reflections of an overweight public official. Ryerson, who had spent a lot of time before crowds, tried the trick that usually worked among the young – looking people in the eye. He moved from face to face, staring down the devil of unrest in each soul, talking all the time – that is, until he came to me. Then he literally jumped. I was afraid he had seen through my disguise and recognized me as Eliza. Instead, he shook his head as if puzzled, then offered up an abrupt extempore prayer for the success of this mission. Finally he took his leave, looking over his shoulder with a fearful glance.

His fear was groundless. The Reverend Mr Ryerson had taken his place in my past. It was the future to which I was looking now.

"The two young squaws who were the principal performers in this travelling Indian opera, were the most beautiful Indian women I ever beheld." The voice was that of Susanna Moodie, her subject, a Mohawk family named the Lofts who lived in Tyendinaga township. They were Christian but also very proud of their native customs and religion, and they made it their mission to preserve the old ways by performing Mohawk songs, rituals, speeches and dances before native people and white men alike.

Mrs. Moodie was reading from the first copy of a book that her publisher, Richard Bentley of London, had recently posted to her. It was January 1853, and to celebrate its publication I was attending a literary soirée at the Moodies' house. This, a substantial stone cottage at the corner of Sinclair and Bridge streets, combined Georgian symmetry and Upper Canadian materials, and it was, to use Mrs Moodie's favourite words, charming and homely.

Susanna Moodie stood at the peak of her career. *Life in the Clearings versus the Bush,* which she was reading from, was only one of several of her books in the process of publication. "There was no base alloy in their pure native blood" she continued. "They had the large, dark humid eyes, the ebon locks tinged with purple, so peculiar to their race and which gives such rich tint to the clear olive skin and brilliant white teeth of the denizens of the Canadian wilderness."

I listened raptly. Never before had I seen a real writer, and now I sat in the same room with one. Mrs Moodie was describing persons I myself had encountered, and as accurately as if the Loft sisters were in that very room. Over in the corner, holding a glass of Madeira in a manner suggesting he was more accustomed to crystal than to beer tankards, was Mac Bowell. He had arranged my invitation.

Mrs Moodie read with the same clarity of expression that ladies visiting the spa in Donegal town had adopted when speaking to locals. The woman was not physically striking – in her late forties or early fifties, I adjudged, stoop-shouldered, with two coal-black hairs sprouting from a mole on her cheek. But she commanded attention like a schoolmistress at the blackboard.

"Susannah Loft and her sister were the *beau idéal* of Indian women; and their graceful and symmetrical figures were set off to great advantage by their picturesque and becoming costumes..."

Next to Mac stood a large man who looked more like an institution than an individual. This was George Benjamin, founder of the *Intelligencer* and now Worshipful Grand Master of the Grand Orange Lodge of British North America. Across the waistcoat that spanned his massive trunk he wore a gold key chain carrying the Orange and Masonic symbols. This was the first time I had directly encountered Pope Benjamin, as Ogle Gowan called him ("Warden Benjamin" was my respectful name for him, for at present he served as warden of Hastings County); in the social hour that preceded Mrs Moodie's reading he had made a point of meeting me. Mr Benjamin may have looked like a bank, but in fact he was an excellent politician and learned names and faces quickly. He had marked me as a sensible young man with a future. Now he was listening to Mrs Moodie with as much respect as if she were proposing a scheme of roadworks.

"... and becoming costumes, which in their case was composed of the richest materials. Their acting and carriage were dignified and queen-like, and their appearance singularly pleasing and interesting."

In the corner opposite Mac, as far from Mrs Moodie as possible, leaning heavily on a walking stick, was her husband. "I am John Weddeburn Dunbar Moodie," he had announced to me earlier, "and, if memory serves me, and usually it does, you are Mr John White from Ireland." He shook my hand firmly. "You must call me Dunbar Moodie, however. Can't bear that long handle." He had the tired eyes of someone who has seen too much and remembered too well things that he would rather forget. "As I recall, you praised the *Victoria Magazine.* Do tell Mrs Moodie that you liked it, won't you? She still regrets its failure and tends to blame the vulgarity of local taste."

The authoress, who had almost reached the end of her per-oration, paused for effect. The room was dead silent as she concluded her vignette of the Loft sisters. "Susannah, the eldest and certainly the most graceful of these truly fascinating girls, was unfortunately killed last summer by the collision of two steam carriages while travelling professionally with her sister through the States." The reader's voice dropped, her last words uttered with the slow cadence of a funeral drummer. "Those who had listened with charmed ears to her sweet voice, and gazed with admiring eyes upon her personal charms, were greatly shocked at her untimely death." Silence, and then the room burst into applause. One young woman, a Miss Johnston, was so moved that she began to weep and had to be taken from the room. Mrs Moodie curtsied modestly and promised to read more later in the evening.

I did not then know that the Miss Johnston who hurried from the Moodie drawing room under the touch of tender emotions was the lady who would share my life as wife and helpmeet. I did not know that the robust woman who arrived late to the soirée was Mrs Moodie's sister, Catherine Parr Trail, whose *Backwoods of Canada* had so strongly influenced my father and, as much as anything else, led to my being in the Canadas in the first place. Nor did I know that Mrs Moodie and another of her talented sisters had written *The Little Prisoner,* which I had studied as a child – like scripture. How could I have known? Their names were not on the title page.

Yet I went away from that literary evening knowing that I was not alone in being a woman who saw a world of beauty in such members of the fair sex as the Loft sisters, for Mrs Moodie, a woman of highest artistic genius, had seen the same truth.

8

Emancipation

When duty calls, you must answer the trumpet.

That was what Ogle R. Gowan, visiting Belleville in late May 1853, told me. Of course, he meant that when Gowan calls, you must answer the trumpet.

"Your reports have been quite useful, Eliza, altho' they have rather trailed off into prattle of late," he said. They had, indeed, for not only did I consider myself a good friend of Mac Bowell, but I could not see that George Benjamin was such a terrible man – quite affable, in fact, once one got past that bearish exterior. So my reports to Gowan had become mere tittle-tattle and invention, not the steaming malicious gossip that he wanted.

Gowan was on the verge of a war with George Benjamin and Mackenzie Bowell. He still wanted to regain control of the

Orange Order whose Grand Mastership he had resigned in
1846. He had just gone bust as a newspaper publisher in Brockville and was now operating a paper in Toronto. He had been
elected an alderman in Toronto, hoped to be elected an M.P.,
and was trying to recapture what he called his rightful place
in the Order. When he told me these things he fairly bristled
with the injustice that had been done to him.

"Still, Eliza, you can be of use to me in the great approaching
contest." He used my female name to punctuate his sentences,
reminding me that he and I shared a secret which bound me
to him like a prisoner. "In your capacity as *Mr* John White, you'll
accompany me to Kingston as I prepare to unseat Pope Benjamin from his alabaster throne." Thus was I press-ganged into
acting as a combination outrider and aide de camp. I would be
Mr Gowan's secretary, errand boy, confidential assistant and,
in the contested election for the Grand Mastership, a floorman
rounding up votes. I was not keen on any of this, but what
could I do?

"Won't Mr Bowell and Mr Benjamin see me with you? And
won't that end my intelligence-gathering for you?"

"Never mind, my dear Eliza. Your use in that field is now
done. That was reconnaissance, this is war!"

So I accompanied him to Kingston early in June. The great
gathering of the Loyal Orange Institution of British North America was scheduled for the middle of the month, and like a general
walking a prospective battlefield, Gowan wanted to get the feel
of the place first. He set up headquarters at the Grimason House
and also took a room in the Queen's Hotel, near where the
actual contest would take place, at Kingston City Hall. Mrs
Grimason fussed over him and said Mr Macdonald would be
so very glad to see him and wasn't it nice that young Mr John
White was with him again and everyone obviously prospering?
Anything Mr Gowan wanted would be made available. If there
was a God in heaven, he would win back his Grand Mastership.

In fact, Mr Macdonald was not as happy to see Gowan as
Mrs Grimason had suggested. When they met, he was reserved.
He looked sleeker than when I had first seen him. His shirtfront
was well starched and perfectly white. He still sniffed his fingers, however. I was gratified to discover that he remembered
me and my name at once. "I hope that you prosper and that

you always vote Tory," he said to me. In his mind, a strong link bound the two conditions. As for Ogle, he assured him he would do nothing on either side to affect the outcome between him Benjamin. "I'm a good Orangeman and I've done my duty in arranging for the Grand Lodge to use the House of Lords without fee." This was how he referred to Kingston's city hall, a building constructed when the city fathers had visions of their metropolis becoming the Rome of the Canadas. It was large enough to house a full one-quarter of the population of the city. "But, Gowan, I am also a politician, and a good one. The Benjamin people are strongest in the east of our province, the very part that I represent. And you and your people are for the most part from Toronto and the west. That is true, isn't it?" Ogle nodded. "What should a good politician do?" Mr. Gowan suggested that he remember old frendship and loyalties. "And that, Gowan, is why I'm remaining completely neutral. Politics tells me to go for Benjamin, and it is only for the sake of my old friendship with you that I have decided to remain neutral. I won't attend the sessions. In fact, I'm sure that urgent business will call me out of town." After he took his leave from us, Gowan turned to me and said to me that Macdonald was an ungrateful Scotch whelp who would come to no good end.

I had one bad moment during this period. I was descending Princess Street in the direction of city hall to check on some arrangements when at a corner I crashed into a portly man who was in a great hurry and knocked him over. "Watch where you're headed, you ignorant young sod!" he said, picking himself up and brushing the dust from his trousers. It was Mr Schuyler Shibley, whose trousers I had seen on and off several times during my Classon days. He bent over and retrieved a silver-handled cane. I thought he might take a swing at me with it, but instead he peered at me. "Don't I know you?" he said. I replied that I thought not and was sorry to have inconvenienced him. "Well, I guess I would not have had occasion to meet such an ignorant lout as you! Good day and good manners, young man!" And he disappeared in a cloud of indignation. I had to lean against the building to stop myself from collapsing. My heart raced, my face burned.

That was a valuable lesson. If you are dressed as a man you are thought to be one, and that is how you are treated. When

I reflected on that it made me feel more confident. I *am* John White.

Working for Gowan I found to be increasingly distasteful, especially because of his habit of calling me Eliza when we were alone. There was no comradeship in this trick of his, only threat.

The day before the Grand Lodge opened I met Mac Bowell near city hall. Mac was County Grand Master for Hastings and one of Mr Benjamin's chief lieutenants. He took me into an inn for a smoke and a talk. He had taken to smoking a large Meerschaum pipe that he thought gave him a sagacious air. "John," he said, "we – Mr Benjamin and I – were very disappointed to learn that you're an assistant to Mr Gowan in his bid to recapture the Grand Mastership of British North America. Of course, a man must follow his conscience, but John, I thought you and I were friends." I tried to explain that I was helping Mr Gowan only because I owed him a debt: he had found me employment when I was just starting out in the Belleville area. That was plausible, and Mac accepted it as a genuine reason. But he argued against it and went into detail about Gowan's crimes against the Orange Order – including dismissal from the order in Ireland for being of bad character. Mac had a satchel filled with documents and pamphlets about Gowan and they seemed convincing. He talked to me for an hour and a half with the earnestness of someone trying to save his brother from a grievous error. For the good of the Protestant cause in Canada, I had to forsake Gowan, he said. "This is one of those times in your life when you have to decide whether you're a man or not."

I said that I would consider the question.

Two days later the election took place for the Grandmastership of British North America. Mr Benjamin was renominated, Mr Gowan's name was placed in nomination. The Kingston City Hall council chambers reminded me of a cock-fight. Orangemen might all be brothers and might all want the Lord to bring peace, but that was only some of the time. Now they wanted blood. Mr Benjamin, in the chair, had a hard time keeping order. Cries rang out all over the room, curses flew around, in that sort of half-whisper that carries as far as a shout, delegates were in and out of their seats like obstreperous children. The election came down to whether or not proxy votes would be permitted. The Benjamin people had collected a lot of proxies from the eastern part of Canada West and from the Montreal area. If they were valid, Benjamin would win; if not, Gowan would. Mr Benjamin, who fancied himself a parliamentarian, fell into a trap. He permitted someone to move a resolution limiting each lodge to one vote, which was the same thing as saying no proxies. The debate turned into a shambles. There was pushing and shoving and Gowan's supporters began threatening Benjamin's, making them fear for what might happen later on. When it came to the vote, Ogle's camp won. So proxies would not count.

The handwriting was clear, and at this point Mr Benjamin and all save three of his followers left the council chambers. As the walkout began, Mac Bowell tugged my sleeve. "Well, John, this is the Rubicon. Are you with us or gainst us?"

I was the last brother to follow Mr Benjamin from the room. The Gowan men were yelling and tossing their hats in the air and slapping each other on the back. Ogle ascended the podium and stood full centre, surveying his victorious field of battle. He watched our group retreat. Just before going through the door, I turned around and caught his eye for a long moment.

Our association was over. But like many failed partners we still were joined, for each had a hold on the other's throat. He knew of my past, I knew of his passions and political methods. From that day on, we honoured a compact of distant silence.

Soon after that the Orange Order split and Avignon Papacy, as some bitter wit called it, commenced. There were two Grand Masters – for Mr Benjamin claimed that Mr Gowan's election was illegal – and thus two orders. In 1856 when the order reunited, both Mr Gowan and Mr Benjamin had to stand down. That was the price of peace.

But all this mattered not a fig to me, for I had found my future. I was captured by a sweetness, by a happiness, by a reverence for life that has filled all my days since with profound satisfaction. It was in the spring of 1854 that I met Miss Esther

Johnston, whose lissome form I had fleetingly glimpsed at the Moodies' soirée.

The previous winter I had again spent as an itinerant metalworker in Tyendinaga township, for the most part among the Mohawks, but now I spread my trade farther north where immigrant farmers made up the majority. Most of them were Irish and not a few of these popish. By the time I returned to Belleville in March I had put aside one hundred fifty pounds. This brought my personal savings – mostly acquired in my Classon days – to over one thousand pounds, which amount I lodged with the Bank of Montreal, having admired the institution ever since seeing its great headquarters in Montreal soon after arriving in this country. I lived simply, but I knew I could buy a farm or a business if the notion took me.

Mac Bowell invited me to his house for an evening whenever I visited Belleville. He was proud of his house and family and still painted the glories of domestic life in expansive strokes. I envied him. "Meet a nice girl, marry and settle down," he advised me frequently. But where could I meet the right person? Picking up working girls was one thing, finding the right sort was quite another. "Try joining the Belleville Reading and Literary Society," Mac suggested.

The society rented two rooms above the office of the *Hastings Chronicle*. It shared these rooms with the Belleville Branch Bible Society. The literary club was modeled on a very well-known Irish one, the Doagh Book Club. Members of the group paid a shilling a month and the society bought books, mostly of the improving sort. Each fortnight the group met. Sometimes there was a formal debate on a particular literary theme. At other times, a book was assigned and we all gave our views on it. The society functioned under the patronage of Sheriff and Mrs Moodie and, tho' they never appeared their presence was felt. They had donated copies of each of Mrs Moodie's works to the society library. Together with the Bible group and various churches, our literary club was one of the few places a respectable young woman could attend without a female companion or chaperone.

I was welcomed into membership by virtue of a short note of introduction written for me by Mr Benjamin at Mac Bowell's request. During the first meeting I concluded that I had made an error. We spent the entire evening discussing whether or not Milton's *Paradise Lost* was an attempt to replace the Bible, since it claimed to explain the ways of God to man. The group consisted of older women with strong opinions, office boys with delicate opinions, and the ugly daughters of the women with strong opinions, who themselves had no opinions of any sort.

The second meeting changed my mind. We had as a guest lecturer one of the inspectors of the common schools, and his consuming passion was the mythology of the Scandinavian nations. He accented the first syllable of Scandinavian making the word sound as if it would explode. For some reason that he never explained, he refused to use the word Norse. He was quite engaging on the subject of early *Scan*dinavian belief and its bloodthirsty side. The best part of his lecture concerned the Norns, personifications of fate who usually appeared to men in the form of virgin goddesses.

This same night Miss Esther Johnston attended the literary meeting. Tho' the first time I saw her she had left little impression on me, this time Cupid's arrow struck right in the center of my heart. My goddess! My fate!

What I remember best about that meeting was a wonderful line of buttons that ran down the front of her prim black dress. They started at her throat, and like a tiny army of ebony beetles marched between her breasts and disappeared into a bright waist sash that accented her otherwise severe garb. I could not help but imagine where the small army would have ended its march had not the sash intervened.

I asked Mac Bowell for advice. He laughed when I told him that I had been unable to bring myself to speak to Miss Johnston. "Go to the next meeting and ask to walk her home, silly man!" Easy advice to give, but for the first time in my life I was afraid of talking with a girl. Me, who at one time could blarney my way into the good graces of any young thing from Montreal to Buffalo and have my hands up her petticoats after two meetings! Me, tongue-tied and afraid!

I decided to lay siege to my goddess, and very carefully. I took a job at the Victoria Foundry on Pinnacle Street in Belleville. I swore to live in Belleville for at least the next year, or until I had completely failed or succeeded in my quest. The next meeting of the Reading and Literary Society seemed far, far away. In anticipation of an encounter with Miss Johnston I made a list of questions to ask and topics to discuss as I walked her home.

And when the meeting finally came, I made a terrible fool of myself, as a few snippets from her responses will show:

"Yes, you may, see me home, thank you."

"Yes it is a warm evening for this time of year."

"No, I did not know that the population of Belleville had grown from 4,000 in 1850 to over 5,600 today."

"I think it is a good idea, yes, that the railway is coming to Belleville. It will bring mercantile benefit and cultural and literary improvement."

"No, I do not think the sidewalks are particularly good."

"No, I am not Church of England."

"I am pleased you do not mind Methodists and Presbyterians. Very good of you, I'm sure."

"No, you do not need to walk me any further. My lodgings are just up the street."

"No! Good night!"

Oh my God! How could I be such a clothead? The memory alone makes me wince. Not only had I failed to make good conversation, but I had insulted her religion. I might as well put my head on the anvil and have a trip hammer drop on it for all the good my brains do me, I thought.

That passed. Mac Bowell listened to my humiliating story and said that I should try again, then went on about that damned spider and Robert the Bruce. He reminded me, too, of something that I knew but, being smitten, had forgotten – that most people would rather talk about themselves than about things, ideas or even other people, and that flattery is the universal social solvent. At the next meeting of the society I did much better:

"Yes, I suppose you may walk me home."

"Why thank you! I am pleased you thought my reading of Mr Tennyson so effective."

"Oh, indeed! Well, you are correct. I do take an informed interest in fashion. Actually, I am not merely a seamstress any longer. I make complete copies of London designs. And sometimes do my own dress designs for ladies of the highest quality."

"Thank you, I will take your arm. These potholes can be dangerous."

"It was good of you to see me to the door. Teatime next Saturday? Yes, that would be fine."

Thus began a courtship as slow as the mating dance of the pharaohs. To make myself agreeable I went so far as to attend divine services with her at the Wesleyan Methodist Church on Bridge Street. Nay, I went farther. On one occasion Esther mentioned the Reverend Mr Ryerson as being the great lynchpin in the Methodist connection. I praised the man fulsomely, claiming to have read the newspaper reports of his activities, and said he was a true Christian example to us all.

So circumspect was I in courting my Norn that it was not until the spring of 1855, a full year after I had encountered her, that I essayed to do more than touch her sweet hand. During the times when we walked-out of an evening, our conversations became more and more confidential in nature and one time she confided to me that I was the first member of the opposite sex with whom she felt at ease: I was not so hard in manner as other men, and I seemed intuitively to understand a lady's humours. "Come to think of it," she said, "except for you, I don't like men at all."

I said that I could understand that.

Not long after that I touched my sweet Norn's flesh for the first time, and the thrill of it rises in me even now. The dear angel is wearing an outfit of a style popular about the time Victoria acceded to the throne and that Esther, ever conscious of fashion, says is on the verge of coming back: a one-piece outfit with a tight waist, puffed sleeves and a full skirt plumped out by pettitcoats. The design shows the lines of the female form to perfection if, indeed, by exaggeration. An innocent straw hat with a large brim coyly contradicts the wordly contours of the dress. On two previous occasions we have kissed lightly, but this is different. I kiss Esther and she showers kisses back on me. I believe it is mutual love. I venture to touch her limbs. She presses against me and makes noises that have no words. My hands explore her and soon I touch everything that I have worshiped so long from afar. The movement of my hand upon her most private person leads her to gasp and, finally, to say enough.

She kisses me over and over, and I know that we are each other's forever. My joy becomes despondency, my happiness hell. Esther and I fall fathomlessly spinning into love, tumbling over each other's souls through the heavens. The darling adores to have me touch her and now, when we walkout alone, she wears no chemise under her outfit, so that pleasing her is easier, movement less restrained.

The hell that tears at me has two parts. Together, they work back and forth across me like a double-handled rasp, never ceasing, always abrading. One is Esther's family. They do not take to me. The Johnstons started out as bush savages, and Mr Johnson looks half Indian, even, though he is not, but now they have a wee farm and a small cheese factory, near Roslin. That little bit of enterprise has made them think of themselves as substantial citizens. They have no idea that I have savings in the bank and I am too proud to tell them: no truckling, my father often said. I am common, Mrs Johnston says, and Mr Johnston says that there is something not quite right about me.

That is nothing compared to the other source of pain. I want Esther for my wife, our fates entwined. She loves me. But, while I know that she would be a perfect wife, I realise that at best I would be a singular husband. The problem haunts me day and night: if I do not tell her of my particular circumstances, we can never marry – and if I do, she might leave me for good. Dear God!

Daniel Defoe saved me. I think literally, he saved my life, for without Esther I did not wish to be alive.

It was the custom of the treasurer of the Literary and Reading Society to report at each meeting the state of funds and also to read out the titles of new books purchased and any donations received. At our mid-September meeting in 1855 he read off the purchases for the library – Mrs Gaskell was just becoming popular – and added that Sheriff Moodie had graciously sent along a volume acquired from a barrow stall in the Toronto market. The volume was in terrible shape, the front cover attached by only a few threads and many of the pages water damaged. But that mattered not. What mattered was that it was a mid-eighteenth-century edition of *A General History of the Robberies and Murders of the Most Notorious Pyrates* by "Charles Johnson." "Of course we must send this out for rebinding right away," the treasurer said. I volunteered immediately. I was intending to visit Kingston the next week, I said, and should be happy to take it there for mending. Esther looked at me in surprise, as I had not mentioned such a journey, and indeed I had none planned. But, by some God-given instinct, I knew that if I could just lay my hands on that book, the greatest problem of my life would be solved.

"Why did you want that book?" my angel asked me as we left the society.

"Because I want to read parts of it with you," was my answer.

We entered my lodgings discreetly – my landlord was a bluff German and cared only that I paid my rent on time and kept the place tidy – and sat down to read by the coal-tar lamp. I steered Esther to the chapter on Mary Read and Anne Bonny. She gasped as she saw the Dutch engravings of two women dressed as male pirates. She flipped the pages quickly and then came back to look again, like a moth to flame. Then she read every word about the two women's adventures. As she read I kept my hands busy beneath her clothes. She was very excited and had a spasm.

"Esther, I said, "has it ever occurred to you that women might make much more satisfactory... be more attractive... gentler than... than men?" She blushed deeply, thanks be to God. And then my secret tumbled from me, along with a declaration of my soul's pledge to her.

She stands up and, dear God, she is intending to leave, and to leave forever. But thanks to Heaven for miracles, she only gets up, walks to the bed and sits on it demurely. She pats the place next to her, indicating that I should sit there. I obey, speechless. She kisses me on the cheek, more a sisterly peck than a lover's endearment, and raising one hand to my shirtwaist says, "Well, John White, I think it's time we make your secret into *our* secret."

My dear Norn did to me with her hands what I had long

done to her, and more. We played with our tongues and our lips and learned that we were not just twin souls but twin bodies. Merciful God! could there ever be such happiness?

"John, I think we should marry."

"What about your parents?"

"They're just poor people who are proud. You said you have savings; money will buy their acceptance."

I nodded.

"And I think we should have a large family."

Part Three
My Own Man

9

Home and Hearth

I require and charge you both, as ye will answer at the dreadful day of judgement when the secrets of all hearts shall be disclosed, that if either of you know any impediment, why ye may not be lawfully joined in Matrimony, ye do now confess it. The words were frightening, but neither Esther nor I flinched. We knew what we were doing. Though not a deeply religious person, I had insisted that we be married by a priest of the Church of England, not a Methodist preacher; ever since my experience with Egerton Ryerson, I had found Methodist ministers to be full of cant. For the occasion I had rented a tailcoat, double-breasted, with a collar high behind such as Wellington had worn. The coat was pinched and rather short, the shoulders padded, creating a masculine effect. I had spent considerable care attaching a set of longish sidelocks from my theatrical kit and applying a hint of dark around my chin line, suggesting that my razor was not quite sharp enough. Esther, in white, looked crystalline. Her complexion, naturally fair, was nearly translucent, like a piece of fine alabaster held up to the light. Any observer could see that she was wholly and deeply in love.

For be ye well assured, that so many as are coupled together otherwise than God's word doth allow are not joined together by God; neither is their matrimony lawful. Sitting in a front pew, Esther's parents appeared to savour the idea of God's judgement. They had given their consent to the marriage only after prolonged negotiation, demands and threats. Even now, in the middle of the ceremony, Mr Johnston was scowling. The priest noticed this and almost stopped the service. The arrangements, made around the Johnston family's kitchen table, were simple: I would pay them an excessive rent for the occupancy of their small farm and cheese factory, and would take over both as going concerns. In return, the Johnstons would not stand in the way of the marriage. In the end it was Mrs Johnston who turned the bargain. She told her havering husband that the terms were generous enough, and if he did not take this chance to move off the farm and into the comfort of Belleville, she refused to do any more of the heavy work in the cheese factory. Then where would the profit be?

John, wilt thou have this Woman to thy wedded wife, to live together after God's ordinance in the holy estate of Matrimony? Wilt thou love her, comfort her, honour and keep her, in sickness and health; and, forsaking all others, keep thee only to her, so long as ye both shall live?

Esther, wilt thou have this Man... so long as ye both shall live? The assemblage was small, no more than twenty persons, but very respectable. That was guaranteed by the presence of George Benjamin who recently had been elected member of Parliament for North Hastings.

I, Esther, take thee John to my wedded husband, to have and to hold from this day forward, for better, for worse, for richer, for poorer, in sickness and in health, to love, cherish and to obey, till death do us part... and thereto I give thee my troth.

It was the late fall of 1856, and honeymoons were popular. The word had changed from its original meaning – the first month after marriage – to mean a post-nuptial holiday. At that time the most exciting way to take a honeymoon from Belleville was by train. The Grand Trunk railway had opened its local station in October and, suddenly, this miraculous mode of transport put the town in touch, comfortably and quickly, with Toronto, Kingston and Montreal. Esther danced about the room when I told her that the honeymoon would be a train trip to Toronto and that we would stay in a first-class hotel. She had never been farther away from home than Kingston. This would be an adventure.

I had not been completely honest with Esther about my past, and so when we checked into our reserved suite in the Classon Hotel in Toronto it was with some trepidation on my part. There was always the chance that someone might blow the gaff. As it turned out, the domestic staff had changed completely since my day there. Only the Faithful Retainer remained. When I announced to him that Mr John White of Belleville and his wife were checking in, he looked up from the glasses he was polishing, blinked once, twice, and then with the true professionalism of those who have seen every aspect of human nature and who judge nothing, he said, "Yes sir. Welcome to the Classon!"

A day later I went down to the bar while Esther rested in the room and had a confidential and pleasant reunion with the Faithful Retainer. He was pleased for me and approved of my new identity. As for Esther, he thought her a great beauty. A prize.

"I always knew you had the urge to leave the sail and go into steam," he observed. "Have you had this marriage all done up right at a doxology works?"

"Yes, it was a church wedding."

"Well, in that case," the Retainer concluded, "those whom God has joined together, let no man put asunder."

The spring of 1855 had seen an economic bust, and things did not get much better until the end of the decade. This was not a good time to be starting a family business, and it was grudgingly that I paid the Johnstons 40 pounds a year in rent when a decent house in Belleville was going for 15 pounds a year at most. But I realized that I was not so much renting a farm and cheese factory as paying the ransom for my beloved Esther.

Still, hard times are good times for those with money in the bank, at least if they have a good nose for investment. Esther and I worked out a plan. On our twenty-five acres we grew almost everything to meet our daily needs, and thereby saved. Twenty of the twenty-five acres went under cultivation; the remaining five spread over a rocky, hilly stretch that descended towards a fast-moving river. When the census taker came around in 1861 we were putting in three acres of spring wheat, four of peas, three of oats and two of potatoes. ("My God, this is a lot of potato-land," Esther said, and I replied, "I know, I dug praties as a child till there wasn't a muscle in my body that wasn't sore!") We had two horses, about one hundred pounds, worth of farm implements and six pigs – a nice small holding, self-sufficient and running at the peak of its capacity.

Esther and I planned to earn our cash elsewhere. One source of dollars in the pocket (and it now started to be dollars, not pounds, we talked in, for British North America was just switching to decimal currency) was the cheese factory. In reality, *factory* was too proud a term for it: Esther's parents had set up in an unheated building, twenty by twenty-five feet, with a hard-packed gravel floor and vats and presses for cheese production. Some of the equipment was dented and rusty, all of it was filthy. Our first task was to polish everything until it shone, replace those items that could not be fixed, and put in a cobbled floor, a labourious job. We spent dollars to make dollars, calculating that the real money was in hard cheese, not the soft, perishable varieties the Johnstons had manufactured. Cheddar especially travelled well and could be sold as far away as the southern United States or even the British Isles, where Canadian butter and cheeses already had a good name.

The work was hard but not back-breaking. Late every afternoon a neighbour delivered twenty to thirty gallons of milk. This we left to settle overnight; in the morning the cream was skimmed off, heated, and reintroduced into the milk, along with some starter – milk high in lactic acid – and a bit of rennet, found in the stomach of calves, which makes milk curdle. Soon curds formed; when warmed and stirred properly, these formed larger curds. These were put in a spiked cheese roller that broke them into an even-textured mass. Usually Esther did the processing work, and I the heavy lifting. Next everything went through a "cheesit," a device that looks like a wooden hatbox with a cover that fits inside rather than on the top of the box. This cheesit was placed under a press, which pushed the top down and thus forced any residual water out of the cheese. The machine exerted half a ton of pressure and had to be kept in place for at least a day. Finally the cheese was taken out, wrapped in calico, and put aside to cure.

Our cheeses soon gained a reputation for quality and we found that we had more calls for cheese than we could produce. We doubled the size of our factory and hired a strong local lad to do the heavy work. Soon we added an older woman to the operation who knew how to control cooking fires. The result was that we had a very efficient little business, one that Esther could manage, leaving me free to make money elsewhere.

I played to my own strong suit. In a disused smithery in Roslin (we were living in the far northwestern corner of Tyendinaga Township and Roslin was just across the township line in Thurlow) I began a small foundry. It made parts for farm implements and small tools for the mining industry that was opening up in the northern part of Hasting County. In the early days I spent some time at the forge myself, but my goal here was the same as with the cheese factory – to get something going where other people would work for me. By 1860, my little foundry was producing two thousand dollars worth of goods each year and doing the heaviest work with steam power.

A nice young couple on the way up, that is what everyone saw. I made a point of showing the flag, particularly being active in the Orange Order. When funds were collected to build an Orange hall on the concession road just south of my farm, I contributed money and labour. Gradually, as our businesses grew, Esther and I began to see hats doffed to us during marketing days in Belleville. We were promising young citizens, energetic people, good examples. Under the sponsorship of Mackenzie Bowell and George Benjamin, I was admitted to the Freemasons in Belleville. Socially, this was a step above the Orange Order, for it was limited to the area's more substantial citizens. Mr White and his wife, everyone said, would be somebody, someday.

If I remember anything nearly as much as the happiness of those first delicious years with Esther, it is the worry. We laughed and we worried in equal measure. Of course we worried about money, for in setting up our businesses we were taking big risks with my savings. But money worries plague all young couples. My darling Esther and I always had the further fear of discovery, and tho' we learned better and better to cope with it each year, it never left us completely alone. We established some guidelines to reduce the risks. Most important, I tried never to go any place where I might be injured without first arranging that Esther be within fifteen minutes of me. This way we avoided incriminating medical attention. I tried also to refrain from physical work, especially the smithing, because the chance of injury was so great.

We transformed our worry into laughter, or at least made a game of fear. I bought several travelling kits of theatrical paint and various facial hairpieces. Of an evening, Esther practised applying these to me so that I could appear to be anything from boyishly clean-shaven to swarthy and bush-weary. In these, our young years, I did not sport anything save sidelocks, but later upon entering public life I found that a nicely trimmed moustache and chin piece gave a modestly Solomon-like quality to my utterances. Esther became fascinated with the potential of grease paint and adhesive, and one of our games on a winter's evening was to pick out an engraving from a newspaper and transform me into the person in question. Then I would act out the subject's mannerisms until we both became hysterical with laughter. I made a particularly good William Ewart Gladstone, and I like to think that my later political success was in part due to my ability to walk as he did, with the world on his shoulders and Christian duty written all over his face.

I found that Esther, poor darling, was given to fits of melancholy religion. These cast a shadow over our first years together. Although the Johnstons were an Irish family, they had given up the Church of England and Ireland in their early days on the Canadian frontier – that happened to an awful lot of Irish people in the early days, when the church was weak – and taken to following the circuit-riding Methodisticals. Esther had been baptized in the Church but was at heart a Dissenter. Sometimes when she was in a melancholy mood, I found her reading passages in the Bible that could be taken as condemning our marriage, such as Our Lord's saying "Neither doth a corrupt tree bring forth good fruit" (St Luke 6:43). Then she would start weeping and wailing, banshee-like; we were corrupt trees and would never bear fruit, she moaned.

These moments were deepest and most wrenching after Esther paid visits to her parents in Belleville. They made her dip into some well of perpetual guilt – one, I suspect, they had dug for her years before, in childhood.

The worst moment, tho', occurred in Kingston, after which for a brief time I thought that I had lost my heart's treasure. Once a month we took a load of hard cheese to the shops there. Most times we made a little holiday of the excursion and had a meal in a hotel or eating house. By way of some brothers in the Orange Order, we had a regular contract to deliver cheese to the military barracks. The storehouse where we took the goods was under the commissariat and served both the active-duty barracks and the hospital. We had just finished unloading the hard cheeses from our four-wheeled wagon when a demonic figure appeared. It – not he or she, it – was no more than five feet high and, although spring had arrived, was wrapped in two black overcoats, a muffler, and a tall stovepipe hat of the sort just starting to be called a Lincoln. In a high, squeaky voice, this gargoyle demanded to inspect our goods, which were described as being delivered for "ingestion" by hospital patients. The word was new to me, but what the person wanted was clear enough. It ordered the commissariat-keeper to find a corkscrew. "Bore in there!" it pointed to one of our cheeses. The soldier obeyed. "And there too!" it commanded in a voice like a bosun's whistle. "And there!" Soon holes riddled our hard cheeses. The figure bent over and applied its nose to each cheese in turn. In order to do this, it removed the Lincoln hat and revealed an old, lined face that could have been a full seventy or eighty years. The skin was red and blotched and its owner was continuously squinting and blinking. "Well, these are good enough," the person pronounced, and turning from the store-keeper to Esther and me, waggled a finger. "Don't think you can cheat the hospital department!" it piped, then turned and was gone.

"That's the inspector-general of hospitals for the army, Dr James Barry," the store-keeper explained. "Just down from Mon-treal, and just back from being with Florence Nightingale in the Crimea. Damned strange officer." The storeman shrugged and gave me some chits to indicate that delivery had been completed, and we went about our business.

"Odd," I observed to Esther as we left Kingston.

She reacted unexpectedly. "Don't you see, John, that that... that *thing* was sent to us as a warning?"

"No," I replied.

"That was no man! The face had no hair. And the hands, when the creature took off its gloves to tap the cheeses, those were not the hands of a man! They had the lines and veins of an old lady."

She was right, I realized.

"It's a warning to us, John – a warning of what will become of us if we continue the way we are! We'll both become horrible little creatures, ugly and frightful. Oh, John! God is going to punish us!" And with that she burst into such a loud wailing that the horses were frightened and it took a quarter of a mile before I could rein them in. "Oh, dear God, don't kill us now!" she screamed as the wagon careened along, almost out of con-trol. "We repent, dear Lord, we repent before Thee!"

Finally I managed to stop the wagon and began comforting her. It was all that I could do to convince her to stop crying. I used everything – a warm embrace, kisses, old private jokes, tender words. Finally she quieted down. With my arm around her the rest of the way, we made the long trek home. She was exhausted when we got there and fell to sleep on the bed with all her clothes on.

That passed, but something had to be done to cement our marriage. Esther had said that she wanted a family. She began a collection of porcelain figures, most of them from Europe, and gave each a them a name.

Yes, we needed a real family. But how? Here my winters doing metalwork amont the Mohawks in the south of our township provided salvation. I had good friends there, the more so because when, in January 1856, our pompous Hastings County council had petitioned the government to take over more of the Indian lands, I stood out against it. Local politicians claimed that Mohawk lands were uncultivated largely because of indolence and intemperance. I knew this was untrue and had Mac Bowell insert items in the *Intelligencer* saying that there was more than one opinion about such things.

I was especially close to half a dozen young Mohawks who were Orangemen – as strong a hand of Loyalists as ever existed, I might add. So now, in 1858, I went to my best friend among them, a man who went by the English name William Martin. He had a brother, Peter Martin, who became a famous doctor after training at Oxford University, but William was more of a traditional healer. He was my age, very intelligent, and frequently he was sought out for counsel by band members, despite his youth. He and I talked. I explained that my wife had female debility and that we could not birth a child of our own. After one of those silences that are so common when discussing matters of import with a Mohawk, he said, "John, when things are meant to be, the knife cuts two ways." In other words, things ordained in the heavens are usually of mutual benefit to everyone involved. He explained that he was frequently asked counsel by girls who were pregnant. Usually this posed no difficulty: the right thing was done. But now and then a Mohawk girl went off to work in a hotel or inn in Belleville or Kingston and returned with a white man's baby inside her. That was a doubly ignominious business. Not only was there no one to marry the girl, but the child would have no right to land or to a share of the common band property. These rights passed through the male line – no Mohawk father, no Mohawk inheritance. Killing the babies was a common practice and accepted, tho' not talked about, William said. Normally the young mother took the baby to an exposed place and left it. Both boy-babies and girl-babies suffered, but the infant girls were most apt to be dispatched. Everyone knew when a young woman was setting off on such a terrible errand; everyone knew and no one said anything. She went out silent and she came back silent. Many girls, William

said, were torn up inside by this cruel necessity. So the blade
would be cutting both ways if he could find a good home for
even one of these white-fathered infants, especially the girl-
babies.

Esther and I talked for a long time. While we did so, she
arranged and rearranged her collection of tiny porcelain figures.
Was William Martin to be trusted? Yes. Could he keep a secret
for his entire life? Yes, and beyond. Would the baby look white?
Mostly. Would I love the child? With all my heart, I replied.
Could we have a girl? Of course. Would Esther become "pregnant"? Yes – the neighbours would start talking if a child just
appeared on our hearth one day! Could we name the girl Eliza?
Perhaps. It was a lovely idea.

Two months later William Martin and I had another talk. He
knew a fine Mohawk girl who was four or five months pregnant
by a Belleville hardware merchant, whose housekeeper she had
been. Instead of having her come home infant in arms, William
would arrange to have her lodge with some friends of his near
Cornwall. I would pay all the expenses, I said, and, boy or girl,
would accept the child. It just had to be a girl! I thought to
myself.

To say that my darling Esther and I waited expectantly for
the baby sounds like a music hall joke, but in a way it was
theatre. We were very excited, which helped us carry out our
deception. Esther became pregnant; at least that is what she
told her parents, and what she whispered to two or three of
the women in our concession road. Soon people were coming
up to me in the street wishing me the best. Esther affected all
the mannerisms and ailments of pregnant women, and I think
she came to have them in truth. She took to waking up in the
middle of the night and to clumping around the house on
swollen feet.

We did everything right, and as the time approached we
prepared our bedroom for birthing. Towels were laid out and
basins and ewers made handy. We arranged to call a trusted
neighbour lady when the moment came; but the delivery, we
would say, was quick and unexpected and occurred before the
message could be sent. Esther and the baby would spend at
least a week together in complete bedrest, so that no one would
think the little one looked more than just newborn.

Finally the good news came – we were parents of a girl! William Martin accomplished his mission with silent efficiency. He came through the front door and handed us the baby with the words, "You have a lovely girl; I am very happy for the mother, for the infant, for you, John, and your wife." And then he was gone.

In a fit of cowardice – which we later regretted – we christened the child Mary Eliza. We never called her anything but Eliza, however, which is the name everyone uses. And rightly.

In 1859 we "adopted" a second child, Sarah. William Martin again acted as intermediary.

"I see that your old friend Mr Gowan has made the newspapers again," Esther said. In the evenings we took turns reading various weekly papers aloud, and occasionally we looked at a Toronto paper. "It says here that Mr Ogle R. Gowan, M.P. for Leeds North, is to be tried before the police magistrate to Toronto for criminal assault on two young girls."

"How young?"

"Twelve years old." Esther glanced protectively at the room where our own baby girls were sleeping. "I wonder if they liked it."

I mused, then declared abruptly, "One thing is certain – Gowan enjoyed himself. And I'd bet money that he's clever enough to beat the charge."

On this I was right in the short term but not in the long. Ogle suborned witnesses, vituperously attacked the child victims, and gained a verdict of not proven. This beat the charge in a technical sense, but it did not amount to a verdict of innocence. The evidence against him had been overwhelming, and it terminated his political career. I regretted seeing him end this way, but in truth, he got no more than he deserved.

"It's a good thing you backed Mr Benjamin and Mr Bowell instead of Gowan, isn't it, darling?" Esther said.

Indeed it was.

10

Civic Sense

"But why is the man called Prince of the Whales?" said a barefoot lad of about six, who was talking to a friend at the junction of Dundas and Front streets in Belleville.

"Don't know." They were awaiting the biggest event of 1860, the visit of the Prince.

"It's *Wales*, young man," corrected Esther. She was standing on the board sidewalk behind them. "Wales is a small place; whales are big fish."

"Mammals, actually," said Mackenzie Bowell. He, along with the wealthy distiller Henry Corby, was head of the St George's Society of Belleville, a group whose members shared English origins, royalist enthusiasms, and social pretensions. "Whales are mammals, Mrs White," he smiled, tipping his top hat. He had a bright blue sash laid across his long-tailed frock coat.

When he bent forward, his starched shirt front sent forth the faintest creaking sound. "They were mammals long before they swallowed old Jonah."

"Not actually whales." This time it was George Benjamin making the correction. As warden of Hastings County he was one of the leaders of the official reception committee. He bore two sashes running in opposite directions across his broad shirt front and at a distance resembled a Union Jack. "The Scriptures don't say that Jonah was swallowed by a whale; they say he was swallowed by a big fish. Is that not correct, Mr White?" Benjamin was a bit on edge; he had been on a first-name basis with me for quite a while, but now in his nervousness had lapsed into formality.

I nodded agreement. The various medals on my Orange sash tinkled in the light breeze like a Chinese glass hanging. I was deputy grand master of Hastings County, an indication of rising influence in the community.

"Where is the big fish now, sir?" one of the urchins said, turning and tugging at my sleeve.

Esther interpreted. "He means where is the Prince of Wales."

"Ah that, then is the conundrum," pronounced Benjamin.

And indeed it was. That morning, Thursday the sixth of September, was to be Belleville's big day. Royalty would appear in the person of Albert Edward, Prince of Wales, eighteen-year-old heir to the throne of the British empire. The visit was occasioned by the opening of the Victoria Bridge in Montreal and by the laying of the cornerstone for the new parliament building in Ottawa. Also, with the Americans certain to become involved in a civil war, it was thought useful for someone from the empire to show the flag on the Great Lakes. Thus, accompanied by the beginnings of a formidable stomach, one mistress, and the fusspot colonial secretary, Henry Pelham Fiennes Pelham Clinton, fifth Duke of Newcastle-under-Lyme, the Prince had steamed up the lakes. The citizens of every city, town, harbour and hamlet vied with each other for the opportunity of presenting him with a loyal address. "Cleopatra on her barge never had such attention," John A. Macdonald had observed earlier in the week, and as the leading figure in Kingston's observance of the royal progress, he was well posted to know.

In Belleville, the citizens had prepared for the event with

characteristic loyalty and equally characteristic bickering. The centre of the town, from wharf to merchant district, was a great riot of patriotism. There were nine arches spanning the main streets, and the two largest of these had been constructed by Orangemen. One said NO SURRENDER and the other FAITH. Everyone knew which faith. The pathway at the wharf where the Prince was to land was covered with a scarlet carpet. Small balsam trees sat in rows of pots at intervals of a few yards. Forty-foot-high flag poles lined the main street of town, and at the top of each a Union Jack fluttered in the breeze. From a distance this was impressive, but up close one could see that the poles had been hastily thrust into the ground and some were beginning to lean dangerously.

"I don't think it will happen," Mackenzie Bowell pronounced, surprising the rest of us. We had been waiting for an hour and had run out of small talk. This prophecy, solemnly uttered, came after a period of restless silence. "You see, I think those yahoos in Kingston will muck things up. John A. can't control them."

In Kingston, two days earlier, things had gone sour. The city had been decked out as every bit as lavishly as Belleville, and most of the citizenry were out in force. So too were fifty-four Orange lodges, with over four thousand Orangemen in full regalia. And there was the inevitable Orange arch. The Duke of Newcastle, acting as combination consort and protector of the prince, had learned a week before that the Orange Order was to be represented on the official welcoming committee at various stops as the royal party steamed up the lake. In response, he dealt with the Canadian colonials in the supercilious manner of a Roman proconsuls dealing with the Gauls. He proclaimed that since the Orange Order was illegal in the British Isles, the prince could not consent to meet anyone from the society or to walk through one of its arches. John A. Macdonald, now ranking cabinet member in Canada West (he was attorney general), took a deputation to Brockville to try and convince Newcastle to relent. The Orange Order in Canada was completely independent from its counterpart in the British Isles and was quite legal, even respectable, here. Macdonald failed to add that the order was the backbone of the conservative party in Canada West. The Duke said no. Macdonald argued. The

Duke said no. Macdonald pleaded. The Duke said no. Macdonald said good day. The Duke said yes.

When the royal vessel anchored off Kingston, the duke spied not only a massive Orange arch but also large groups of men strutting about in the regalia that he had declared prohibited. Ever the proconsul, he gave Kingston's city fathers sixteen hours to clear the area of insignia offensive to His Britannic Majesty. The Orangemen refused to cooperate, insisting on their civil rights as British subjects to parade peaceably and to endorse any association of society that was not illegal. The Duke ordered the Prince's vessel – the unfortunately named *Kingston* – to steam off. And so the Prince of Wales had visited Kingston while not setting foot ashore.

"The same thing just *can't* happen here," said Esther. In a white dress, even though it was after the first of September, and carrying a pastel parasol, she looked like one of her delicate porcelain figurines. "I must see royalty once in my life!"

"It would serve us right, though," I observed. "All that bickering yesterday was frightful." A comic opera fight had taken place over the loyal address to the Prince. A subcommittee of Belleville's town council had drafted the speech, but the full council had rejected it and put out a version of their own. The mayor, William Hope, had refused to sign the new version, and after a barrage of name calling the council asked the reeve of the township to sign it instead. The joys of small-town life.

"Still", Mac said, sounding doubtful, "we did the right thing about the decorations. And quickly enough." Having heard of the debacle in Kingston, and wishing now more than ever for the Prince to step ashore in Belleville, he and his fellow Orangemen had agreed to camouflage their arches by painting over the slogans and to mask some gaudy paintings of King William that adorned the gable ends of two large houses. "But I think that the royal party was wrong, George, in gratuitously insulting you."

Mr Benjamin dit not respond. At seventy-thirty that same morning an official from the Prince's party had asked Mayor Hope to come out to the royal vessel and discuss arrangements; he, George Benjamin, warden of the whole County of Hastings, had not even been consulted, and he was aggrieved as a result.

In sum, everyone's nose was a little out of joint.

By noon, the royal personage still had not appeared and a group of Orangemen were beginning to make trouble. They had come up from Kingston in a belligerent mood and now they were stirring up the Belleville Orangemen. Soon all the Orange banners, which had been so carefully hidden away, were broken out. Bands played "The Protestant Boys" and "The Loyal Orange Lilly-O" while the Duke of Newcastle stood on deck no more than a hundred yards from the town wharf. Hearing and seeing all this he ordered the captain to raise steam. The anchor was hoisted and soon the *Kingston* could be seen cruising up Lake Ontario to Cobourg.

Mr Benjamin tried to be philosophical. "Oh, well, perhaps it's all for the best."

"Bloody hell, it's an insult," said Mac.

"I suppose I'll never see royalty," sighed Esther.

"Then perhaps we should go home and feed the children." I placed Esther's arm into mine and down the flag-lines avenue we strolled to where our brand new Democrat would take us home.

By the time Esther and I were home we were laughing hysterically. It was funny, we had decided in retrospect. And the Prince's nonvisit left small eddies such as you see after you throw a big rock into a calm lake. The strangest, to me, was that William Martin's half-brother, Peter, who was known in his own language as Burning Cloud (Oronhyatekha) received an Oxford education. He followed the Prince's Nile barge to Toronto and there made himself known to the royal courtiers. He so impressed them as an example of a pure native inhabitant of our land that they brought him in to talk to the Prince. His Majesty equally taken, invited the young man to study in England. William kept me informed of Peter's progress. He received an Oxford degree and then a medical degree at the University of Toronto. He practised medicine near us for a while but later moved up near London, Canada west. William was extremely proud of his brother.

The old order was changing in our home county. Esther and I changed along with it. During the summer of 1861 old Sheriff Moodie, as decent a gentleman as ever lived, took a stroke and his left side was paralysed. It was a sad thing to see him dragging himself along the sidewalks as he tried to perform his duties. His left leg would swing in a half-crescent as he hirpled down the road. For all that, the people he arrested or served papers on kept suing him in civil court, and finally he lost a malfeasance case in 1863. That forced him to resign as sheriff. He had not been dishonest, just inept.

I saw him now and again. Unable to find employment, he could often be found sitting on a bench or an old crate in the sun watching the activity in Belleville Harbour and reminiscing about his old days as a soldier in the Napoleonic Wars, as a settler in southern Africa, as a magistrate in Natal. The man had lived.

That he had suffered marital bliss with Mrs Moodie with such Christian resignation was a great wonder to me, but, then, he had once killed a lioness with a wooden spear, and he must have had wonderfully steady nerves.

That Mrs Moodie was a great artist is a conviction I have never lost, but the odd social encounter with her taught me that greatness could be grating. Mrs Moodie's writings were no longer selling very well, and without money from the sheriff's post the two of them had suffered a great financial come-down. They sold their elegant stone house and bought a tiny cottage outside of Belleville, where I called sometimes. Mr Moodie was always pleased to see me. At first his wife was cool, but when she realized that I knew something about local land prices, she grew friendly. She and the ex-sheriff were using what money they had in hand to play the land game. For old Dunbar's sake, I was glad to help.

Another change was the wasting illness that suddenly hit George Benjamin in 1863. He was an M.P. one day and less than a year later he was dead. Mr Benjamin had been like a father to Mac Bowell and his last months wrenched Mac something terrible. Sometimes I would join him in visits to Mr Benjamin, and I don't know what was harder to take – seeing this once-vital man, the embodiment of solid self-confidence and vigour, now thin, pale and wasting, or Mac trying to cheer him, on the verge of tears himself. The funeral drew more mourners, Orange lodge representatives and Tory politicians than anyone had ever seen. John A. Macdonald walked with the Benjamin family. The only notable Orangeman missing was Ogle R. Gowan, who, it was said, did not even send a letter of sympathy.

Meanwhile Esther and I decided we had had enough of her family. Despite the regular ransom I paid then, Mr and Mrs Johnston still made it clear that they did not entirely approve of me. And they were meddling old fools. Every time Esther and I altered an outbuilding or did something new at the cheese factory or made a change inside the house, they came and inspected it with disapproving clucks and whines.

That was vexing, but in the heel of the hunt I could have outlasted them easily enough. The trouble was that old Mr Johnston, once a temperate man, had taken to drink. It got so bad that even his wife started calling him a drunken Indian. She said that a black Irishman in drink is just another savage. Indeed, when he was in his cups, his hair long and greasy, Johnston did look like a reprobate Mohawk. In 1859 he had mortgaged the farm that Esther and I lived on, and by 1863 was on the verge of defaulting the mortgage. That meant that everything Esther and I had worked for might disappear: anyone who foreclosed would take the farm and cheese factory and leave us out in the cold. And just because the old fool could not resist ardent spirits. So Esther and I scraped up enough money to buy out the mortgage. We could now call the land and all we had put into it our own, but on circumstances were straitened. Thank God for Mac Bowell. When he found out he tided us over with a loan.

Darling Esther, characteristically, was pulled in two directions. She hated the way her parents had acted, especially her father, but she would not bring shame on her family. I respected that. So we agreed to tell everyone that we had inherited the farm by way of a generous gift from Mr and Mrs Johnston.

Everyone told us how lucky we were, and in the long view, they were dead right.

11

Gathering Force

"Right, lads. By the numbers now!" Mackenzie Bowell had a great parade-ground voice. He was running through the manual of arms with a group of men usually called the Belleville Rifles. I was with them as a supernumerary. It was 1864. The company, originally raised in the troubles of 1837–38, had been reorganized in 1862 largely by Mac's initiative. He was not the official commanding officer, only the lieutenant, but he usually ran things. Mac had put on weight and grown a full beard and massive handlebar moustache. When drilling troops, he wore a Persian lamb officer's cap in the Russian style. The mid- and late-1860s were heady times; both Mac and I seized opportunity by the throat.

"Right wheel!" Mac ordered as he moved the men onto the parade square. "And keep it smart, laddies!" George Benjamin's death had come as great personal blow to Mac, but it opened up a line of succession in the Orange Order and in local politics. Mac was determined to follow in the footsteps of the man who had been a virtual father to him. And, later, as he rose, I followed him like a younger brother following an older.

"You never know if, or when, those Yanks will invade!" Mac told his men when they were at parade rest. "We must be ready to fight for Queen and Empire!"

This was during the American Civil War, and everyone was afraid of an invasion. It was a great time for anyone who trafficked skillfully in the symbols of empire – the crown and, especially, the Queen, – and no vehicle was better for such a business than the Orange Order. Mac realized this. In 1862 he had become Grand Master of the Orange Lodge of Ontario East, which meant, roughly, that he controlled the same territory George Benjamin had held sway over in the days of the schismatical fight with Ogle Gowan. In Hastings County alone there were forty or more local Orange lodges, and anyone with a political career in mind could use these as a base. Mac had run for the North Hastings riding in 1863 but lost because his move was premature. They still did not know him well enough that far north. But given his work in the Order, and now his efforts in the Belleville Rifles, they soon would.

Exactly what the people of Hastings County had to fear from the Americans was not clear, but fear works that way – like a fine fog vaguely clouding the vision. "And another thing, lads – if you want to know what we're fighting against, you should read this book!" Mac was shamelessly promoting a volume that he had just printed at the *Intelligencer* office and which was for sale there, George Taylor's *History of the Rise, Progress, Cruelties, and Suppression of the Rebellion in the County of Wexford in the Year 1798*. This was one of the books Father had given me to warn of the danger of the papists. It was worthy reading. Very instructive.

The Belleville Rifles thought that their big moment had come in 1865, when Canadian spies in the United States learned that American veterans of the Civil War, Fenians, mostly Irish in origin and fanatically anti-British, had planned a three-pronged attack on Canada. An attack on Canada would be a severe blow to the British empire, they thought. "Those bastards aren't at all for freeing Canada," Mac Bowell argued in a conversation with me one night. "Mark my words, John, they just want to continue 1798."

"You mean, Mac, they're all Catholics and would not mind killing a few of us Irish Christians. And any freeing of old Ireland would be a bonus." Religious hatred was the silent foundation of the American Fenian movement. The chance to get a bayonet into the old Protestant enemy was too good to miss.

Mac leaned back in his chair and twirled his handlebar moustache. "That is why our own lads will do so well, if it comes to battle. They know what this is really about."

"The unit is True Blue all the way, isn't it, Mac?"

"Absolutely. Nine out of ten of the lads are Orange. There are only the two Catholics in the Rifles and both of them are Frenchies, not Irish papists."

"Does John A. know what's going on with the Fenians?" As attorney general for Canada West, Macdonald was minister for militia and thus in charge of the civilian defence forces.

Mac bent forward and tapped me on the knee. "Confidentially, laddie, John A. tells me that he has spies in the Fenian camp. In Chicago, Buffalo, New York. And he knows what they're thinking the day after they think it!" He sat back, pleased. "Now, what do you say to that?"

I was impressed, and when in November 1865 the Belleville Rifles were part activated, I knew it must be for a good reason. Mac Bowell took about half the Rifles – now, officially, the Fifteenth Battalion of the Argyll Light Infantry, but still the Belleville Rifles to everyone who knew them – up to Amherstburg, near Windsor. Men with regular jobs or families were excused service. It being the beginning of winter, there were plenty of able-bodied men who had no employment; the money for active service suited them fine. Mac made a great drama of going back and forth between Amherstburg and Belleville, drilling men half of his time, editing the *Intelligencer* the other half, and playing the local hero all the time. But no attack came. In spring the men went home.

John A. either knew something or was playing at something, for on March 1866 he sent this message by telegraph to the adjutant general of the militia: "Call out ten thousand (10,000) men of Volunteer Force... They must be out in twenty-four (24) hours and for three (3) weeks and whatever further time may be required." Mac now was promoted to captain. He calculated that if his luck held he would be a colonel before the papish bastards finally gave up. Because of their long service the Belleville Rifles did not have to go on active duty immediately, but early in the morning of 3 June 1866 they received their marching orders. A band of Fenians had crossed the Niagara frontier the previous day, and though they had been beaten back, more attacks were expected everywhere along the border. When the news arrived, Mac issued a special broadsheet number of the *Intelligencer* with the headline "CROWN AND HOME THREATENED, Republican Invasion Repulsed, More Attacks Imminent."

People spilled into the streets of Belleville. An Orange band marched up and down playing patriotic songs and Orange tunes. Stores stayed open into the gloaming hours, their lights filling the streets. Esther and I were part of the crowd. I told Esther that if the Rifles marched, I would be going along with them.

The call to arms came at two in the morning. My battalion left Belleville the next noon in cattle cars on the Grand Trunk Railway. One half of the unit went to Prescott, the other to Cornwall. Invasions were expected at each place. For many of the country boys, this ride was the first time they had been on a railway train. It was an exciting trip, but then, once we reached our destinations, nothing happened.

John A. Macdonald became convinced – rightly – that the Fenians were not inclined to try again, and he ordered everybody home.

Mac Bowell sat next to me on the flatbed railway car as it moved slowly through the countryside towards Belleville. He was resigned to the lack of battle and waxing philosophical about the virtues of peace. Wistfully, he added, "Though, to tell you the truth, John, I think if they'd invaded I would have ended up a general."

My darling Esther once told me that John A. Macdonald and I

were the only two people in Canada who understood the outcome of the Fenian raids. If that's true, Macdonald has forgotten.
The raids led to Confederation. I do not mean all by themselves;
they set a line of skittles falling, and the final pin in the sequence
was the joining of four British North American provinces into
the Dominion of Canada.

John A. forgets this fact because, to be honest, remembering
it loosens his pedestal. Oh yes, I know my man well, on that.

And the Fenian movement is something that most people do
not want to acknowledge anyway. The main emotion in those
days was not so much love of the new-nation-a-forming but joy
at sticking a finger in the eye of the loudmouth republicans to
the south, the worst being that bunch of papish louts from
Ireland who showed us why the crown should always rule and
who ran like a flock of she-goats when faced by True Blue
Britons. It is something I think we should remember.

Still and all, it was a time of great confidence in this country.
Our own family was growing. In 1864 my third daughter, Ida,
was delivered (in every sense) by William Martin. Earlier we
had worried that the half-Indian blood of our daughters would
some day betray them. But slowly our fears ebbed. As I myself
long had known, people see only what they are told to see,
and we took care to dress the girls in frilly things when they
went out in public.

Our girls gave us such pleasure that we wanted more, and
this led to a domestic crisis. In 1865 William Martin had another
likely candidate for us. An Indian girl was pregnant by a big
Irish lumberjack who had gone missing. "What if it's a boy this
time?" Martin asked. Were we still so very keen on girls? Yes,
Esther said, emphatically. She did not want any little tadpoles
around the house. I agreed with her that girls are nicer than
boys – any sane person would agree with that – but I thought
maybe we should consider a boy if that was the way things
worked out. Esther promised to think about it. This time, as
her "pregnancy" progressed, she grew more and more edgy. "I
just know it will he a boy," she said often, and added that she
did not want one in the house. Though she would not say it, I
think she feared that a half-Irish, half-Mohawk boy would be
spotted, while a girl would not be. That is why she hardened
her heart.

The pinch came when William Martin appeared at our door one night. He knocked softly. It was after midnight. He had a baby with him. He addressed Esther directly. "Don't be upset, Mrs White. Look at this perfect boy." Esther refused. She lay in her bed and turned her face from the child. "No, I will not have it." I tried to reason with her: the boy-child was beautiful; he was in the peak of health; he would add a whole new dimension to our family. She would have none of it. "Take it out!" she ordered, and William Martin obeyed. His eyes told me that he did not understand.

To keep the neighbours at bay we declared that Esther had experienced a late miscarriage. Like the decent people they were, the women expressed sympathy but did not press for intimate details. Most of them had experienced a miscarriage or two. They told Esther to be especially careful to keep cheerful, as a miscarriage often brought melancholy.

And she did grow melancholy, in her characteristic way. What I mean is that at times of great disappointment or great tension Esther took to religious melancholy. Her sense of sin – always just below the surface – came out. This reminded me of an engraving Mac had printed in the *Intelligencer* of the birth of an underwater volcano. When Esther's conviction of sin surfaced, heat, light, steam and molten rock flew about. It took me a whole week to calm her down and talk her out of the idea of confessing our sin to the preacher of the Wesleyan Methodist Church in Belleville. She wanted to ask him to lead us to God's mercy seat. She was dissuaded only by my argument that our darling daughters would be treated as freaks by everyone if word ever got out. She accepted that. And when I told her that until now I had not fully understood her spiritual needs and that I would become a Methodist myself, she settled back and allowed herself once again to accept our happiness together.

Less than a year later, in 1866, we had another daughter, our dear Anna. Esther said that God's giving us a daughter showed that he approved of our staying together and keeping our secret to ourselves.

When a fifth daughter arrived, late in 1870, she took up my suggestion that we name the child Esther in her honour. And so our first daughter was Eliza, our fifth, Esther. No woman, or man, ever had better girls. Under their mother's tutelage they became modest and refined young ladies, always helpful and never prying into other affairs, including their parents'. They never so much as asked either of us an awkward question.

We were growing in our mercantile status as well. The cheese factory was doing so well that we bought a hundred acre lot two miles to the east of our house and put up another cheese factory there. More important, after a great deal of thought we sold the foundry in Roslin and set up a really going concern in Madoc, to the north. That was one of the luckiest things I ever did, because in the autumn of 1866, not long after I had set up the new foundry, gold was discovered nearby. A small gold rush ensued. There were other mines there too, copper and lead, which meant, all in all, that there was a rush on foundry goods. We stamped out picks and diggers, mended almost every kind of tool that broke and custom-made anything the mine owners would pay us for. Father would have been proud! I was also lucky in finding a good foreman and an honest works manager – both of them Irish and both Orange – so that I only had to visit the works once a week. The Madoc works was the making of us. Before we had just been doing well; now we landed on the far side of comfortable. I should say that the mortgage to make the Madoc investment came from Mac Bowell. Esther and I never had a better friend.

The Madoc venture had a happy side product. It gave me a chance to see something I had forgotten, that Esther was a compassionate person and no coward. This got me over being vexed at her lapses into religious melancholia. I had told her of my three brothers, of course, because I wanted no secrets between us. The two older lads had disappeared, one to the States, the other to the western parts of Canada, but the third one, the one with the sad eyes and misshapen head, was still in our part of Canada. He wrote me a letter every now and then in his large childish hand. The Burtons in Montreal had treated him fairly, but he was not sharp enough for any skilled trade and now he needed work desperately. I explained this to Esther, and with no hesitation she said that of course I must help him.

So he came to us, but he only stayed one night. Though he knew our secret he refrained from mentioning it. He kept his knit cap on throughout the evening and did not apologize for this breach of manners; nor should he have, for he was entitled to his own secret. He praised the food set before him in that slow way of his. In the morning he thanked Esther gravely and said that he could not stay any longer, but would remember our kindness always. I walked down the road with him to the Roslin coach stop. All he had in the world was a small sack tied to a stick and carried over his shoulder. He was as serious as a pallbearer at a funeral. Would he like work? I asked. Carrying things and sweeping up at my foundry in Madoc? Yes, he said. So I gave him a note to hand to my works manager and he went up to Madoc. There he stayed until 1868. I saw him each week usually, and always slipped him a dollar. He would look at it puzzled, and I would remind him that for almost ten years now dollars had taken the place of pounds. I made a point of asking him regularly if everything was all right. "Yes, brother, I'm very happy here. I am in luck." There was no danger of him giving away my secret. He remained as silent as ever.

That word: *luck* – my brother used it every time I saw him. Esther and I talked about it a good deal, as well and the way we each thought about it tells a lot about the difference in our characters. I think that, for the most part, people make their own luck. If they keep their head up and eyes open, they cut down the chance of falling into a bog hole and increase the chance of finding a ten-dollar bill blowing across the fields. It is not just dame fortune that has given me a fine family and business success and a respectable place in the community, it is also will power, making luck, keeping my eyes open. Esther has always believed just the opposite, that a person should sit still and take what comes along – that luck is what happens *to* you, not what you make yourself.

In those days we used an unpleasant former client of mine, a man from my Classon days, as an arguing point. This was Schuyler Shibley, and he was as big a land speculator, farmer, conservative politician and general gasbag as the Kingston area possessed. He had high political ambitions, but in 1866 he landed in court. In addition to his wife in the Kingston area he kept a mistress (poor thing!) near Sarnia, and in this western outpost of his empire he fathered a bastard daughter. That was not so uncommon in and of itself. But in the early fall of 1866 the child died, an inquest was held, and it came out that the wee girl had been underfed to the point of malnutrition. On several occasions – tho' not on the eve of death – Shibley had severely whipped the poor thing. There was a big public uproar, a great scandal, and when he ran for Parliament in 1867 he lost. Esther argued that his luck was God's will. I said that he brought it all on himself, he made his own luck.

Neither of us could have guessed that Shibley would be resurrected. This Mormon prophet, as the papers called him, easily won the wardenship of Frontenac County the very next year and then, in 1872, was elected a member of Parliament. I suppose that doesn't change either Esther's or my view on the nature of fortune.

"So, men. Future prosperity and the election of Independent Conservatives are linked; good times and Mackenzie Bowell are tied. Vote for Bowell and do your duty!" Thus I concluded my first political speech. It was given in the early autumn of 1867 in aid of the candidacy of Mackenzie Bowell for Parliament of the Dominion of Canada, the first assembly elected under Confederation. I was in my mid-thirties, a confident speaker, and though my speech was not brilliant it had most of the characteristics that would later make me – if I may be so bold – an effective political speaker in rural constituencies. I did not have my booming voice – in fact, I feared that if I spoke too loudly my long-cultivated tenor would break – but I made up for this with dramatic gestures. I found that an effective device for addressing a crowd of farmers or mineworkers was to put on a little play. I would cast myself two or three parts, both asking questions and answering them, employing different voices and gestures for each. Unlike most political orators I avoided sarcasm and instead used jokes, many of them adapted from musical variety shows I had seen in Toronto or in the Belleville playhouse. And I had another good trick, which was always to pay more than the obligatory passing notice to the ladies in the audience, even though they did not have the vote. I would point out how my candidate, or the project I was pushing, would benefit women. On the rare occasions when more women than men showed up I vowed that some day women would vote – this with a smile, almost as if it were a joke. Most of the audience smiled with me.

"What about John A. Macdonald?" someone called from the crowd at a meeting in the north riding of Hastings County, where Mackenzie Bowell was determined to follow in the footsteps of his mentor, Mr Benjamin. The questioner was a miner.

I raised my hand in an extreme gesture, then abruptly dropped it, as if having forgotten something. "Oh, my dear sir... I almost forgot, as did you. It is *Sir* John A. Macdonald now!" The crowd laughed and someone called out "Three cheers for Sir John!" Macdonald had just received a KCB in London for his work on Confederation. "I must add," I continued, "that Sir John has the more important recommendation of having just this spring remarried." I turned to a group of matrons in the crowd. "And we know how that improves a man's behaviour, don't we ladies?"

I had avoided telling a direct lie by telling an irrelevant truth. While in London to negotiate the details of Confederation Macdonald had fallen head over heels in love with one Susan Agnes Bernard, twenty-two years his junior, the sister of his personal private secretary and the daughter of the former attorney general of Jamaica. He had followed her and courted her with all the awkward energy of a puppy. This piece of news drew attention away from another fact – that Mac Bowell was not willing to tie himself too closely to the coattails of Macdonald. Mac styled himself an Independent Conservative and intended to keep his freedom of action.

"Well done," Mac told me later. "God, I thought they were going to start that bloody with-John-A-through-thick-or-thin nonsense." Bowell's keeping his distance required some courage, for Macdonald was riding a large wave. On the first Dominion Day, 1 July 1867, he had put on a party bigger than the country had ever seen and made himself the guest of honour. In English Canada, especially amongst the Protestants of Ontario, Confederation was extremely popular, for it meant that the danger of being swamped in a Roman Catholic tide was forever put aside. Ontario (as Canada West was now called) celebrated wildly. In Ottawa, balls, parades, a 101-gun salute and a military tattoo marked the occasion. That same day it was announced the Macdonald had been made a Knight Commander of the Order of the Bath. "They probably had two-score trumpeters on hand for that announcement," Mac muttered.

The election in which we were engaged was messy, but that's the way most elections are. This particular general election took place during late August and early September. Voting was not done by the cowardly secret ballot which soon was to corrupt our national politics. Bowell pulled a victory out of the morass of Hastings North by nearly 300 votes. "You must follow me into the House, John," he told me at the victory rally. "We would make a great team."

That had been on my mind for a long time. I had been active in Orange affairs, accepting all the middling jobs of my lodge, "outside tyler" and the like, and had eventually become deputy master, then master. From that point I went on to hold district and county posts. Finally I was elected Deputy Grand Master for the County of Hastings, the perfect platform for a political career. "Fully three-quarters of the Protestant families of this county have one of their menfolk in a lodge, Esther," I explained. "If I'm ever to become a member of Parliament, these are the men who will carry me on their shoulders."

"Of course, dear. It's the men who have the vote. But remember this: always pet the women."

I did. I went to every Orange funeral, wedding or soirée in the riding and not only shook hands with the men but gave the widows cream-thick sympathy, praised brides as the most beautiful creatures on earth, and told their mothers the same. Hostesses were asked for recipes to be taken home to "my dear wife Esther, who told me you are the most marvelous cook in the county." I was not subtle.

"I'd rather talk to the women anyday than suffer some of the gobshites we have on the township council," I told Esther one day. It was 1868. I had served faithfully on the township council for several years, building on a record of selfless service by sitting patiently through long inane debates about minor patronage posts – viewships of fence lines, keeperships of the town animal pound – and interminable discussions of road repairs. "I am fed to the teeth with this business. I've a mind to pack it in."

Esther knew that I wanted encouragement to fight. "Perhaps, dear." She was working on a sampler that said God Bless our Happy Home. "But why don't you run for reeve in the winter election? Then you'll be able to chair the meetings and have everything done quickly. Besides, the reeve's chain would look good on you. It's a striking ornament, you know." Esther knew I loved to dress up. And that I coveted that chain.

So I ran in 1869 and became reeve of Tyendinaga Township, a post I kept all through the 1870s except for 1873–74, when other calls on my time drew me away. I quickened the pace of township government, and I looked good in the reeve's chain.

Yes, I believe that for the most part people make their own luck, but I am not crazy. Nobody is God, especially not me, and if more than most I have created who I am, I have always recognized that people have their limits.

I knew in my heart that some day I would work my way into Parliament, so becoming reeve in 1869, rather than surprising me, merely confirmed something I had foreseen. It was like going to a play a second time: the story is good, but not startling.

And I knew that it is all right to say "I" a lot, even if the very best people say "one" all the time. "One thinks... One feels... One knows..." Nobody makes luck for himself unless he knows how to use *I*. That's right. "*I* think... *I* feel... *I* know..."

Yet, as I said, human beings have their limits, and I paid attention to them. There were warnings that required notice, especially warnings about becoming too prideful. One was the death of John Wedderburn Dunbar Moodie. He had conducted himself with dignity through countless trials, including the frustrations of serving as sheriff for a crowd of savages. Yet, even after his stroke and loss of employment, he kept his head high and looked at the world with sad and sensible irony. After he died, Mrs Moodie took me aside and asked that I continue to give her advice on mortgages she might invest in. I did, and in fact put her in the way of a good mortgage on the other half of the lot where Esther and I had our second cheese factory.

After her husband's death Mrs Moodie never wrote a thing, I think, except maybe a few little articles (her last novel came out in 1868). And I will tell you why. Once, when we were drinking some potsheen whiskey in their wee retirement house, old Dunbar told me a secret. He would have an idea for a story and get it going, and when he was about halfway through Mrs Moodie would take over and finish it. Then they would put her name on it. That, Dunbar said, was the way his wife had worked in the early days when she wrote children's books with her sisters, and later with a prig named Thomas Pringle, secretary of the Anti-Slavery Society. She had been infatuated with Pringle in her mid-twenties and under his direction had turned out children's books and antislavery tracts. Dunbar carried on from there. It worked, he said with pride. To me, this was a real lesson: I recognized that I could no more have a successful political career without the support of my darling Esther than Mrs Moodie could write a book under her own steam.

The other person whose life reminded me of the limits of humankind was my brother, who went as far as God would let him, poor soul. I last saw him in 1870. The circumstances were these. A chum of his, a big handsome Irishman named Thomas Scott, got himself in some trouble in Manitoba. It was just at the time that Macdonald was trying to make a deal with the Hudson's Bay Company for what was then called Rupert's land and what really was the middle of this whole blooming country, whatever you want to call it. Anyroad, that insane Louis Riel and his thugs grabbed what is now part of Manitoba and said they would become Canadians and citizens of the British empire over their dead bodies. I think that offer should have been taken up. Sir John A. temporized, but out there on the site a decent man, John Christian Schultz, argued against Riel and his half-castes, and they had the decent man arrested. Now Thomas Scott was a young buck who loved action and who had good values. He was from County Antrim and as True Blue and Orange as a man could be. For a while he farmed near Belleville, but he was happiest as a miner. The roll-of-the-dice character suited him. He moved to Madoc and he and my brother became good friends, or at least close acquaintances. When Thomas Scott heard what had happened to Schultz he joined a party to rescue him. But, as luck would have it, Scott was caught by

Riel. Happy-go-lucky chancer that he was, Scott did not keep quiet and play the odds; he ran his mouth and got himself executed. A shot in the back of the head and no ceremony, was the way the saintly Riel worked.

The people of Ontario were scalded when they learned this, and the government of the province – a liberal government, no less! – put up a five thousand dollar reward for Riel. A party of volunteers from here went out to try and find the elusive devil, which they never did. Almost to a man, the volunteers were Orangemen. My brother went along. When he told me what he intended to do I felt a cold hand on my spine, a premonition, but I did not try to dissuade him. Tom Scott had been a friend, after all, and besides, how can you tell someone not to bother fighting treason? No, I said nothing, he went, and I never heard a word from him again. Nor have I met anybody who could tell me what happened to him after getting to rebel territory. He must have died out there on some prairie, alone and lost, having run into a band of Roman Catholic rebels. I like to think that he took one of those bastards with him.

There is no human who does not have limits. Not even the most powerful of leaders. In 1869, Sir John A. Macdonald went bankrupt. That same year he and his new wife had a baby girl. He was bursting with pride. Slowly over a couple of years they realized that their child was crippled and retarded. A girl who should have been the joy of his life became a helpless, lifelong dependent.

Dear God.

12

The People's Choice

I came close to losing Mac Bowell as a friend in 1871, but it was worth the risk.

A week or so after our fifth daughter came to us, I had a long talk with Esther about the future. There were rumours going round that Robert Read, who was M.P. for East Hastings, was about to be paid off by John A. Macdonald with a seat in the Senate. The riding was one of the best around, a heavily Orange constituency that the Tories could lose only if they split the vote, or became overconfident and lazy. Most likely the Grits were dead in the riding, and just as well, I thought. Esther and I talked about this. She said that I ought to go for the seat if it came open and I said maybe. "You *have* to run, dear. It's the way to a richer future for us." I remembered what the Faithful Retainer once had told me: "Some day, every dog gets its kick at the cat. It struck me that my turn for a kick had come. I would try for the Conservative nomination.

So in January 1871, before any official announcement was made, Esther and I began to campaign. She attended every church social, card fest, soirée, and temperance meeting that she could and talked me up among the ladies. The idea was to get them to bring the matter up with their husbands, which they did. Having been reelected reeve handily – 464 votes to 132 – I went about my new campaign with confidence. Every township reeve sat on the Hastings County Council, and there I played well. Without wishing to sound smug, I should add that I shaped things, offended no one and made friends. For example, I seconded the nomination of old A.F. Wood from Madoc for county warden, while saying in my seconding speech that I supported him because my friend Thomas Emo of Huntingdon was not running, and that I would nominate Mr Emo the following year. That way, two sets of people were obligated to me, Mr Emo's friends and Mr Wood's. That was a minor commitment on my part, but if a person makes enough such commitments they add up like straws in a barn.

Our county council meetings ran for two days, and at them I scored other small points, such as seconding a motion to give a hundred dollars to the Hastings Rifle Association. People remember that, at least if they belong to the association benefiting, and I was smart enough not to point out that this would come out of the common tax revenues, raising everyone's rates slightly.

But, Lord, the best meeting was a glorious supper in honour of A.F. Wood, Esquire, Warden, County of Hastings, held in late January at the Huffman House in Madoc. Despite short notice, we invited one hundred guests to a massive oyster supper and had toasts until nearly 2 in the morning. This was much more fun than the usual municipal banquet, for someone proposed the idea of our giving a song after each toast. After toasting the Queen and singing the national anthem, we raised our glasses to the Governor-General and belted out "For he's a Jolly Good Fellow." After about half a dozen toasts the party was thoroughly enspirited, but we ran out of songs that we all knew and could sing together. So we took to doing individual turns. When the time came for the ladies to be toasted, I sang "Eve Had a Roving Eye." That brought the house down. They made me sing it all thru three times. It was good fun, and it reminded all the important people of Hastings who I was.

A few nights after that I worked the other side of the street, joining Esther at a lecture presented under the auspices of the Young Men's Christian Association, "Woman: Her Position and Influence." That was early in February. The paper had reported that the temperature would fall to 12 degrees below zero that night, so you can see how keen I was in getting to the voters thro' their wives. The lecturer was the Reverend William Stephenson from Ottawa. He began with a prayer, then continued with a reference to the Garden of Eden as the cradle of human existence. Eloquently he depicted those happy scenes in paradise that nothing but the presence of woman was required to render complete. I clapped loudly at that. Whatsoever might be urged or adduced by the advocates of women's rights, the reverend lecturer proclaimed, God's own estimate of woman's sphere remained to this day unrepealed and unaltered. "It is not good for man to be alone," he quoted. "Woman's mission is to cheer and brighten the lot of man." Esther nudged me, and I put my arm loosely around the back of her chair in a protective gesture. "There is a difference in the love felt respectively between man and woman," Stephenson declared confidently, resting his hands in his waistcoat pocket from which a large gold watch chain hung. Esther leaned forward, curious what he would say next. "Man loves woman because he could not love himself: woman loved man because her life would be aimless and desolate without someone to cling to and comfort in peril or prosperity." Esther murmured something under her breath that I did not hear.

"The intellectual status of woman is in harmony with the peculiarities of her sex in other aspects. It is less vigourous and powerful than man's, but more warm and truthful to the impulses of the heart. As for the influence of woman, it is one of the mightiest instruments for good or evil in existence. Woman's influence is less ostentatious than man's, but unseen and unobtrusive, it virtually rules the world." The reverend gentleman finally concluded by suggesting to the young women present that they should never go out into the terrestial world with the sole aim in life of being "clotheshorses." He sat down to great applause.

I had been asked by the convenor of the meeting to move the usual vote of thanks to the lecturer, and I did so in the most flattering of terms, expressing agreement with his estimate of woman's unseen influence and suggesting that the day would come when it would be more visible. "Some day women will vote," I declared and received applause from the majority, along with one or two catcalls. "There are stranger things in heaven and earth," some Bible reader called out, to what intent I know not. Then I moved the formal vote of thanks, and afterwards everyone congratulated themselves on having such advanced but sensible views.

Meanwhile, the Grits met and grew despondent. They too had heard the rumours of "Read's beatification," as Mac Bowell called it. They thought things over and decided to sit out the dance: it wasn't worth running a candidate.

I kept my Orange colours flying with a trip to Brockville near the end of February to attend a meeting of the Grand Lodge of Ontario East. Mac was no longer Grand Master of Ontario East, for in 1870 he had the honour of being chosen Grand Master of all of British North America – which meant that countrywide he was head Protestant, head Loyalist, head defender of the British empire. It was the next best thing to being prime minister. In fact, when I saw him after his election I told him he would be prime minister of the dominion some day.

At our Brockville meeting in 1871 the important business was to keep Tom Scott's martyrdom in everyone's mind and to remind the people of Ontario what a vicious serpent that rebel Riel was. We passed resolutions about the "cruel murder of the late Thomas Scott" and called "upon every good subject of Her Majesty to use all proper means to bring the perpetrators of the bloody deed to condign punishment."

Finally, all the nervous pacing about and waiting ended: the government announced that the polling would be on 17–18 March (the first day being St Patrick's) and that a nomination meeting would be held on the tenth. Not a moment too soon; I was growing edgy. Not much time remained, but that worked in our favour, Esther rightly observed, for we were ahead of everyone else in our organizing. I already had an electoral lodge, as I called my workers and trusted friends. They knew what was required of them.

I had better stop here and explain something. You may have heard that I conducted myself in a dishonest and ungentlemanly fashion in this, my first, electoral contest, so I should make clear what happened. Mac Bowell, as chief Conservative in the county, had a great (and very silly) worry that the Grits might win. He dropped a note asking me to call on him at the *Intelligencer* office to talk about the approaching bye-election in East Hastings. I went to see him, ready to act modest when he asked me if I would run for the nomination, and to agree to do so as if it were some big sacrifice. What I heard from him instead was most extraordinary. Would I, for the sake of Conservative party unity, engage not to run? Wellington Frizzell, longtime party stalwart, wanted the Conservative nomination, and he deserved it because of his past loyalty. I was shocked, to say the least. Mac contended that if two Tory candidates ran in the bye-election, the hated Grits would squeak into the crack and grab the seat. I should have told him that the Tories could run a pig and it would beat the Grits – but in my surprise no words came. All I could think of was Esther and how crushed she would be, and me playing a tinpot local politician all my life. Good seats like East Hastings come up only once in a generation. Mac went on and on about the need for us all to be True Blue, to stick together and sacrifice for empire and the Grand Old Cause, and before I left his office I had written him a letter – actually, Mac dictated it – promising that I would not run.

"It's not fair," was Esther's reaction, and she was right, of course. But what could I do? I had given my word.

Had William Martin not visited I would have stayed out. He came to see us, as always, at night and unannounced. He was disturbed about something. He had a letter from his brother, the Oxford-educated doctor, about a matter with which he, William, was in complete agreement. He told us so solemnly that it could have been a declaration of war: Wellington Frizzell had to be stopped. As the local Indian agent for the Mohawk reserves, Frizzell had made life hell for the Tyendinaga band. He was a land-grabber, William told me, and wanted to sell all the Mohawk property to white men. A rat. If he ever became a member of Parliament, William adjudged, the Mohawk band could say goodbye forever to their home.

I took what he said very seriously.

He came back a little more than a week later, just after the bye-election notices had officially gone out. He stayed only minutes and his message was brief: "Trap a rat."

"William's right," Esther observed after he left. She, darling wife, was quicker than I about such things. That night we laid new plans.

I stayed out of sight for a few days, but Esther as my deputy went about the riding gingering up the members of my electoral lodge. On Saturday, 4 March, I made a point of going to Belleville and walking about. I ran into Mac, as I knew I would, and we stood in the middle of the half-frozen road talking, almost posing, so sure were both of us that we would be seen and noted. A number of the solid men of the community came up to join us, and in their presence I promised Mac that I would keep the spirit and the letter of my promise and not be a candidate.

I lied.

When the Conservative nomination meeting was held on Friday the tenth, at Chisholm's Mills in our township, two or three hundred electors showed up, many of them with their wives and children. I let myself be nominated. A good Irishman, James Fargey, did the honours. He proclaimed that I had lived in his community for fifteen years and he dared anyone to utter one word against me. He looked around after he said this as if he really would fight them. He went on to say that I was a working man, one of themselves, and they could not do better than to elect me. When it came time for me to make a speech, I said it was not necessary to say what I would or would not do if elected. I would be in the future what I had been in the past – an honest, straightforward man.

Wellington Frizzell, the fool, made a long speech, by which he did himself no favours. He supported reciprocal trade with the United States, thought the Confederation Act one of the best measures ever introduced, wanted a railway to go to the Northwest Territories, and heaven knows what else. As he wound down he added that the Indian lands in the township of Tyendinaga were available at too high a price. "Something must be done to bring the price down so that they can be sold to Europeans, cultivated and made a source of revenue to this great country."

William Martin had been right.

The trap was sprung.

Only seven days remained until polling started. I had a great lodge of workers already quietly at work, and now they could go full steam ahead. Frizzell had not even bothered to put together a team, so sure was he that Mac had pulled me from the race. Mac went mad! The *Intelligencer* denounced me. My actions were certain to bring a Grit victory, the paper said. No chance: the Grits did not even have a candidate. My workers went from elector to elector in town and country. The day before the election Frizzell, seeing the handwriting on the wall, quit. Just plum backed down. I was the only candidate.

That is how, on St Patrick's Day 1871, I became the first woman elected to the Canadian Parliament.

It was late March. I was bouncing painfully in a railway car on the Brockville-Ottawa line. This badly maintained spur of the Grand Trunk did not even make it all the way into central Ottawa. So underfinanced was the line that its roadbed could not be used until a month after the spring thaw began. "Next time, I'll take a coach – or walk!" I vowed.

"Too right, John. Too right!" The words emanated from the noisome pipe smoke enveloping Mackenzie Bowell. We had made peace. Mac had been quick to forgive; he realized that he needed an ally if he were to keep his own semi-independence from Sir John A. Macdonald, who had been attempting to impose rigid party discipline.

"I'm glad you decided we're still friends, Mac."

"Of course, my boy, of course." More smoke poured forth, so that Bowell's pronouncements were like those of Jehovah, coming as they did from a dense cloud. "It's for the good of everyone. Party. The Loyal Orange Lodge. Our constituencies. The empire. And, besides, I could hardly forget our years. We're old partners, you and I. Know each other's secrets and all."

I nodded agreement and thought, how little you know. "Where are we staying in Ottawa, Mac? You're the old hand."

"Ah, now, I've given this serious thought," he said, as if he were about to deliver the Judgment of Solomon. "And I've decided on Mrs Ferguson's boarding house. It's convenient enough, cheap, and you'll meet some of the lads that way."

Parliamentary sessions are short – two months at most – and ordinary M.P.s do not keep their own flats unless they are rich. Most stay in boarding houses. These can be a great place for a new member to make acquaintances and pick up tips on parliamentary behaviour. There are Liberal houses and Conservative houses, some for English-speaking M.P.s and some for French-Canadians. "The food is passable, the rooms clean," Mac continued, "and the company profitable."

Just like the Classon, I thought.

Once we were settled in Ottawa Mac let me shift for myself. "Call me when you need anything. For a start, just shake as many hands as you can." He meant M.P.s' hands, but I was more interested in talking to factory hands. At heart I was still my father's apprentice. My interest lay in how real things, physical objects, were made. And that was fortunate, for the more I kept in touch with artisans and manufacturers, the more adept I became at selling people dreams and ideas.

Ottawa was still a raw city. It had a new street railway that ran along Duke, Wellington and Bank streets to Sparks and then along Rideau to Wurtemburg. Horses drew wheeled cars along rails. In the winter, sleighs replaced cars. I studied this system intensely. It could easily be adapted to foundry work and used for moving heavy pieces of machinery from one work station to another. When Mac inquired how my first day in Parliament had gone, I replied, "Grand! I had a long talk with a city railway train driver."

One of the great sights in Ottawa was the new dam at the Chaudière Falls, just a short walk from Parliament. There was a huge sawmill there. I skipped my second day in Parliament – a new member had precious little to do, I had already discovered – and like an ordinary tourist visited the mill. There nearly forty sawblades all whirled at once, each served by a chute, two feedmen and a sawyer. Out of the noise and the curving yellow arcs of sawdust emerged square logs, planks and massive beams. While I was watching, a man with an American accent asked what I thought of it. When I expressed great admiration for the works, he introduced himself as the owner and offered a complete tour. That night, at the lodging house Mac asked me again if I had met any useful politicians. "Not really," I replied. "But I met a man named Ezra Eddy, and he makes things."

My introduction as a member of Parliament was accomplished with a minimum of fuss. The Canadian Parliament does not make an event, as the British do, out of a new member's maiden speech – which is just as well, because most first speeches should pass mercifully unnoticed. Instead, Parliament simply has someone introduce the new member to the house, after which he signs his name in a book avowing allegiance to the crown. The signing is done in the clerk's office. I had my introduction and signing in on 27 March 1871, and the proceedings took place more celerity than ceremony. Sir John A. Macdonald, in Washington D.C. as part of the United Kingdom delegation trying to settle some residual issues of the American Civil War, had deputized Sir Francis Hincks to introduce the new Tory member for East Hastings. Hincks was minister of finance and a former Reformer. What I remember most about him is that he was once challenged to a duel by Ogle R. Gowan.

"I think the reason they introduced you so quickly," Mac told me that evening, "was that the House was in the middle of a debate on fire insurance and the urgency of the subject precluded their taking much time over you." He smiled wryly.

"Well, I do hope they get my name right." There was another John White in the House of Commons, and henceforth whenever either of us said or did anything our geographic origin had to be noted: "John White (Holton)", or "John White (East Hastings)." My counterpart from Holton usually voted against the Macdonald government, whereas I supported it.

Every once in a while I would meet some man or other on the streets of Ottawa whose face was familiar. One day one of them came up to me and I realized where the faces came from. "Good day, sir," a man of about thirty years of age said, tipping his hat. He appeared to be a respectable clerk or lower civil servant. "We met in Prescott. You remember. The lads from

Ottawa were sent to Cornwall and Prescott during the Fenian trouble, just like you Belleville folks." We shook hands. The man was impressed to learn that his fellow volunteer was now an M.P. Would the member of Parliament like to see the new offices of the Montreal Telegram Company where he was chief telegrapher? Of course. Seeing the flow of business that went through that office, I recognized that very soon every village would have a telegraph office or be consigned to commercial oblivion. That is why, within a year, the firm opened an office in Roslin with these words in gold leaf on the front window: "Montreal Telegraph Company – Roslin Office – John White, Founder."

Of all the diverse things that caught my eye in Ottawa, the most intriguing was the doorstep of the lodging house on Sparks Street, not two hundred yards from where Mac and I lodged and the very spot where Thomas D'Arcy McGee had been assassinated by Fenians. McGee was a rare man. An Irish Catholic, he had been a man of violence in the 1840s, later an enthusiastic admirer of the American republic. But his time in the United States and Canada taught him that Irish people would be better off on the farmsteads and in the small towns of Canada than in the slums of the United States. Under the crown or under the Stars and Stripes – to him that mattered less than the well-being of Irish emigrants. The more radical Irish nationalists could not forgive his abandoning republicanism and becoming a minister of the Canadian government. They wanted his blood and they got it, at the very doorstep I passed each day. Will it always be such with the Irish?

The big debate of the 1871 session was whether or not to admit British Columbia to the Dominion of Canada. I sat quietly and voted the Conservative line. When, on 20 July 1871, British Columbia became part of Canada, I remarked to Mac, "Well, that's about all I did in this session. I imagine that it all would have happened without me."

Although national politics could be a profitable business it was not a full-time job, and without a general election pressing,

Mac and I had other things to tend to – our businesses and the Orange Order. Bowell was spending half his time serving as Grand Master of British North America, while I was being primed to become Grand Master of Ontario East. Moreover, we had hatched a scheme to bring to Canada an elite phalanx of the Orange Order called the Royal Black Preceptory. From the viewpoint of an ambitious man, the trouble with the regular Orange Order was that its base was too wide. We wanted an Orange equivalent of the Masons (to which, not so incidentally, we both belonged), that is, a club limited to the wealthier and more influential members of each local community, our own version (though we never would have called it this) of the Family Compact. The two of us spent a good deal of time traveling separately about the countryside – Mac went as far as Nova Scotia on one trip – talking to the wealthiest Orangemen in each locale, telling them about the Black Preceptory's origins in Ireland and its promising future in Canada. What appealed most to these men was the nomenclature of the preceptory and the fact that it was socially exclusive and each member was given a titular knighthood. For example, the master of a local lodge would be known as The Most Worshipful Sir John Doe, or whatever.

Taxed by Esther with spending too much time away from home, I replied that the various Orange activities laid the base for re–election. "Besides, I enjoy the pageantry. The dressing up in various regalia."

"The vanity of man hath no limits," Esther intoned in her Methodistical voice.

"And for that we must be truly grateful," was my liturgical reply.

13

Loyalties

I must confess something – I never really liked sitting in Parliament. The House of Commons was full of men who smiled like old meerschaum pipes and who had big tufts of hair growing out of their ears. Some of them were drunk, others half-witted, all forever pounding their desk and crying "Hear, hear!" at the wrong time, then falling asleep; or taking out a newspaper and reading the market prices at home. I would have preferred a Wesleyan Methodist service any day. That is how bad it was. Commons business, I had thought, would be conducted with pageantry, but except for the throne speech each session the whole performance resembled a session of the Hastings county council – with the slanging, if anything, being of lower quality. I voted the Tory line faithfully and kept my mouth shut. Mac Bowell was gone half the time, on Orange business, and I had no other real friend in Ottawa.

I suppose I would have done more in the House if I had felt more secure in my guise. I was perfectly at ease with myself – to repeat, I *am* John White, not just someone dressed up to play his part – but there are limits to the trustworthiness of theatrical cement. I was now wearing a well-trimmed set of becoming chin whiskers, and the fear of having them work loose on the Brockville-Ottawa Railroad, or worse, in the House, with a gallery of newspaper men in attendance, dogged me.

The hardest part of that unforgivably long session – my God, it ran from mid-February to mid-June, and I was there at least half of the time – was listening to John A. try to sell the Commons a load of old rope, the Treaty of Washington. It was daylight robbery. Washington and Westminster had come to a deal, and Ottawa was forced to accept the scraps from the table. We got nothing from the Americans for our claims in the wake of the damned Fenian raids; the inshore fisheries battle with them went to arbitration for settlement sometime in the future; in exchange for our surrounding fishing rights they gave us bugger-all; and the boundary between Vancouver Island and the United States, it was decided, would be settled by the German emperor. The German emperor for heaven's sake! We might as well have employed Genghis Khan! Watching Macdonald peddle this merchandise was like seeing a costermonger try and get rid of rotting fruit. Yet the old magician did it, in part by votes, in part by that strange charm of his. It is hard to put a finger on exactly what he had that allowed him to talk people into his way of doing things when it went against their self-interest. His power of being an admitted rogue who – just this one time – was being honest (what a theatrical performance!) went down a treat with your average member of Parliament.

Not me. For the first time I bucked the Tory line, casting my vote against the Treaty of Washington. That is why, just a little later, John A. tried to have me dumped.

But if the Commons was no joy, I enjoyed – no, adored – playing the politician. That is the real thrill of politics – standing up in front of crowds, going down the street shaking hands with everybody, flattering housewives, bouncing babies, telling jokes, asking after everyone's problems, and doing all that better than the next man. I was as addicted to all this as a Manchoo is to opium.

I suppose everyone remembers that the general election of 1872 ranks as one of the dirtiest ever. "Hotly contested," they called it at the time. They meant crooked. Macdonald took money from everyone save the Society of Good Templars, and that only because it was broke and in favour of temperance, two severe drawbacks in the view of our Conservative leader. He got a big lump of money from Sir Hugh Allan, in exchange, as I recall, for permission to build a railway to British Columbia and visiting rights to the emperor of Japan. Sir John put the money into election propaganda, Tory picnics, brass bands and wholesale bribery of voters.

If I sound a wee bit jaded about our leader, it is because during this election Good Sir John turned on me. I knew he was suspicious on account of my friendskip with Mac, who, though a Conservative, was an Independent, and also because thro' the Orange Order Mac exercised influence over Tory voters that Sir John could not control. Still, except for that vote of mine on the Treaty of Washington I had been a good servant – dear Lord, I had voted with Sir John on things I would be embarrassed to tell my creator – and I thought that would stand me in good stead. Not a bit.

So, instead of a nice easy campaign, I ran into a trio of turd-punchers (if Father could only hear me talk!): old Senator Campbell, Gombeen Man Rathbun and that corrupt Indian Agent Frizzell, whom I had tanned in the previous election.

Alexander Campbell, a former law partner of Sir John's, was now the Conservative paymaster in eastern Ontario. He was a terrible old humbug but he had influence, serving simultaneously as minister for the Post Office Department (which might as well be called the Ministry of Patronage) and dean of the law school at Queen's College in Kingston. He subverted the law with one hand and interpreted it with the other. In the 1872 election, Sir John put him in charge of several projects in the Kingston region, one of which entailed replacing me with a safe partyman.

Campbell would have been willing to pour thousands from the party chest to defeat me, but because of E.W. Rathbun, that was not necessary. This pillar was the son of an American lumber magrate who had founded the town of Deseronto. I had nothing against the old man, he was an honest sort of the old school. But the son wanted to buy his very own member of Parliament and, on top of that, had developed a hatred for Mac Bowell. So young Rathbun poured thousands of the family fortune into beating me. He and Campbell maintained a secret correspondence. I learned that later. And I learned that Macdonald knew all about it and approved.

A local Grit named Holden was running in the election, but that was just a complication. He did not have a hope.

The real trouble came from Indian Agent Wellington Frizzell, who wanted another shot at being M.P. and helping his cronies grab as much Indian land as possible. When Frizzell announced his candidacy I had a visit from William Martin and his brother Dr Oronhyatekha, who had been educated at Oxford and Toronto and was now practising medicine near Belleville. He surpassed even his brother William in solemnity, by which I mean he was the gravest man I ever met. He greeted me as a fellow Orangeman and paid formal compliments to Esther and each of the children. The cadence of his speech had been altered by his years in England; so one heard a slow-talking Indian pronounce words in the manner of an English gentleman. He insisted on standing until Esther and the children left the room. Only then would he sit down and chat. He called me Brother White and explained at great length what I already knew, that Frizzell was a crook and would roll the local Mohawks into Lake Ontario if he had his way. Nothing new there. What was new was an idea of his for vengeance. He said when – not if, when – I won the election, I should use my influence to get rid of Frizzell and appoint a suitable new Indian agent, namely, him. I whooped with joy. What a splendid idea – Dear Lord, that would be real vengeance, an Indian in the job of Indian agent! I passed the idea on to Mac Bowell and he liked it as much as I did.

As usual, I prepared for the election by beating on my Orange drum as hard as possible. I stood on the reviewing platform for the twelfth of July parade 1872. That day everyone from Belleville to Brockville staged demonstrations in Kingston, and it was an amazing event. The parade alone took four hours to wend its way past the reviewing stand. John A., eschewing

Orange demonstrations now that he was getting on so well with the French papists, was absent, but he sent a fraternal greeting on very thick yellow paper, which just goes to show that a man can walk both sides of the street at once.

Three days later, on Monday evening, 15 July, a torchlight procession wound through Belleville in honour of William Johnston, M.P. for Belfast in the United Kingdom Parliament and Deputy Grand Master of the Orangemen of Ireland. This great tall man with a flowing beard, this Methuselah, was drawn through the streets of Belleville in a carriage pulled not by horses but by enthusiastic junior Orangemen, and during his patrol he held a pose with one arm out as if to cast forth some utterance about the future. No, on second thought, he did not look so much like Methuselah as Elijah, and I half expected his chariot to rise up in the air to meet the Lord. The fine spectacle eventually ended up at the Masonic Hall where, with Mac in the chair and me on the platform as senior Orange representative, Mr Johnston gave a speech warning that every nation governed by the papacy would in time succumb, that the thrones of Rome and Babylon were numbered among the dead, and that we should all continue to live happily under the old banner and the crown. Great stuff it was. I led the applause at several points. Take that, Thief Frizzell, thought I.

These public appearances of mine must have frightened the Rathbun-Campbell–Sir John A. people, for less than a week later an old acquaintance of mine called on me at home and after a long chat conducted in the way that country people have of circling before they start to strike a bargain, he slapped his hand on his knees and said abruptly, "Well, I'm here to sound you out."

"Oh?"

"Nothing official, you understand. Nothing official."

I nodded and waited.

"But, in the interest of keeping the Grits and the papists out of office, in the interests of party unity, would you..."

"Would I what?"

"Consider standing aside." He took a quick breath and continued before I could say a word. "Of course, we realize that such an act would entail quite a sacrifice on your part. And that you already have spent a good deal of money in election expenses. And we wouldn't expect you to lose money now, would we? Heh Heh!" The laugh was more of a hiccup.

"How much?"

"Let's say, a thousand dollars. Cash. This week."

"Two thousand," I replied. I wondered how high he was authorized to go.

"One thousand five hundred."

"Two thousand." I folded my arms across my chest and looked straight at him.

"John, old friend, I'm sorry, I can't go that high. But I'll be back to you directly, with word from my principals."

"Do that."

And off he trotted. He failed to show up again, so I guess I was not worth 2,000 dollars to the Tories. Not that I would have taken any amount of money to step aside, but it was interesting to measure my value. Besides, sidetracking my opponents with the question of a bribe kept them from the hustings for a little while.

As the election approached we – Esther, the girls and I – worked out a dandy little technique of campaigning. I had often told them how sad it was that something like the Christmas mumming I had enjoyed as a child did not exist in Upper Canada. Well, for this election we created the "family tableau," which we presented any place we could gather an audience of ten or more people – schoolhouses, Orange halls, temperance buildings, and so forth. We were a troupe of seven – Esther, myself and the five girls, Eliza being 14, Sarah 12, Ida 8, Anna 5, and Esther a year and a half. We gave the audience a mixture of jokes, songs, patriotic verse and a short serious speech from me about the importance of the approaching election. I always mentioned the martyrdom of Tom Scott and the need to capture and punish the rebel Riel. Sometimes I mentioned the disappearance of my brother.

We were not serious for too long or people would leave. I had the girls, who did a good brogue, trained to tell a couple of Irish jokes in dialogue:

Young Eliza (a judge): Now, Patrick, what do you say to the charge before you? Are you guilty or not guilty?

Sarah (a prisoner): Faith? But that's difficult for your honour to say, let alone myself. (Pause) Wait till I hear the evidence!

Great howls of laughter from the audience.

Ida (acting very exasperated, hands on hips): I'm an Irish attorney. And there's one of my clients (points).
Anna (five years old, but with a great loud voice): Good day, your honour. Long life to you.
Ida: Pay me that five dollars you owe me.
Anna: For what?
Ida: For that opinion you had of me.
Anna: Faith, I never had any opinion of you in my life!

If there were two or more ladies present, and usually there were, my darling Esther gave a short talk aimed at them about the dignity of Parliament and the importance of sending a responsible family man to represent our values. "I promise you that my husband John is always willing to listen to the opinion of the ladies of Hastings County. Most politicians ignore us women, because we do not have the vote. My John considers the opinion of each of you as important as if you did vote. And some day we *will* have the franchise! But until then, it's by talking to John White that you can make your opinion count. And make sure that your husbands remember to vote, won't you, ladies?"

The Family Tableau and my other activities bearing fruit, the Frizzell camp panicked. They should have known better than to court the Catholic vote out of fear. That was very stupid. The Catholics numbered about one out of three voters in the riding and they always voted Grit. Rathbun and Sir John A.'s henchman Campbell saw how strong the Orange's backing of me was and somehow convinced themselves that there were as many R.C.s as True Blues. Silly lads. So perfidious Frizzell went about currying Papist favour. For every Roman he attracted, he lost a Protestant.

The actual polling was set for the last week in August. Earlier that month Macdonald appointed Samuel Shaw Lazier as returning officer. That was a strange move. He must have thought Lazier, whom I knew well from my early days in the Belleville area (and, for that matter, whose brother and cousins I knew), would keep me in line. There was no need for that. I was not planning violence. Because I had first met Macdonald in the company of Ogle Gowan, Sir John, I suspect, felt that I would resort to electoral violence, as Ogle had done so often.

I reckoned that old Sam Lazier would be an honest returning officer, but just in case the government tried something funny I had Mac Bowell deliver a message to the meddler Campbell: if I was defeated by government influence, I and my friends would rush to the Prince Edward riding, which voted a few days later than East Hastings, and do everything we could to turn out the government candidate and put in a Grit. I was not bluffing.

The election turned out to be deuced close, and nasty. The nastiness was right out of 1798. There is a Catholic belt in our township of Tyendinaga, to the south of where Esther and I live, and a more unpleasant bunch of Fenian bastards would be hard to find. The polls were scheduled to open on Monday, and on the Thursday before that Fenians, led by a local thug, Dominick Tighe, murdered an Orangeman, a good man by the name of Winters. This happened in the little hamlet of Lonsdale, a Catholic place where Protestants go only in twos and threes if they have any sense. On the fatal day, Dan Winters drove alone on his wagon to the Lonsdale Post Office. As he pulled up, a crowd of papists started to hoot at him and threatened a fight. "Boys, I don't want anything to do with you," he said, meaning that he was not looking for trouble. He bent over the dashboard of his wagon to secure the reins when Tighe, the leader, shot him three times in the back. Poor Winters staggered off down the road in the direction of some Protestant friends. The Catholic gang pelted him with rocks as he dragged himself up the road and he had to be carried off by his friends who rescued him. One of them, John Garret, a fine, courageous man, had his arm broken by one of the rocks. With Winters gone, the papish savages took out their venom on Winters's horses. They stoned and beat the poor creatures until they collapsed on the ground, unconscious and covered with blood. It took fifty Catholics to stone two horses!

Winters was buried on Sunday, and that day every Orangeman in the county stalked the area. Not one papish coward showed his head. Orangemen understood exactly what had happened. Most of them had heard from their own parents or grandparents what Catholics had done to the Protestants of

Wexford, Waterford and Kilkenny in 1798. In some ways this New World of ours is just a weary continuation of the old.

One thing, so strange it makes my skin crawl: the name Dan Winters was not just any name, it was a sacred name to Orangemen. You see, it was at Winters' Inn, at the Diamond in County Armagh, in the Old Country, that in 1795 the Orange Order was founded. So when the local Papishes killed our own Dan Winters, they hit bone.

I won the election by forty-four votes, and I am certain failure would have been mine had the papists not killed Dan Winters. But with his ghost walking beside me, neither they nor that fraud Frizzell was going to beat me.

What a sweet victory! Mac Bowell told me about the excitement in Belleville as the results came in, a crowd of several hundred besieging the Montreal Telegraph Company Office. The returns trickled in, and it was not until 10 o'clock in the evening that my triumph was sealed. Cheers could be heard all the way across Lake Ontario, Mac claimed.

Esther and I heard the good news at the home of one of my election agents in Shannonville, whereupon we set off for Belleville. A torchlight procession met our carriage on Dundas Street. What a fine sight. Hundreds of cheering people. Lots of ladies. And some hearty lads who unhitched our horses and pulled the carriage themselves. Mac joined Esther and me in our moment of triumph. The procession stopped at the *Intelligencer* office, where Mac and I both made speeches. Then, with three cheers for the Queen, the crowd dispersed. We shook hands with all our well-wishers and then watched the last of them disappear into the darkness.

It finally dawned on me what this meant: I was the people's choice.

It is nice to have the people's confidence. Not everyone in the Commons enjoyed that security. Take Sir John A. Macdonald, for example. He kept his seat, of course, but lost Ontario and damned near lost the whole election. His government stayed in office by a thread, the six British Columbia seats. I will credit Macdonald with one thing: he knew how to eat crow. Less than a week after my election victory he had old meddler Campbell ask Mac Bowell (whom Sir John was now courting too) what it would take to keep me supporting the government. Nothing much, just something symbolic, Mac told him – a new Indian agent in Tyendinaga. Done! But then Campbell learned that I wanted an Indian, Dr Oronhyatekha, for the office. He went mad! You would have thought I had suggested electing a woman to the Freemasons. The matter was referred to Solomon, that is, Sir John A., and he decreed that I could have anyone I wanted as Indian agent, but not Dr Oronhyatekha, not a Mohawk, not an Indian. In the end we replaced Frizzell with a decent Orange-man, Matthew Hall. Rathbun took care of his failed candidate, who now was out of a job, by giving him a position in one of his lumber businesses. Oronhyatekha's response upon hearing of Macdonald's decision was that a drunken Scotsman was less trustworthy than a wild cur.

In my Toronto days I had come to the conclusion that politics makes strange bedfellows, and now I learned that bedfellows make strange politicians. Schuyler Shibley was elected from Addington as a Conservative. I was worried that he would recognize me, but he rarely showed up in the House, and when he did he was so engrossed in backroom deals that he never looked me in the eye. The funny thing is, in 1873 he jumped to the Liberal side of the aisle and stayed there until he lost his seat in 1878. It always struck me as appropriate that a man tailored by nature to be a libertine in a common-house would become a Liberal in the House of Commons.

As for Sir John A., the few times I encountered him personally in Ottawa he was heavily under the influence. The Grits had uncovered some letters showing that he had taken huge amounts of money in return for rigging the rail line to British Columbia. Maybe he had not: shorn of its wool, his defense was that he had taken the money but not made any promises about who would build the rail line. This, the Pacific Scandal, blew up in April 1873, and in the late fall the government tumbled. An unsufferable little Scot, Alexander Mackenzie, took over.

The next year Mackenzie called an election for January 1874, the first to be held in the Dominion under the Secret Ballot Act. (I gave a good speech in the Commons against it. No decent voter should be afraid of voting openly, and this business of retreating into closets and marking pieces of paper, as if one were ashamed to be voting, was unworthy of the British empire. I lost my case), Mac and I kept our seats easily enough in this election. Sir John A. won Kingston, but a complainant proved that his election agent had bribed voters, so the election had to be run all over again. Sir John A. won by only seventeen votes the second time. That should teach him some humility, Mac commented, and it did. Macdonald never again treated secure and trustworthy Conservatives like Mac and me with anything but the utmost civility. Moreover, the old rascal was totally broke. He moved to Toronto to practise law, mend his finances and sober up a bit.

Meanwhile Louis Riel, the man who had killed Tom Scott and my brother (at least indirectly, if I am not mistaken), resurfaced. He had won a bye-election in some godforsaken place in the middle of Manitoba in 1873 and again in 1874. This with a murder warrant out against him and a $5,000 reward on his head! Now, Riel, using all the resources of the papish underground, including renegade and treasonous priests, made his way to Ottawa in late March 1874, just before the opening of the parliamentary session. His friends hid him in a convent in Hull, across the river from where Parliament sat. On the very last day of the month, the 31st, Riel slipped across to Ottawa. He was in the company of Eugene Fiset, a schoolfellow from a Catholic college in Montreal who had just been elected M.P. for Rimouski, in Lower Canada. Fiset had not yet signed the members roll. He went to the office of the clerk of the commons and said that he wanted to sign and so did a friend of his, a new member also. The clerk said fine, bring your friend in, and Riel, who had been skulking outside, hustled in. Fiset took the roll-book and signed his name, then handed it to Riel, who did the same. They both bowed formally to the clerk and hurried away. When the clerk checked the names, one of them was Louis Riel.

Word spread quickly, and every M.P. was glued to his seat for the next sitting. We waited to see the face of the villain. Of course, the Quebec members secretly thought of him as some sort of hero. In Ontario we knew him for what he was, among other things, a coward, which is why the daring rebel did not show up. He did a bunk. The attorney general of Manitoba stood up and formally read out Riel's arrest warrant, then gave in detail the man's ravenings, his crimes, his murders, his treasons. The House ordered Riel to appear after the Easter recess, but he remained in hiding. So Mac, to his everlasting credit and to the credit of all Orangemen everywhere, led a move to expel the murderer of Tom Scott from the House. This issue galvanized me more than any issue in my political career. I acted as Mac's lieutenant and went from member to member explaining how dangerous the treasonous papist was. I am proud to say that every Protestant and every English-speaking member, with the exception of two from Quebec, voted for expulsion. And is it surprising that every Catholic and every French member voted against expulsion? That tells you where loyalty lies. Where treason lurks. We won, thank God, and the ghostly presence of that murderous scoundrel no longer tainted the Canadian House of Commons.

I need to stop here. What I have just written is true. *Too* true, that is the trouble. You see, when I look back, I am not embarrassed by my part in the Riel expulsion, but I am reminded how little joy my days in the House of Commons gave me. Unlike my businesses, the foundry and the cheese factories, and my work with the order, the Royal Black Preceptory, and the Masons, the House of Commons turned me into a person I did not like. Either the work there involved serious matters of unhappy moment, like the Riel affair, or snapping and snarling on matters of no importance at all.

The Commons made me understand men better than I ever wished to. People in leather chairs and walnut-paneled rooms are just like sled dogs. They pull together in one direction if some giant with a whip lays on them, but the minute discipline relaxes, they growl and snarl at one another. That that is the nature of the beast.

For a time, the Commons made me like that. So engrossed

was I in the fighting that in 1873 when our sixth girl, Emma, arrived, I did not even come home from Ottawa for the occasion.

Then the gods, or God, spoke to me. Darling Esther took ill, seriously ill. It started with a cough. We were attending a social evening at the lodge. She wore a white blouse with a high ruffled neck and kept a large cambric handkerchief in her sleeve. She coughed and held the handkerchief over her mouth. There was a little rattle of phlegm and Esther looked at the handkerchief. Sitting next to her, I caught the puzzled look on her face – and then saw the small pink spot. Later in the evening she coughed quite violently, this time bringing up bright-red spots of blood.

We both knew what it meant. Any nitwit would know what it meant: tuberculosis, the most melancholy of diseases. Foolishly, we thought we had slipped by it. There was a saying abroad at the time: "No TB by twenty-five, you'll live the rest of your life alive." All you had to do was walk in the burial ground and look at the gravestones to see how many young people, men and women at the prime of life, had been snuffed out. That night Esther and I went home in our Democrat, I with one arm around her, the other holding the reins. Neither of us said a word. She prayed, I cried.

William Martin came and examined Esther, then said he would summon his brother, Dr Oronhyatekha. Dr Oronhyatekha prescribed the standard treatment: rest in bed, walks in the open air, sleep in a cold room. Esther was to stay out of the cheese factory and any other place that had damp air.

One of the tortures of tuberculosis is that it is not a dramatic disease. Watching its progress or retreat is like observing the freezing of a lake or the melting of ice in spring: it is so slow that you cannot see what is happening unless you check at distinct and distant intervals. For a long time nothing seemed to happen, but Esther's coughing became gradually worse. Soon my love could only sleep sitting up; rarely was she able to get out of bed. She read the Bible constantly.

Evenings I found myself touching, arranging and rearranging Esther's collection of porcelain figures. She had kept adding to their number during the years, and there must have been four dozen little people, precisely painted, delicate and translucent. One of our girls would sit with me in the parlour for a time, then leave me alone with my thoughts. The porcelains came to fascinate me, I think, because the disease was making a porcelain figure out of Esther. Her skin, always fair, grew translucent and extraordinarily beautiful, and her features sharpened as she became weaker. Forty-eight figures... I did not want forty-nine.

The improvement came so slowly that I nearly missed it. After six months of paling Esther took a turn for the better. One morning I visited her after having checked on my workers in the cheese factory and she asked me for a cup of hot broth. That was unusual, for her appetite had virtually disappeared. When I returned with it I noticed just the faintest trace of colour on her cheek. I said nothing, for to talk about hope is to kill it, but unmistakably my darling had started to improve. In a month we were able to talk about the future.

Meanwhile Esther announced that she was converting to Presbyterianism. That is the direction in which her recent Bible reading had taken her. I agreed to follow, having long since learned that changes in religion always accompanied any serious crisis in her life. Without qualm, I had moved from the Church of Ireland in the old country to the United Church of England and Ireland in the new, then to the Wesleyan Methodist Church and now to the Presbyterian Church. For Esther's sake, I think I would have even turned papist!

As Esther improved, we spent the evenings in each other's company. We talked more than we had done for several years. Sometimes we just read or silently reflected. During this time together I came to realize I had almost lost my soul to gain the world. That sounds rather Biblical, perhaps, but sitting with Esther did that to a person, put one in mind of the Scriptures. I decided, in other words, that I would not let the House of Commons harden me. I would attend and perform my duty, but I would resist getting entrapped by the inmates of that snarling kennel.

One thing we talked about besides religion was children. Did we want more? Yes, we agreed, and here was the important part: out of the blue Esther said, "You know, I think we should just let nature take its course."

I was not sure what she meant.

"That is, we should tell William Martin that if the next infant is a boy, that would fine with us."

For her, it was an epic decision. Finally she had accepted that we were a real family. If nature gave us a boy, or boys, we would raise them just as any other married couple would.

In fact when, in late 1875, William Martin again served as our family angel, he brought us a boy. We named him William, in gratitude to our friend and also after King William of Orange. Two years later we received another son, our last child. We christened him John, after me, after John Oge, after my father. Everyone said how much the boys looked like Mr Johnston, their maternal grandfather.

Part Four
Changing Fortunes

14
Lapses

This history would not be completed lest I tell you, albeit with hesitation and not a little embarrassment, about a peculiar interlude that occurred in the late 1870s. At that time I came to know a student at the women's branch of Albert College in Belleville, one Mary Edwards Merrill, a girl of nineteen years, tiny and frail but possessed of an incandescent quality that was all the more striking for emanating from such a small frame. When first introduced to her I thought that Miss Merrill had emeralds, not eyes, set into her face; they were hard, shining and unsettling.

Mackenzie Bowell was one of the larger contributors to Albert College, a Methodist institution that ran both a high school and a university course for the apple-cheeked offspring of eastern Ontario's farms and small towns. The women's branch, Alexandra College, had about five dozen young ladies in attendance, polite, dutiful, and every one of them an advocate of temperance. At the annual Prize Day Bowell learned of the Merrill girl, who was more gifted in mathematics than her own instructors. She was distinguished in the writing of essays and in the practice of oratory as well. "The interesting thing, though," Mac told me, "is that she seems to have a sixth sense. Mind you, she's a good Christian girl and all. Yet..."

"What?"

"Well, at Prize Day, she gave an oration on the press. I thought when she started that we were going to hear another childish oration on how the press keeps us informed and is that not a wonderful thing. No. She did something amazing. She gave a condensed history of the press, with numbers – she explained how it had developed by using exponents and logarithms, among other things – and then, as if she were solving a mathematical problem, she predicted how and where the press would develop in Canada in the next ten years! It was uncanny. I'd have paid a hundred dollars just to hear that. I wish my block-headed associate editor had been there! You really have to meet this child, John."

This was arranged easily enough. When the principal of Albert College found out that a member of Parliament wished to interview one of his students, he readily agreed, and I was given the use of the headmaster's study to conduct a private interview of the young lady.

The meeting was most unsettling. To start, Miss Merrill refused my offer of a chair. "I prefer to stand, if you do not mind, sir." She formed her words so clearly that she sounded foreign. "You see, I know that you want me to predict the future, and I can only do that if I am perpendicular to the horizon, considered hypothetically as a flat surface. You were going to ask me about the future, were you not?"

"Well, yes," I said, disconcerted. Do you predict by mathematical principles?"

The girl replied in measured tones, but with a hint of impatience. "Somewhat. Certainly you know, sir, that mathematics is the most accurate and pure of the sciences. And, yes, one can prophesy through mathematics."

"But there is more?"

"Of course. Anyone can predict through mathematics. All that is required is information and intelligence. I do something more." There was no hint of pride in the girl's voice. She was merely stating fact. "I prophesy through the spirit."

"Really?"

"Would you like me to do that? Or would you prefer that we discuss some academic subject of your own choosing? I am quite pleased to comply in either case."

I threw prudence away. This child had something. "The future. Please. Can you prophesy on any subject at all?"

Are you interested in election results, Mr White?"

I had been about to ask for that, and nodded agreement.

"I could predict those. But of course I won't. Nor will I abuse my gift by predicting the results of horse races or cockfights."

"Well, then, anything at all. If you please."

The girl smiled as if to the tune of some sweet and distant song, then slowly raised her hands over her head. Her mouth gaped; she was utterly frozen. Not a sound. No apparent breathing. I sat nearly as motionless as the girl herself, transfixed by the force that emanated from her. A fly buzzed momentarily in the sunlit corner of the study, then it too became silent.

A full five minutes later, the girl came out of the trance and smiled sweetly at me, as if to say that we shared a secret and it was good. "I will tell you some strange things," she said.

"Please."

"Firstly, the group of which you are the head is almost complete. You will add another boy to it. Secondly, you will never become known as a great man in our national history. Nevertheless, you will have your successes." I was about to say something but she held up her hand. "Do not interrupt. Thirdly, in the long years after your departure, you will be a light to future generations. They will call you blessed. Fourthly, Mr White, a piece of economical advice: to remain successful, you must increase your land holdings. It is what Jehovah has always told his chosen people. And, finally… your most important secret is safe with me." And with that the tiny oracle turned and left the principal's study. There was no question in my mind that she had seen straight through John White, M.P.

Over the next three and a half years I held interviews at monthly intervals, whenever possible, with Miss Merrill. Sometimes I received hour-long lectures on spiritual energies, other times specific prophecies about how individual members of the House of Commons would behave – and they, sometimes, were very helpful to me.

Our relationship ended in 1880 with Miss Merrill's mysterious death. So strange were the circumstances of the gifted girl's demise that it became a serialized item in Mac Bowell's *Intelligencer*. She went into a state of suspended animation one day in April. Her sister discovered her and brought in the family physician and the Belleville coroner, who pronounced her dead, her body pulseless and cooling. Yet, more than twelve hours later, an examination showed a faint heartbeat, and in another twelve hours the temperature was found to be rising, even though the room was cold. It continued to rise, but then all other signs of life vanished. More medical authorities were called in. After long argument, they pronounced Mary Merrill dead.

The pastor of the Baptist Church in Belleville preached a sermon on this topic to his congregation: "The death of this young lady teaches us there is no comfort but in the religion of Christ. Spiritualism and infidelity had not given her any comfort, but true religion would have achieved that end."

"Pious, heartless nonsense," was my comment when told of this. Mac Bowell and I agreed to serve among the girl's pallbearers in protest against such evangelical intolerance.

What I remember of the little psychic's burial service was the preternatural heaviness of the coffin. Although she had not weighed more than a single hundredweight, if that, six pallbearers could not budge the coffin, and it was only after enlisting the extra help of two strong farm lads that we were able to carry away the physical remains of Mary Edwards Merrill.

If I told you the story about my interest in the psychic with some hesitation, it is with remorse that I admit the following fact: some of my political methods were unethical. In fact, the Commons unseated me, albeit briefly, in 1879, for electoral corruption.

I loved being popular – which is why I loved electoral contests and why the memory of close calls disturbs me so. When the election of September 1878 was called I had responded like a veteran steeplechaser approaching the first fence on a fast course. "We'll have some fun this time," I told Esther confidently. "All of us, the whole family. We'll do the family tableau. The boys can be part of it!"

"A crèche, maybe?" Esther teased, but she sounded skepticial. "Don't you think that the voters are going to be a bit bored by the old routines? Why not just run for office the way everyone else does – shake hands, bribe the voters and put up lots of posters?"

No, I had to do it my way. In other circumstances my unique mixture of music hall and political burlesque might have worked, but I was up against W.R. Aylsworth, a popular local man who was also the protégé of the reeve of Thurlow Township, Harford Ashley. I still held my post as reeve of Tyendinaga Township, and so what started out as parliamentary election degenerated into a dogfight over the most insignificant local matters: the location of animal pounds, the appointment of fence viewers, and road repair. In this local mire the family tableau counted much less than whose cousin had been given a job with the county council.

When the polling results were announced, I nearly went into shock. The Liberal candidate had a majority of twenty votes. "A Grit for East Hastings!" I exclaimed. We might as well have a Catholic as District Grand Master of the lodge!"

George Dickson, one of my electoral agents and also my lawyer, immediately demanded a recount. Voters had been bribed, he said, some intimidated, others misled by shady returning officers – all the usual charges in contested elections. A recount was carried out before the county court judge.

"They're numbered, the ballots are numbered!" electoral agent Dickson shouted time after time during the recount. And they were. As it happened, several officers at the various polling stations had confused the laws for provincial elections, which require numbered ballots, with those for federal elections, which require clean ones. They had numbered the ballots in order to check who had voted against the polling list and thus to avoid double-voting. The stations where this happened were those where my opponent had won a majority. And so a large number of votes were thrown out, which worked to my benefit. I was declared the victor, by twelve votes.

"None of this would have happened if we had not adopted the cowardly secret ballot," I blustered. "Voting in public, as we did in the old days, is the only honest and manly way to hold an election."

"You're quite right, dear," Esther said. "But, then, if it hadn't been for the ballot mix-up, you'd be out of office."

I almost was anyway. My opponent formally charged me with electoral corruption, a matter that had to be adjudicated under federal law. When the case was heard the judge voided the entire election, thus unseating me. The election had to be rerun. Sick of the whole business, my original opponent stepped down and a local nobody, a Grit named Willet C. Farley, came forward. Despite his lack of political experience, in the new election of February 1879 he almost put me out. I won by only 74 votes in a poll of over 2,600, and I lost my own township.

That is when the fun went out of electoral campaigns. Because of this and a deepening commitment to the family, I began to stay closer to home.

The electoral case cost over a thousand dollars, most of which went to the Toronto barristers who argued it. With thorough ill grace I let them stew, until in the end they had to execute a writ in order to get the money.

I now devoted more attention to what mattered – ceremonies, and my home circle. By ceremonies I mean the Orange Order and the Royal Black Preceptory. For a time I served as Grand Master of Ontario East, the post Mac Bowell once had held, and in the Black Preceptory I eventually became Deputy Grand Master. The ceremonies of the preceptory were elaborate affairs. I am not ashamed to say that I loved the ritual even more than the camaraderie existing among our elite Brother Knights. In another life, I would have been a great actress.

One of my greatest pleasures as the boys grew older was to

take them to the foundry in Madoc and teach them about metal-working. I even had the old hearth and bellows from the little foundry I had first operated in Roslin moved to our farm and reconstructed. There, on autumn afternoons, I passed some of the most satisfying hours of my life. I would have a hired man set the fire in the morning and look after it until early afternoon. Then, following in my father's footsteps, I taught the lads how to do simple things well – how to shape a horseshoe and, when they had mastered that, how to join two pieces of red-hot iron. What I was doing was reenacting the way my father had taught John Oge and me. It was my way of saying that I was proud of what father had been and of what I had become.

I only wish Esther and I had not been afraid of teaching the girls about how we lived – that is, about my personal identity. I never had the courage to tell them, tho' I longed to do so. They had grown up normal girls, doing everything society expected of them. Esther's and my decision may have been a prudent one, but nonetheless I regret it now. My being different cheated them, and cheated us, too.

Sometimes I think had I not been so unusual, my political career would have been longer and more illustrious. Not, mind you, that I would have wanted that. But think, when in 1878 Sir John A. Macdonald returned to office, he had to woo eastern Ontario back into the fold, especially those Orangemen who formed the spine of the Tory party in English Canada. One shrewd move of his was to appoint Mac Bowell as minister of customs, a post with lots of patronage. Mac stepped down as Grand Master of the Orange Lodge of British North America so as not to be charged with holding two incompatible posts. From then on Mac remained in the cabinet. If I had dared be more prominent my own path would have been to go for the Grand Mastership myself – as you know, I had followed Mac's steps as Grand Master of Ontario East; the progression was a natural one – and to throw myself more enthusiastically into the game that was the House of Commons. But always in the House there was that terrible scrutiny of the press and of opponents, always the chance of making a mistake and revealing myself. Sometimes I envy the women who will come after me, the ones who will not only vote but also sit in Parliament as females.

Not unhappily – for, as I have mentioned several times, Commons politics could consume a man and leave him no time for the happier things in life – I resigned myself to my role. Once I had given up any thought of cabinet office I had the freedom to serve my constituents, and that I did well. I did everything for them from winning judgeships (from Macdonald, of course) to sponsoring the incorporation of the business of my old enemy, Rathbun. And, since I allowed myself no higher ambition, I could speak out on matters of principle.

One of these was temperance. Sir John A. did not like my backing it. I agreed on that single issue with the poe-faced little Scot who headed the Grits, Alexander Mackenzie. People in the Canadas were too much drunk and therefore too often violent. I favoured the 1878 Temperance Act and it nearly cost me an election – but no matter, principle counts sometimes.

Those who, decades from now, go through the Commons debates will see that whenever a matter concerning the Indians came up, I energetically defended their interests. I am proud of that. In fact, when the band chiefs arrived in Ottawa at the time the Indian laws were being revised, they made a point of visiting me. My opinion on the subject can be summed up by two points I made in an 1880 debate: "We should no longer treat the Indians as children... Had they the responsibility of members of this House they could fill the position here with credit to themselves and to the country." In 1884 Macdonald introduced a bill to give the Indians on reservations – not the treasonous metis, the *real* Indians – the vote. I worked the halls hard, telling my eastern Ontario colleagues that this was the right step to take and not to confuse tribes like the Mohawks with Louis Riel's sort. I argued that when any band of people – even Hindoos and Muselmens, if it came to that – acted loyally and responsibly, as the Mohawks had, then they possessed the right to full citizenship. The bill passed and went into effect the following year, and I am happy to report that almost to a man, the Tyendinaga braves voted for me in the next federal election. Better a loyal Mohawk than a disloyal papist!

Another issue I got involved with was the franchise laws. In 1883 Sir John A. tried to straighten out that tangle – every province had its own law – by introducing a standard federal franchise. At the same time he wanted to include more voters.

The bill was complicated one, and since voters are what make M.P.s everyone in the Common joined in the debate of it, each thinking that his was the ox that would be gored. It was a messy debate.

Sandwiched between provisions in the middle of the bill was one of its most important clauses, that women heading their own households and owning a certain amount of property would be able to vote. I was one of the few M.P.s to show any interest at all in this issue and to endorse it. "The time is not far distant when the women of this country will have a vote," I said in debate. "I am glad the Hon. First Minister has introduced a bill which will give the right of suffrage to a good many women." It is all there on record. I said a good deal more, and I am proud of it. My only regret is that right after my speech a coalition of frightened M.P.s led by a renegade Irishman voted to give the bill a six-month hoist, and Sir John had to drop it. The franchise he got through in 1885 turned out to be good for the working man, but it did nothing for women.

That issue, and temperance, and supporting the Orange Order in its quest for a fair deal – for the right to be incorporated – consumed my time in Parliament. I managed to avoid most of the turbulence of Commons politics. And I stayed at home as much as I could – more, certainly, than most members. In the long run how you take care of your family is what counts.

Now that I am totting up life's ledger, I feel compelled to admit that one of the ways I tried to support my family involved some unsavoury land speculations. "You must increase your land holdings," Mary Merrill had advised me. Thus when, on a rainy Ottawa afternoon in 1881, Mackenzie Bowell said, "We really must think about going seriously into the land business," it was as if someone were uttering a familiar command to a well-trained draught animal.

"Of course," I replied without hesitation. "Land is the future. That is what God told his Chosen People."

"The first step, John, is for you to repay to me the money you

owe me. This was the $1,300 he and a fellow investor had lent
Esther and me in 1867 so that we could expand our businesses.
"Don't worry, I won't see you short for cash." And he did not.
Mac arranged for the Real Estate Loan and Debenture Company
to remortgage our farm for $2,600. I paid Mac off and had some
money in hand to start playing the real-estate game.

But where? The West was the only place, Mac informed me,
as sure of this as he was of everything in life. If he pronounced
that tomorrow the sun would rise in the west, his confidence
alone would make a believer of you. "Our grand leader, Sir John
A., controls half the land in the country now, and if we're
discreet he'll not object to our having some of it!" Prime Minister
Macdonald had been acting as his own minister of the interior
and of indian affairs. "He's letting his department slide; we have
a great opportunity."

I agreed, especially since Lawrence Vankoughnet, senior deputy minister for indian affairs, was running the department on
a daily basis. He came of Alsatian loyalist stock and his family
had been staunch Tories since the early days of the province of
Ontario.

"Mind you, John, as a cabinet minister I'll have to keep my
hands clean."

"Of course, Mac. I'll take the lead. But I'll have to be discreet
too."

In the following months Mac and I put together a series of
colonization companies, that is, businesses that settled white
people on the vast lands of the Canadian West. The first and
most successful of our firms was the Prince Albert Colonization
Company, which operated mostly in what is now Saskatchewan
and Alberta on lands claimed by the metis. "We've got 51,200
acres!" was the good news Mac brought to me one spring day
in 1882. "Near Batoche, on the Saskatchewan River."

"It's a license to print money, Mac!"

But it was not so easy as all that. We needed to cover our
tracks. We had obtained a grant from Macdonald's own department of Indian affairs which, confirmed by Privy Council order,
gave us the tract in return for our settling "agriculturalists," or
white people, on it. The Prince Albert Colonization Company
was a wonderful front. Mac and I had secret "blind shares" that
gave each of us one-twelfth of the expected profits; these had

a face value of $33,000, a bargain considering that neither of us had put a penny of direct investment into the scheme. Other shareholders had to shoulder nearly $20,000 each for considerably smaller parts of the enterprise. "So far, all we've spent is $700 taking Vankoughnet and a few privy councillors drinking and dining," was Mac's comment.

"And our promise to vote for anything John A. proposes for the rest of our parliamentary careers."

"Still, it's a bargain."

Such a bargain, in fact, that Mac began to worry. For $500 he transferred his blind share to his son-in-law, a Belleville businessman named James C. Jamieson, and arranged with him to split future proceeds. He even asked for a canceled promissory note from Jamieson so that later, if critics started to investigate, he could say that he had nothing to do with the Prince Albert Colonization Company in its formative stages; if they found out about the $500 from his son-in-law, he could claim that it was a repayment of a debt, not a sale of stock. Mackenzie Bowell had a Canadawide reputation for honesty, and he protected it.

So profitable was this scheme that less than a year later, in 1882, I applied to the government for another tract of land, this one surrounding Edmonton. "It's just a fort now, but in twenty years it will be a hub," I told Mac. This time, tho', Macdonald's government said no. The plum was too choice to give away.

"One door shuts, another opens, right Mac?" That was my response. I lost no time forming another company, this one called the Shell River Colonization Company. It operated the way the Prince Albert Company had: blind shares for myself and for Mac's son-in-law, public subscription for the rest of the shares, a big government grant and profit for all. This worked. The company received a grant for a chunk of the Northwest Territories that was as large as that given to the Prince Albert Colonization Company. The paperwork passed quickly through the Indian affairs people, through the Interior Ministry, and was confirmed by a Privy Council order. Macdonald put his signature to the deal in several places. Not surprisingly, I stood to make a lot of money.

One evening Esther and I sat in the drawing room of our large farmhouse. I was combing the local newspapers, a habit maintained since those days long ago when I was an intelligence-gatherer for Ogle R. Gowan. Esther was arranging and rearranging her porcelain figurines. "I wonder sometimes dear... How is it that you can be so keen on the rights of Indians and yet use your colonization companies to take land from the natives? Isn't that wrong?"

I responded with the heavy patience of a adult dealing with a child. "In the first place, we're not taking land from real Indians. Real Indians, like the good Dr. William Martin, and the Mohawks here in Tyendinaga, are some of God's finest creatures. They're loyal. They fought for the Queen against the Yankees a hundred years ago and have been steadfast ever since! Why, right here they have one of the strongest Orange lodges in the entire dominion. As long as they're True Blue, who gives a damn if they're red? They've earned all the rights of any white man."

"But the metis..."

"The metis are scum, droppings, dirt! They're half-French, half-Catholic, and worst of all, rebel. They're like the Celtic savages in Ireland in 1798, disloyal and dangerous. Remember, they killed Thomas Scott... and my poor brother too! The best way to order society is to take away the land of treasonous Catholics and plant it with Protestants."

The motives of fair profit, just revenge, rewarding loyalism and punishing treason all came together at Batoche, on lands held by the Prince Albert Colonization Company, in mid-May 1885. It was the occasion of the last significant battle of the Northwest – or Riel – Rebellion. About 800 white soldiers, mostly Orangemen from Ontario, fought fewer than 200 Metis in a battle that lasted four days. Against an enemy well-equipped with carbines and Gatling guns the Metis were reduced to firing stones and nails in their rifles. The victory was never in doubt.

A few days later Louis Riel walked up to some scouts of the Northwest Mounted Police and surrendered. He was convicted of treason, but the judge added a recommendation of mercy. Eventually, after two unsuccessful appeals, the decision was passed up to the prime minister and his cabinet. The question was a simple one: to hang Riel or not? Mac Bowell and I were among the most active canvassers against clemency: Treason

Must Not Be Tolerated: Loyalty Shall Not be Mocked, was our slogan. The Orange Order brought all of its pressure to bear on the Ontario members of Parliament.

John A. Macdonald counted the votes, and on 16 November 1885 Louis Riel was hanged.

At the time, Wilfrid Laurier, who like Mackenzie Bowell was destined to become prime minister of Canada, shrewdly observed that Louis Riel was executed not for the Northwest Rebellion but for the killing of Tom Scott. Privately I amended that: Riel was hanged both for the murder of Scott and for the disappearance of my poor deformed brother.

15

Assay

In 1885 I bid fair to increase my fortunes further. Esther and I took out another mortgage on our local properties, this time four thousand dollars, and put the money into land ventures in British Columbia. We now had three big land projects on the fire, the two Northwest colonization companies and the B.C. speculation.

This, I now realize, invited political danger. In July 1885 a Grit newspaper in Ottawa picked up bits and pieces of the story of the Prince Albert Colonization Company, and the following winter the Toronto *Globe* took up investigation of it. By April and May 1886 the Grits had stored up enough fodder to attack me and my partner Mac in Parliament with a series of highly embarrassing allegations. Mac's defense was that he had never had a pecuniary interest in the Prince Albert Colonization Company. It was impossible for the Grits to prove otherwise, since he had used his son-in-law as a catspaw. And therefore I took most of the heat. "You ought to have given your share to *your* son-in-law," a Grit needled me during the debate.

The parliamentary attack resulted in a motion to refer the whole Prince Albert business to a select committee. Sir Hector Langevin, leader of the Quebec wing of the Tory party, moved that instead the matter be looked into by the Standing Committee on Privilege and Elections, which the Conservatives could more easily control.

At this point I gave one of the best theatrical performances of my life. In a speech lasting an hour and a half I played the bluff and honest Irish Protestant immigrant to the hilt. I stated my opposition to the standing committee investigating the accusations on the grounds that it would take too long to report. A quick report was required, I said. The sooner the truth was out, the better. Then I shifted ground. The charges in the newspapers and now in Parliament had upset my wife, I announced. "She has had to read these matters and has had to notice the cowardly, mean and contemptible correspondents that attack a man, and have not the moral courage and independence to put their names to the attack. She has had to read all these things, but I said to her, 'All right, Esther, take it quietly. It is all right. I have never surrendered and I never will…'"

I went on to evoke the workingman image that had worn so well throughout my political career. "There is one thing I can say… No man ever had to write a letter to ask the people of East Hastings to elect me. They know who I am. They have known me now for thirty-eight years… I am not ashamed to state that I landed in the town of Belleville thirty-eight years ago with a York shilling, and that I worked on farms for 3 and 4 dollars a month in that county… I got the seat in 1872 [my dates were a bit off]… At the time I speak of, it was thought that it would not answer for me to try unless seven or eight hundred Roman Catholic votes went for me, and I only got two out of seven hundred voters. I had the banks against me, the commercial men against me, I had the Tories under Sir John A. Macdonald against me, and I had the Grits against me – but I got the seat and I will hold it…"

At the end of my performance, I voted in favour of the main

motion calling for the select committee investigation.

Sir John A. Macdonald, however, knew the difference between political theatre and parliamentary reality, and he was not about to have a select committee look into what he, as minister of interior and of Indian affairs, had approved. All of us – he, his senior officials, his Minister of Customs Mackenzie Bowell and myself – would have been caught with our hands in the biscuit tin. He made certain that the matter went to the Standing Committee on Privilege and Elections, which never issued a public report. Everything was quietly swept under the rug.

The electors of East Hastings were less easily controlled. Throughout the rest of 1886 our local Liberal paper frequently reminded its readers of the creative use I had made of their political trust. As always I read the newspapers carefully, but now I was less interested in politics than in diversion. Mackenzie Bowell's paper was serializing *Little Lord Fauntleroy*. I read it aloud to Esther, putting great feeling into the more melodramatic parts.

Although now and again the Toronto *Globe* would snipe at me, I began focusing on those odd fugitive items that make newspapers so fascinating. In January 1887 I read Esther a report from New Mexico of the exploits of Broncho Len, the Female Terror of the West. This desperado had for several years been the bane of southern Colorado. "'In her younger days,'" I read, "'she was a dashing woman, with enough of grace and health, brightness of eye and freshness of complexion to make her pass as reasonably good-looking. She was as queer a compound of ferocity and gentleness, devilishness and decency, brutality and womanliness as ever was seen...'"

"That reminds me of those two women pirates, Anne Bonny and Mary Read," Esther commented. She caught my eye and smiled at our shared remembrance.

"'... She rode her horse like a man. She was strong and lithe and could endure anything...'"

"Just like you, dear husband."

"'... In spite of her hard life, her figure was trim, her voice musical, and her hands deft. She could kill a man with a revolver or knife and nurse a wounded or sick companion with equal dexterity... She is credited with killing two husbands, in Colorado, and nobody knows exactly how many she has made away with here in New Mexico...'"

Esther laughed. "Well, she's not exactly like you."

"'... The band to which she belonged in Colorado became so troublesome that the settlers could put up with their lawlessness no longer, and a posse was organized to go in pursuit... If they had left the country then it is probable that they would not have been pursued, but they remained in the southern part of the state, committing many depredations ...'"

"One should always know when to quit," Esther said, as if she had been thinking about the matter for some time.

"'... She was in Socorro in 1883, and while engaged in a gambling game with Robert Black, she shot him dead...'"

"Did they arrest her?"

"Eventually... 'The jury took the case and in five minutes returned a verdict of not guilty, which was received with wild cheering.'"

"Well, I think that's terrible," Esther said in her Sunday school teacher voice. "The creature doesn't know when to quit, she commits more crimes, and in the end is cleared to great acclaim."

When to quit? The question was relevant to my own situation. The general election was approaching. Should I step down or soldier on and hope for a big surge in voter sympathy because of the attacks by Toronto journalists?

I decided to run, but as the mid-February 1887 election date loomed long-time supporters noted my old campaign energy flagging. I dropped the family tableau and made only token appearances at the lodges and social gatherings that I had worked so assiduously in the past.

And thus the unthinkable happened: by a margin of fifty-nine votes, East Hastings went to a Grit.

I accepted the loss gracefully. "I've been over confident," was my public explanation. In private, I was relieved to be out of the public eye. My success in politics has exacted a great price in strain.

I have spent the last seven years making money, travelling to British Columbia several times to promote my lumbering and colonization projects, and now I am close to being a millionaire.

But as I have so often noted about the course of my fortunes, nothing comes without its price. In the late spring of this year, 1894, while in Victoria negotiating some timber leases, I experienced some mild internal bleeding. At first I thought nothing of it, but the pain intensified. For weeks I put off seeking medical help, spending day after day in my hotel room, alone, in agony, trapped by the secret that has endured for my entire adult life. Finally, I wrote a letter to William Martin describing my condition and asking him to confer with his brother, Dr Oronhyatekha, who is now head of the Order of Foresters and known nationwide. Dr Oronhyatekha telegraphed a colleague and brother forester in British Columbia who provides me with a daily supply of laudanum, no questions asked.

The opiate dulls the pain. I have been able to write cheerful letters to Esther daily throughout the summer, repeating that she should not worry, that I will be leaving for home any day now. But I doubt that, in all honesty, for I fear that my suffering is caused by uterine cancer. I am keeping this hard truth from Esther, instead devoting the space in my letters to reminiscences of our life together. Lovers always, we have managed to touch fingertips in this our most trying hour. That is enough.

16

Postscript

Eliza McCormack White died in Victoria, British Columbia, on 24 September 1894. By Esther White's express order, the body was immediately sent home for burial without being embalmed or medically examined. In Belleville it was quietly made known that John White, former M.P. for East Hastings, had died of kidney stones.

In the ten days between Eliza's death and public burial, Esther Johnston White received numerous sympathy calls at her home. Between visitors she pondered whether, if ever, she should tell the children the truth about their father. This was on her mind late one evening when William Martin arrived, appearingly silently and unannounced, as was his habit. Gravely he accepted a cup of tea. They were alone in the parlour. "Will you ever tell the children?" he asked, referring to their origins.

Esther said nothing for a long time. The kerosene lamp flickered and she looked at it as if it were some distant beacon. "No," she said finally. "No, some truths are better left unsaid."

William Martin rose, bowed, and was gone, silent as the grave.

Mackenzie Bowell's Belleville *Intelligencer* reported the funeral in detail. The heart of that report, which like all such obituaries has very little to do with its true subject, reads as follows:

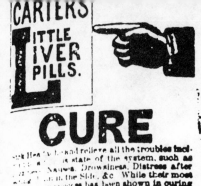
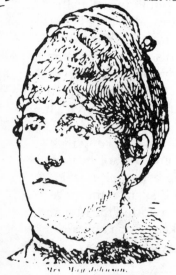
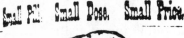
JOHN WHITE'S FUNERAL.

An Immense Gathering.

An Imposing Funeral Procession —
Universal Regret — The Grand Orange
Lodge of Ontario East Conducted the
Funeral — Grand Chaplain Duprau's
Sermon — The Hon. Senator Rowell
Speaks of his Departed Friend — Friend
and Brethren From Near and Far shed
Tears With the Family.

From Friday's Daily, Oct. 5.

But one theme has been the subject of conversation in the county for the past ten days. "John White is dead" were the words on every lip. Like other men who have risen to prominence and "left their footprints in the sands of time," his death has been a revelation of the hold he had on the hearts of the community, who knew him and honored him. John White has not only been a prominent man for a quarter of a century, but he had a striking personality. His indomitable will, his "pluck," his devotion to his friends, his kindness to fallen foes, and his "never say die" in every cause he undertook won people to him in spite of themselves. Commencing the struggle of life amidst the most diverse circumstances, sailing ever against the wind, and with only his nervy heart and his wondrously sanguine nature to aid him, he turned that which would have thwarted a less brave soul, to his gain. The obsequies proved how deep set was the affection entertained for him. The funeral was remarkable above anything else for number of ladies present. This was but their way of showing how much they valued the man "who set such store" on them. How often has he been heard to say "give me the ladies on my side and I don't care much for the men" and he could ever count on them as his staunchest friends and greatest admirers.

A Note on Sources

I should underscore something that the reader will notice: that
Eliza and Esther do not suffer much guilt about their relationship, and what guilt exists is really only Esther's. This is very
important. In her pioneering study *Surpassing the Love of Men:
Romantic Friendship and Love Between Women from the Renaissance
to the Present* (New York: William Morrow 1981), Lillian Faderman demonstrates that prior to the 20th-century, romantic love
between women of the middle classes was frequently and readily condoned. Whether such love involved genital sexual activity
was not a matter widely canvassed at the time, and anyway it
is irrelevant for our understanding of nineteenth-century lesbian relationships. As Faderman establishes, it was only in the
twentieth century that studies of lesbian behaviour, conducted
by heterosexuals, decreed and gained public acceptance of the

belief that love between women was an abnormality to be condemned.

On the other hand, Eliza's transvestism is something she and Esther did everything possible to hide. They arranged their lives to protect their secret. Although transvestism was not uncommon in the seventeenth century through the nineteenth, it was usually severely punished by ostracism or criminal prosecution. Why was transvestism condemned and romantic love between women condoned? "Transvestites were, in a sense, among the first feminists," Faderman argues. "Mute as they were, without a formulated ideology to express their convictions, they saw the role of woman to be dull and limiting. They craved to expand it and the only way to alter that role in their day was to become a man" (61).

Transvestites were punished in a male-dominated world because they threatened male domination. That they could be marvelously successful in male roles is shown in Julie Wheelwright's highly entertaining, *Amazons and Military Maids: Women Who Dressed as Men in the Pursuit of Life, Liberty and Happiness* (London: Pandora 1989). But threaten male domination they certainly did.

Even today, some male historians will resist letting Eliza into the Canadian firmament. But resistance will arise from other sources as well. The novelist and essayist Reynolds Price has shrewdly noted that the blurring of gender is one of the most pervasive fears of modern Western society. "We're generally unnerved, if not routed, by sexual ambiguity," he observes. I suspect that the sexual ambiguity of Eliza will lead even some feminist historians to join their patriarchal colleagues in rejecting her claims. That is their problem, not Eliza's.

CHAPTER ONE

The cholera pandemic of 1832 is chronicled from a Canadian perspective in C.M. Godfrey, *The Cholera Epidemic in Upper Canada, 1832–1866* (Toronto: Secombe House, 1968), and in Geoffrey Bilson, *A Darkened House: Cholera in Nineteenth-Century Canada* (Toronto: University of Toronto Press, 1980). On the Irish cholera panic of 1832, see S.J. Connolly, "The 'Blessed Turf': Cholera and Popular Panic in Ireland, June 1832, *Irish*

Historical Studies 23 (May 1983): 214–32.

Although in various political and other public directories, John White's birth is ascribed to the years 1832 and 1833, it actually was 1831. His baptismal day was 8 May of that year. (See the register, Church of Ireland, Donegal Parish Church, Donegal Town, County Donegal, Public Record Office of Northern Ireland, MIC 1/146.) This matter of the birth dating is revealing, for it was one of the few times that Eliza made what some psychologists call a "diagnostic" or "motiviated error." That is, she gave a birthdate that was closer to her own actual birthdate than to that of her late brother John. Not only did she do this in providing information to the public directory-makers but she did so in the confidential dicennial census returns. Thus in 1871 she gave an age for John White that would have meant birth in 1834. And in 1881 and 1891 she gave the enumerators information that required a birth date in 1835, even farther from John White's real birthdate.

The town of Donegal and its environs in the Whites' lifetime can be studied on a building by building, farm by farm basis by using the first Ordnance Survey of Ireland (version with a scale of 6 inches to the mile), especially sheets 93 and 94. For surrounding topography (which is essentially unchanged since the 1830s), see the 1969 national grid compiled by the government of the Republic of Ireland, scale one-half inch to one mile, Donegal, sheet 3. The best visual presentation of the extent and vulnerability of the Protestant settlements in western Ulster is a map prepared for the 1926 Boundary Commission, based on the 1911 census. This remained suppressed under the Official Secrets Act until 1969, when it was edited by Geoffrey J. Hand and published by the Irish University Press, Shannon.

The entries in the following contemporary guides are germane to Donegal town and County Donegal: *The Parliamentary Gazetteer of Ireland* (Dublin: A. Fullarton 1846), and Samuel Lewis, *A topographical Dictionary of Ireland* (London 1837). The most precise verbal material on the environment in which the White children grew up is the holograph "Ordnance Survey Memoir of Donegal Parish," found in two parts in the Royal Irish Acadmey, Dublin, Ordnance Survey Memoirs, box 21, Donegal I, ix, "Donegal Parish, statistical report," and "Donegal

Parish, memoir with sketches." It is useful to compare these items to James McParlan, *Statistical Survey of the County of Donegal with Observations on the Means of Improvement; Drawn up in the Year 1801, for the Consideration and under the Direction of the Dublin Society* (Dublin: Graisberry and Campbell 1802). Further, highly specific information is found in the great report of the massive Irish Poor Law Commission of 1833–6. The material is best approached through the *Index*, in the United Kingdom parliamentary papers, H.C. 1845 (40) xliii.

The journal of the Ulster Folk and Transport Museum, *Ulster Folklife* (hereafter *UFL*), is a trove of information on the historic province of Ulster, not just the present six counties. On housing, see Desmond McCourt, "Some Cruck-framed Buildings in Donegal and Derry," *UFL* 11 (1965): 39–49, and Alan Gailey, "The Housing of the Rural Poor in Nineteenth-Century Ulster," *UFL* 22 (1976): 34–58.

The problem of representing the language spoken in and around Donegal town is virtually insurmountable. One can know it in a technical sense, but representing it is another matter. Much of the Catholic population was bilingual, speaking the Donegal dialect of Irish Gaelic and a stilted but often highly creative form of English. There are several good articles in *UFL* on the Irish language in Ulster, most of them by the late distinguished scholar G.B. Adams. The inhabitants of the town of Donegal were well acquainted with English. Those of English background spoke with an attenuated west-of-England accent; the majority, like the Whites, traced their roots to lowland Scotland and spoke what contemporaries called broad Scotch. The reader is apt to be acquainted with the form of Lallans spoken and written by the poet Robert Burns, and though the Donegal speech had veered somewhat from the Lallans original, it was closer to the language of Burns than of Goldsmith. For a nontechnical view of the sort of Scotch spoken by people such as the Whites, see Donald Akenson and W.H. Crawford, *Local Poets and Social History: James Orr, Bard of Ballycarry* (Belfast: Public Record Office of Northern Ireland 1977). All of this material helps the historian establish the way people thought in Donegal, for language sets the parameters of human understanding. But still we are left with a problem: even if one could report broad Scotch accurately, most of it would be incomprehensible to us. The Gaelic and Lallans vocabularies are familiar to a only handful of scholars, and even the grammatical structures of these dialects are strange to modern English speakers. Thus we must be satisfied with a rough transliteration of how people spoke.

CHAPTER TWO

For more general and more recent material on Donegal County, see the various issues of the *Donegal Annual*; Stephen Gwynn's chatty *Highways and Byways in Donegal and Antrim* (London: Macmillan 1899), and the serious and serviceable study by Desmond Murphy, *Derry, Donegal, and Modern Ulster, 1790–1921* (Londonderry: Aileach Press 1981).

The question of whether or not Irishwomen were severely mistreated in the nineteenth century is a matter of some scholarly controversy. In *The Irish: Emigration, Marriage and Fertility* (Berkeley: University of California Press 1973), Robert E. Kennedy, Jr. argues that the lot of Irish women was worse than that of women from any major Western European country. He demonstrates that the extent to which women outlived men was lower in Ireland than elsewhere. Because of technical errors in his work, I cannot accept his international comparisons. (see Donald H. Akenson, *Small Differences: Irish Catholics and Irish Protestants. An International Perspective, 1815–1922* [Montreal and Kingston: McGill-Queen's University Press 1988]). But even if one rejects the idea that Irish women were no worse off than women elsewhere, this does not mean that their lives were easy – far from it. See Margaret MacCurtain and Donncha O'Corrahn, *Women in Irish Society: The Historical Dimension* (Westport, Connecticut: Greenwood Press 1979), and Hasia R. Diner, *Erin's Daughters in America: Irish Immigrant Women in the Nineteenth Century* (Baltimore: The Johns Hopkins University Press 1983).

Nineteenth-century Irish farming techniques are described and illustrated in Jonathan Bell and Mervyn Watson, *Irish Farming: Implements and Techniques, 1750–1900* (Edinburgh: John Donald 1986). On potato culture, see especially pp. 43–63 and 112–37. For a major article on the processes of blacksmithing see William N.T. Wylie, "The Blacksmith in Upper Canada, 1784–1850: A study of Technology, Culture, and Power," in D.H. Akenson (ed.), *Canadian Papers in Rural History* (1990), 7: 17–213. This article is profusely illustrated and shows in detail the techniques of smithing as practised in the British Isles in the early nineteenth century and as imported into central Canada.

The Donegal female seafarer who was given a royal pension was real. See the section "Remarkable Events" in the Ordnance Survey memoir of Donegal Parish.

In addition to the pensioned female sailor in Donegal town and the female pirates in Defoe's book, there was also circulating in rural Ireland, especially in seaside towns, a rich tradition of ballads about girls who dressed up in male clothing to serve as soldiers or sailors. Usually, but not always, this was for the purpose of joining their male lovers. See Hugh Shields, "Some Bonny Female Sailors," *UFL* 10 (1964): 35–45. Also circulating at the time was Henry Fielding's *The Female Husband: or, the Surprising History of Mrs Mary, Alias Mr. George Hamilton, Who Was Convicted of Having Married a Woman of Wells and Lived with Her as Her Husband, Taken from Her Own Mouth since Her Confinement* (London: M. Cooper 1746).

On the various Protestant proselytizing societies, including the London Hibernian Society, see Donald H. Akenson, *The Irish Education Experiment: The National System of Education in the Nineteenth Century* (London: Routledge and Kegan Paul 1970), 80–94. On the books circulating in the countryside, see pp. 51–2. On the nature of indigenous education before the national board standardized things, see *The Life of William Carleton: Being His Autobiography and Letters* (London: Downey 1896), 1: 11–23.

For an interesting critical evaluation of Susanna Strickland Moodie, with a commentary on her characteristic feminizing of men and bringing women to life, see Carol Shields, *Susanna Moodie: Voice and Vision* (Ottawa: Borealis Press 1977). The information in the text concerning authorship of *The Little Prisoner* corrects material in the *Dictionary of Canadian Biography*, which states wrongly that Catherine, rather than Elizabeth, was Susanna's coauthor.

The *Irish Monthly* of March 1883 contains an interesting commentary on the fear of the workhouse: "I do not think that Englishmen, who try to do something for the benefit of Ireland, understand what 'going to the poorhouse' means to the people of Donegal. It means degradation in every sense of the word.

It means the breaking up of their homes, and, above all, the contamination of their wives and innocent daughters" ("A Six-Days Trip in the Donegal Highlands," 271).

The dismal Hamilton estate, Brownhall, is described in McParlan, *Statistical Survey of the County of Donegal*, 6. The new island estate is described in the Ordnance Survey Memoirs' section "Gentlemen's Seats."

On modes of transport such as were used to take the children to Brownhall, see George B. Thompson, "Some Primitive Forms of Farm Transport Used in Northern Ireland," *UFL* 1 (1955): 32–6.

On Christmas mumming, see the following by Alan Gailey: "'The Christmas Rhime,'" *UFL* 21 (1975): 73–84; "The Rhymers of South-East Antrim," *UFL* 13 (1967): 18–28; and *Irish Folk Drama* (Cork: Mercier Press 1969), esp. 43–50.

CHAPTER THREE

For an interesting aside on herb women, see Sean Ban MacMenamin, "Life in County Donegal in Pre-Famine Days," *Donegal Annual* 3 (1954–55): 5. The entire article repays study. For information on folk medicine, see the questionnaires in the archives of the Ulster Folk and Transport Museum, Cultra Manor, County Down. The material in this text on the female use of sweathouses is hypothetical but lies within the parameters of recent historical methodology in women's studies.

Carleton's story of Lough Derg, somewhat modified from its original printing in *The Christian Examiner*, is found in the various editions of his *Traits and Stories of the Irish Peasantry*. The context of the story is discussed in Carleton's autobiography, 1: 97–107. Carleton mentions the 1842 Lough Derg fire in the revised edition on the *Traits* (London: Maxwell n.d.), 207.

For an illuminating study of Irish visual symbolism, see Jacqueline R. Hill, "National Festivals, the State and 'Protestant Ascendancy' in Ireland, 1790–1829, *Irish Historical Studies* 24 (May 1984): 30–51.

The French anchor from 1798 was still visible in Donegal Harbour as late as 1899 (see Gwynn, *Highways and Byways*, 45). It now is the centrepiece of a small roadside park.

James Orr's "Donegore Hill," in his *Poems on Various Subjects*

(Belfast: Smyth and Lyns 1804), is conveniently available in the reprint edition (Belfast: Mullan 1935). For the context of this poem see Akenson and Crawford, *James Orr*, 10–17.

The Musgrave *Memoirs of the Different Rebellions* was so popular that it was in its third edition (Dublin and London) by 1802. The Taylor book went through two Irish editions and one Canadian.

Catholic millenarianism, adverted to in the text, is badly in need of study. For a pioneer work, see James S. Donnelly, Jr, "Pastorini and Captain Rock: Millenarianism and Sectarianism in the Rockite Movement of 1821–4," in Samuel Clark and James S. Donnelly, Jr (eds), *Irish Peasant Violence and Political Unrest, 1780–1914* (Madison: University of Wisconsin Press 1983), 102–39.

For general background on the parts of Donegal that John White and his children visited, see T.W. Freeman, *Pre-Famine Ireland*, 296–301. On Gweedore, see *Gweedore, Compiled from the Notes of Lord George Hill, M.R.I.A.*, reprinted in fascimile from the fifth edition, 1887, with an introduction by E. Estyn Evans (Belfast: Institute of Irish Studies, Queen's University of Belfast, 1971). For an elaboration of my comments concerning the false link between Roman Catholicism and technological backwardness, see Donald H. Akenson, *Small Differences*.

The place that illicit distillation played in the economy of northern and western Ireland is succinctly analysed in a classic study by Kenneth Connell, "Illicit Distillation," in his *Irish Peasant Society: Four Historical Essays* (Oxford: Clarendon Press 1968), 1–50.

The standard history of Irish education in the nineteenth century is *The Irish Education Experiment* mentioned earlier. The local situation as of 1855 is covered in "Donegal Schools a Century Ago," *Donegal Annual* 3, no. 2 (1956): 102–7. The Irish predeliction for sexual segregation of school children is documented in detail in Donald Akenson, *A Mirror to Kathleen's Face: Education in Independent Ireland, 1922–1960* (Montreal and London: McGill-Queen's University Press 1975), 135–42. It should be added that Protestants were not as afraid of coeducation as Catholics were. The Canadian appropriation of the Irish books (and of many Irish structures and methods) is discussed in Donald Akenson, "Mass Schooling in Ontario: The Irish and

'English Canadian' Popular Culture," in *Being Had: Historians, Evidence, and the Irish in North America* (Toronto: P.D. Meany 1985), 143–87.

Two revealing articles on the position of farm labourers in Ulster in this period are Jonathan Bell, "Hiring Fairs in Ulster," *UFL* 25 (1979): 67–78, and "Farm Servants in Ulster," *UFL* 31 (1985): 13–20.

The two best works on the Irish famine of 1845–59 are R. Dudley Edwards and T. Desmond Williams (eds), *The Great Famine: Studies in Irish History, 1845–52* (Dublin: published for The Irish Committee of Histoical Science by Browne and Nolan 1956), and Cecil Woodham-Smith, *The Great Hunger* (New York: Harper and Row 1953).

CHAPTER FOUR

Concerning emigration from Londonderry and other northern ports, the best work still is William Forbes Adams, *Ireland and Irish Emigration to the New World, from 1815 to the Famine* (New Haven: Yale University Press 1932).

The "old" Orange Order to which John White, Sr, was inducted is set forth in *The Orange Institution: A Slight Sketch with an Appendix Containing the Rules and Regulations of the Orange Society of Great Britain and Ireland* (Dublin: J. Charles 1813). *The Annals and Defence of the Loyal Orange Institution of Ireland*, by Ogle R. Gowan, was privately printed for the author in Dublin in 1825.

For evocative if not entirely accurate depictions of the famine migration to Canada, see Gilbert Tucker, "The Famine Immigration to Canada, 1847," *American Historical Review* 36 (April, 1931): 532–49, and John B. O'Reilly, "Canada: The Irish Famine and the Atlantic Migration to Canada," *Irish Ecclesiastical Record*, 5 series, 69: 870–82.

CHAPTER FIVE

William Burton's founding work on behalf of Montreal Orangeism is mentioned in William P. Perkins Bull, *From the Boyne to Brampton, or, John the Orangeman at Home and Abroad* (Toronto: George J. McLeod 1936), 72. Burton for a time was First Deputy

Grand Treasurer of the Loyal Orange Order of British North America.

It is not surprising that Eliza's knowledge of Thomas Moore's poetry was limited, despite his being the best-known Irish song and verse writer of his time. He was hated by True Blue loyalists in Ireland for, beginning in 1813 with his satirical "Two Penny Post Bag," he had been a strong advocate of Catholic emancipation and an opponent of Protestant hegemony.

On contemporary modes of travel, see James J. Talman, "Travel in Ontario Before the Coming of the Railway," *Ontario Historical Society Papers and Records* 29 (1933): 85–102.

Most serious readers of Canadian history know Wilson Benson from Michael Katz's *The People of Hamilton, Canada West: Family and Class in a Mid-Nineteenth-Century City* (Cambridge: Harvard University Press 1975), 94ff. Wilson's life is worth studying for itself, however, and one should read his diverting *Life and Adventures of Wilson Benson, Written by Himself* (Toronto: Hunter, Rose 1876).

On John A. Macdonald and Mrs Grimason, see E.B. Biggar, *Anecdotal Life of Sir John Macdonald* (Montreal: John Lovell 1891), 237–38. Macdonald's trip to the United States in the early winter of 1846 is mentioned in Peter B. Waite, *John A. Macdonald* (Toronto: Fitzhenry and Whiteside 1976), 13.

On Kingston entertainment, see John W. Spurr, "Theatre in Kingston, 1816–1870," *Historic Kingston* 22 (March 1974), 37–55.

Eliza's public apprehension and case in magistrate's court were reported in the Hamilton Spectator. No orignals of this paper for the relevant date exist, but the story was reprinted in the Brockville *Recorder* on 7 January 1847.

CHAPTER SIX

There is a massive literature on the history of Toronto in the nineteenth century. I found the following especially useful: Barrie Drummond Dyster, "Toronto, 1840–1860: Making It in a British Protestant Town" (Ph.D. diss., University of Toronto 1970); J.M.S. Careless, *Toronto to 1918* (Toronto: Lorimer 1984); Victor L. Russell (ed.), *Forging a Consensus: Historical Essays on Toronto* (Toronto: University of Toronto Press 1984); Robert F. Harney (ed.), *Gathering Places: Peoples and Neighbourhoods of*

Toronto, 1834–1945 (Toronto: Multicultural History Society of Ontario 1985); and Elmer Henderson, "Bloor Street, Toronto, and the Village of Yorkville in 1849," *Ontario Historical Society, Papers and Records* 26 (1930): 445–60.

The background of John George Hodgins is found in Akenson, "Mass Schooling in Ontario" in *Being Had*, 154–55, 230 *n*38 and *n*39. Hodgins's views on Irishness are developed in his *Irishmen in Canada: Their Union Not Inconsistent with the Development of Canadian National Feeling* (Toronto: Lovell 1875). This was published during his term as president of the Irish Protestant Benevolent Society of Toronto.

The standard biography of Adolphus Egerton Ryerson is C.B Sissons, *Egerton Ryerson: His Life and Letters*, 2 vols. (Toronto: Clarke Irwin 1947). Ryerson's supposed autobiography is a strange production. It was published posthumously in 1884 and was not only edited by John George Hodgins but in part written by him (see *"The Story of my Life" by the late Rev. Egerton Ryerson, D.D., L1.D.* [Toronto: William Briggs 1884]). Neither the autobiography nor Sisson's *Life* mentions Eliza.

The *Victoria Magazine*, edited by Susanna and J.W.D. Moodie, lasted less than two years. It has been reprinted with an introduction by William H. New (Vancouver: University of British Columbia Library 1968).

The three-volume history of Orangeism that Ogle Gowan was working on was never completed. One volume, *Orangeism: Its Origins and History*, appeared in 1859 (Toronto: Lovell and Gibson). Eliza's confession to Gowan is detailed in Don Akenson, *The Orangeman: The Life and Times of Ogle Gowan* (Toronto: James Lorimer 1986), 266–7.

On the Toronto fire, see F.H. Armstrong, "The First Great Fire of Toronto, 1849," *Ontario History* 53 (September 1961): 201–21. The deaths of the Irish immigrants in Kingston mentioned by the ostler went virtually uncommemorated until 6 September 1966, when the Irish ambassador to Canada unveiled a plaque to mark the re-internment of the remains of the 1,400 victims.

On the British American League see Gerald A. Hallowell, "The Reaction of the Upper Canadian Tories to the Adversity of 1849: Annexation and the British American League," *Ontario History* 72 (1970): 41–56, and Cephas D. Allin, "The British North

American League, 1849," *Ontario Historical Society: Papers and Records* 13 (1915): 74–115.

CHAPTER SEVEN

When she later became known as John White, Eliza listed 1850 as the date of her arrival in Canada, not 1847. This covered up her years in the Classon Hotel (see *Illustrated Historical Atlas of Counties of Hastings and Prince Edward Ontario* [originally published 1878, reprinted edition edited by Gerald Boyce, Mika Publishing, Belleville 1977], x, 72). On White's being a choreboy, see ibid., x.

For the important merchants and substantial citizens of Roslin, see *Canada Directory for 1857–58* (Montreal: John Lovell 1858), 641.

The initiation rite that Eliza underwent is spelled out in *Forms to Be Observed in Private Lodges of the Loyal Orange Institution of British North America* (Belleville: published for the Association at *The Intelligencer* office 1860), found in the L.O.L. collection, Queen's University Archives. *The Intelligencer*, it should be remembered, was owned by Mackenzie Bowell.

On the ownership and personnel of the various Belleville periodicals, see J. Owen Herity, "Journalism in Belleville," *Ontario Historical Society, Papers and Records* 27 (1931), 400–6.

There are a number of interesting items (particularly the clipping collection), as well as microfilms of items held elsewhere, in the Mackenzie Bowell collection in the Queen's University Archives.

On the nature of local government in general, see J.H. Aitchinson, "The Municipal Corporations Act of 1849," *Canadian Historical Review* 30 (1949): 107–22, and Fred Landon, "The Evolution of Local Government in Ontario," *Ontario History* 42 (1950): 1–5. On political fever in Hastings County, see the chapter "County Government since 1850," in Gerald E. Boyce, *Historic Hastings* (Belleville: published for the Hastings County Council by Ontario Intelligencer 1967).

On the Tyendinaga Mowhawks, see E.A. Cruikshank, "The Coming of the Loyalist Mohawks to the Bay of Quinte," *Ontario Historical Society, Papers and Records* 26 (1930): 390–403; William Canniff, *History of the Settlement of Upper Canada (Ontario), with*

Special Reference to the Bay Quinté (Toronto: Dudley and Burns 1869), 312–22; Malcolm Montgomery, "The Legal Status of the Six Nations Indians in Canada, *Ontario History* 55 (March 1963): 93–105; and J. Donald Wilson, "'No Blanket to Be Worn in School': The Education of Indians in Early Nineteenth-Century Ontario," *Histoire Sociale/Social History* 7 (November 1974): 293–305.

For material on Richard Lazier, see the Lazier papers in the Queen's University Archives, Kingston.

The house that the Moodies owned at the time can be seen in a line drawing in Nick and Helma Mika, *Mosaic of Belleville: An Illustrated History of a City* (Belleville: Mika Silk Screening 1966), 14. A portrait of George Benjamin is reproduced in W.C. Mikel, *City of Belleville History* (City of Belleville 1943), 28. A photograph of J.W. Dunbar Moodie and Susanna Moodie is found in Nick and Helma Mika, *Belleville: The Good Old Days* (Belleville: Mika Publishing 1975), 24.

The readings about Susannah Loft were taken from Moodie's *Life in the Clearings versus the Bush* (London: Richard Bentley 1853), 195–6. For a discussion of the Canadian settlement of the various Stricklands, see Audrey Y. Morris, *Gentle Pioneers: Five Nineteenth-Century Canadians* (Toronto: Hodder and Stoughton 1968). For a more analytical viewpoint, see Elizabeth Hopkins, "A Prison-House for Prosperity: The Immigrant Experience of the Nineteenth-Century Upper-Class British Woman," in Jean Burnet (ed.), *Looking into My Sister's Eyes: An Exploration in Women's History* (Toronto: Multi-cultural History Society of Ontario 1986), 7–19.

CHAPTER EIGHT

The Benjamin-Gowan war of 1853–56 is best followed in the various printed proceedings of the Grand Lodge of the Loyal Orange Association of British North America. Each faction printed its own version of the events of 1853, and as often happens when dirty linen aired, these accounts are wonderfully revealing. For 1853–56 there were two separate national Orange institutions, each of which printed its own rules, regulations and proceedings. These are found in the Archives of the Loyal Orange Lodge of British North America, Toronto, but can be

consulted with move convenience in the collection of the Bald-
win Room, Toronto Public Library.

Mackenzie Bowell's *Directory of the County of Hastings* for 1860–
61 (Belleville: *The Intelligencer* Office 1861) is largely applicable
to the mid-fifties, at least as far as the business and social
institutions of Belleville are concerned.

CHAPTER NINE

The coming of the Grand Trunk Railwoad to Belleville is
described in Boyce, *Historic Hastings,* 116–9. On George Benjamin's political career see the *Dictionary of Canadian Biography*
9.

The White's homestead was on lot 4, concession 9, in Tyendinaga Township. Curiously, it is not marked as such in the
*Illustrated Historical Atlas of the Counties of Hastings and Prince
Edward, Ontario* (Toronto: H. Belden 1878; reprinted in Belleville
by Mika Editions, 1977). The land records, however, are unam-
biguous on this point (see Abstract Index of Deeds, Tyendinaga,
Archives of Ontario, microfilm). The property and production
reported in the text are taken from the 1861 agricultural census
for Tyendinaga (Public Archives of Canada, film C.10334). For
an interesting comparison to the White's enterprise, see "An
Upper-Canadian 'Bush Business' in the Fifties," by Elsie McLeod
Murray, *Ontario Historical Society Papers and Records* 36 (1944):
41–7.

Through the years the person of Dr James Barry (1795–1865)
has aroused considerable curiosity, consequent upon Dr Barry's
charwoman having announced that she had examined the doctor's body shortly after death and found it to be that of a female.
For early commentary, see "A Female Medical Combatant" in
the London, *Medical Times and Gazette* (July–December 1865),
227–8. By the mid-1860s there was an incomplete bibliography
of 168 items dealing with Dr Barry. (see for example, "A Female
Member of the Army Medical Staff," *The Lancet* 26 [October
1895]: 1086–7). In recent times there has been scrap over the
doctor's corpse between the forces of ideology on the one hand
and those of empiricism on the other. In 1958 Isobel Rae published *The Strange Story of Dr James Barry, Army Surgeon, Inspector
General of Hospitals, Discovered on Death to Be a Woman* (London:

Longman, Green, 1958), a fascinating biography of a woman doctor posing as a male. Then in 1970 a South African medical professor, one Dr Kirby, who had made something of a hobby of collecting everything known on the Barry case, published a short article in the *South African Medical Journal* (25 April 1970, 506–16). He succinctly argued against there being competent evidence in support of the charwoman's claim; the best reading of the medical evidence suggested that Barry was a male hermaphrodite who had breasts and lacked body and facial hair. Charles Roland, Hannah Professor of Medical History at McMaster University, believes this is the most likely case (see the *Dictionnary of Canadian Biography*, vol. 9, 33–4). That might have been the end of the matter had Carlotta Hacker not devoted a chapter to Dr Barry in *The Indomitable Lady Doctors* (Toronto: Clarke Irwin 1974); she simply ignored the evidence: a 19th-century female doctor was required for a book on women doctors, so James Barry was once again declared to be a woman. This little academic melodrama is being fought over the corpse of the person Florence Nightingale regarded, based on his/her service during the Crimean War, as the most brutal person she had ever met (Kirby, *South African Medical Journal*, 513). Dr Barry was in Canada from 1857 to 1859. Why he came here is unknown, but it is known that his predecessor in Canada was recalled from his post to act on Florence Nightingale's Royal Commission on the Health of the Army (Rae, *The Strange Story*, 101–2). One suspects that Nightingale arranged for the hated Barry to be sent – indeed, for a person with chronic bronchitis, to be sentenced – to Canada.

Concerning the name of the White's first child, it is interesting to note that in the 1861 census she is called Mary Eliza but in subsequent censuses simply Eliza. Compare manuscript censuses of Tyendinaga, 1861 (PAC C.1034) and 1871 (PAC C.9992) and 1881 (PAC C.13237).

Ogle Gowan's child-assault case is discussed in Akenson, *The Orangeman*, 294–307.

CHAPTER TEN

On the Prince of Wales's near visit to Kingston, see J.D. Livermore, "The Orange Order and the Election of 1861 in Kingston," in Gerald Tulchinsky (ed.) *To Preserve and Defend: Essays on Kingston in the Nineteenth Century* (Montreal: McGill-Queen's University Press 1976), 245–8. The most evocative picture of the incident in Belleville is given by Nick and Helma Mika in Nick and Helma Mika (eds), *Belleville: The Good Old Days* (Belleville: Mika Publishing 1975), 33–7. A somewhat different version of events is found in Boyce's chapter, "A Prince Is Welcomed" in *Historic Hasting*, 129–33.

Peter Martin – Oronhyatekha – not only was a respected medical doctor but became the head, for 26 years, of the Independent Order of Foresters, which, by the time he left office, had over 250,000 members.

For the land transactions between the Whites and Mr and Mrs Johnston, see the records of Tyendinaga Township, lot 4, concession 9, found in the Abstract Index of Deeds, Archives of Ontario (microfilm).

CHAPTER ELEVEN

There is a large literature on the Fenian invasion. Still fundamental is C.P. Stacey's "Fenianism and the Rise of National Feeling in Canada at the Time of Confederation," *Canadian Historical Review* 12 (1931): 238–61. On the American context, the classic study is Thomas N. Brown, *Irish-American Nationalism, 1870-1890* (Philadelphia: Lippincott 1966). On the Irish background, see Maurice Harmon (ed.), *Fenians and Fenianism* (Dublin: Scepter Publishers 1968). See also Hereward Senior, *The Fenians and Canada* (Toronto: Macmillan 1978); D.C. Lyne and Peter M. Foner, "Fenianism in Canada, 1874–84," *Studia Hibernica* 12 (1972): 27-76; Brian Jenkins, "The British Government, Sir John A. Macdonald and the Fenian Claims," *Canadian Historical Review* 49 (June 1968): 142–59; W.S. Neidhardt, "The Abortive Fenian Uprising in Canada West: A Document Study," *Ontario History* (March 1969): 74–6; W.S. Neidhardt, "The American Government and the Fenian Brotherhood: A Study in Mutual Political Opportunism," *Ontario History* (March 1972): 27–44; W.S. Neidhardt, "The Fenian Brotherhood and Western Ontario: The Final Years, *Ontario History* (September 1968): 149–61; W.S. Neidhardt, "The Fenian Trials in the Province of Canada, 1866–67: A Case Study of Law and Politics in Action,"

Ontario History (March 1974): 23–36; and F.M. Quealey, "The Fenian Invasion of Canada West, June 1st and 2nd, 1866," *Ontario History* (March 1961): 38–66.

Ironically, one of the spies who reported to John A. Macdonald was an Irishman by the name of John White, who sent reports from Chicago (see Macdonald Papers, Public Archives of Canada). This was not our John White.

On Mackenzie Bowell's military career, see the clippings in the Bowell Papers, Queen's University Archives, microfilm. On local matters concerning the Fenians, see Boyce, *Historic Hastings*, 134–8.

Lest anyone think that the resonance of the 1798 Rising was limited to the Protestants of Ontario, note that as late as 1879 one Thomas Bolger, a Roman Catholic of Irish background (he had been born in Ontario in 1851) and the porter at a Belleville hotel, the Dafoe House, was sitting up nights labouriously copying out by hand a pro-Catholic version of the rising published in Ireland, "The Men of '98: The Wexford Insurrection." He would not have gone to that much trouble were the matter not still alive and important. Bolger's copy is in the Queen's University Archives, Kingston.

For the birth of the White daughters in the 1860s, see the census of Tyendinaga Township, 1871 (PAC, MS C.9992). The same source records John White's shift of religion to Wesleyan Methodism and also his acquisition of more land. The second piece of land, for the new cheese factory, was lot 20, concession 8, Tyendinaga, listed in the 1871 census of Madoc, division 1 (PAC, C.9994). It shows $5,000 in fixed capital investment and $1,000 in floating capital. The foundry worked twelve months a year and employed six adult males, with a payroll of $1,600 annually. It made forty tons of pig and wrought-iron a year, plus farming and mining implements and stoves. The gross output was approximately $5,000 a year.

The mortgage loan to the Whites for $1,300 was provided by Mackenzie Bowell and Robert Read, 28 October 1867. See Abstract Index of Deeds, Tyendinaga Township, Archives of Ontario.

The career of the egregious Shibley is found in Donald Swainson, "Schuyler Shibley and the Underside of Victorian Ontario," *Ontario History* 65 (March 1973): 51–60.

The rules of electoral politics at the time of Bowell's first election campaign are described in D.G.G. Kerr, "The 1867 Elections in Ontario: The Rules of the Game," *Canadian Historical Review* 51 (December 1970): 368–85, and in Margaret Small, "A Study of the Dominion and the Provincial Elections of 1867 in Ontario."

The standard biography of John A. Macdonald is that of Donald Creighton (Toronto: Macmillan 1952 and 1955) 2 vols. In many ways more interesting is Donald Swainson's *John A. Macdonald: The Man and the Politician* (Toronto: Oxford University Press 1971), which is full of illuminating, sometimes picaresque, details.

On Mackenzie Bowell's political career, see Swainson, "The Personnel of Politics: A Study of the Ontario Members of the Second Federal Parliament" (Ph.D. diss., University of Toronto 1968), 77–85.

On the Tyendinaga reeveship, see the *Illustrated Historical Atlas... Hastings*, x.

For the record of the mortgage Susanna Moodie held on the lot next to that registered to John White, see Abstract Index of Deeds, Tyendinaga Township, Archives of Ontario, entry for 15 January 1872. The north half of lot 5, concession 8, was owned by John White; the south half of the lot was the portion for which Susanna Moodie held the mortgage. I am at present engaged in writing the creative biography of John Wedderburn Dunbar Moodie and Susanna Strickland Moodie, which will include discussion of their joint literary output.

On the Scott affray and its relationship to Orangeism, see Hereward Senior, *Orangeism: The Canadian Phase* (Toronto: McGraw-Hill Ryerson, 1972), 73–5. The political events are narrated in Creighton, *Macdonald* 2: 38–69.

On Macdonald's family problem see Waite, *Macdonald*, 30.

Thomas Scott's local background is established in Boyce, *Historic Hastings*, 182–3.

CHAPTER TWELVE

Eliza's first election campaigns are well chronicled in the pages of the Belleville *Intelligencer*. Mackenzie Bowell was miffed about the candidacy, but the reports are full nonetheless.

Reports of parliamentary matters for 1871 and subsequent years are taken from the *Parliamentary Debates, Dominion of Canada* (hereafter *Hansard*).

On the city of Ottawa at that time, see A.H.D. Ross, *Ottawa, Past and Present* (Ottawa: Thorburn and Abbott 1927).

For further background on the founding of the Royal Black Preceptory in Canada, see *The Sentinel and Orange and Protestant Advocate*, centennial edition, 3 July 1930, 7 and 23.

CHAPTER THIRTEEN

Eliza's belief that Sir John A. Macdonald's associate Alexander Campbell was plotting with the Rathbun forces against her is, if anything, understated. For an excellent summary of what was happening and of the documentation provided in the Campbell Papers (PAC) and the Macdonald Papers (PAC), see Donald Swainson, "The Personnel of Politics: A Study of the Ontario Members of the Second Federal Parliament," 61–72. For background on Campbell, see Swainson "Alexander Campbell: General Manager of the Conservative Party (Eastern Ontario Section)," *Historic Kingston* 17 (1969): 1–15. See also Mary K. Christie, "Sir Alexander Campbell" (M.A. thesis, University of Toronto 1950).

For the religious composition of the riding of East Hastings, see *Census of Canada, 1870–71*, 1: 168–69. It is worth noting that Eliza had a shrewder sense of how many Catholics there were than Frizzell's backer, E.H. Rathbun, which helps explain why Frizzell's side lost the 1872 contest.

Eliza's summary of the Winters murder is accurate and her speculation about its effect on the election shrewd, if somewhat histrionic. See the *Intelligencer*, 23 August 1872 and following issues, for details.

For background on the 1795 events at Dan Winters's Inn, County Armagh, see Hereward Senior, *Orangeism in Ireland and Britain, 1795–1836* (London: Routledge and Kegan Paul 1960), 14–19.

There are scores of books dealing in whole or in part with Louis Riel. One of the more interesting is the usually ignored effort of William McCartney Davidson, who in 1928 wrote a biography of Riel that was published only posthumously in 1955

(Calgary: Albertan Publishing). Davidson was an old-time newspaper editor in the West, and his book was based on personal interviews conducted from 1926 to 1928 with persons who had been in the West during the Riel years.

The arrival of the two boys and the change of family religion to Presbyterianism are indicated in the manuscript census reports of Tyendinaga Township for 1881, PAC film C.13237.

CHAPTER FOURTEEN

Mary Edwards Merrill is more commonly known as Mary Melville. She was the subject of a fictionalized treatment of her life by Flora Macdonald, president of the Canadian Suffrage Association, entitled *Mary Melville: The Psychic* (Toronto: Austin Publishing 1890). For a heroic if not entirely successful attempt to find the facts behind the fiction, see Cyril Greenland, "Mary Edwards Merrill, 1858–1880: 'The Psychic,'" *Ontario History* 68 (June 1976): 81–92. For a thoughtful commentary on this form of spiritualism, see Ramsay Cook, *The Regenerators: Social Criticism in Late Victorian English Canada* (Toronto: University of Toronto Press 1985), 71–85.

The contested election of 1878 and the bye-election of 1879 in East Hastings can be most easily followed in the *Intelligencer*. For many of the backroom details of the case, see the letterbook in the George Dickson Papers, PAC MG 29 E86. (Note that this is incorrectly catalogued in the *Union List of Manuscripts, supp. 1977–78*.)

On the Rathbun and Son Incorporation Bill, sponsored by the member for East Hastings, see *Hansard, 1883,* 67.

On favours sought for friends and constituents, see the Macdonald Papers, PAC: White to Macdonald, 10 October 1879; White to Macdonald, 15 December 1881; White to Macdonald, 16 January 1882; White to Macdonald, 17 May 1882; White to Macdonald, 18 July 1885; White to Macdonald, 19 May 1887.

The statement on the Indians is found in *Hansard, 1880,* 1990–1. For background on the Indian franchise question, see Malcolm Montgomery, "The Six Nations Indians and the Macdonald Franchise," 13–25. It is worth noting that the franchise granted in 1885 was taken away by Parliament in 1898.

The statement in Parliament on female enfranchisement is found in *Hansard 1883*, 657.

For a fresh assessment of the Riel matter, mostly from the perspective of incidents in 1885, see A.I. Silver, "Ontario's Alleged Fanaticism in the Riel Affair," *Canadian Historical Review* 69 (March 1988): 21–50.

CHAPTER FIFTEEN

Eliza's speech protesting innocence on the land company matter is found in *Hansard*, 5 April 1885, 488–91. The succession of mortgages on the home property are found in the Abstract Index of Deeds, Tyendinaga Township, lot 4, concession 9, Archives of Ontario.

The *Globe* story of Bronco Len is found in the issue of 22 January 1887.

POSTSCRIPT

The obituary can be found in the *Weekly Intelligencer*, 11 October 1894.